THE LAST BIG THING

ALSO BY DAVID MOODY

THE LAST BIG THING

DAVID MOODY

IB

This collection first published in 2019 by Infected Books

A CIP catalogue record for this book
is available from the British Library

ISBN 978-0-9576563-9-0

www.infectedbooks.co.uk

Cover design by Craig Paton
www.craigpaton.com

www.davidmoody.net

"BIG MAN"
first published in "THE MONSTER'S CORNER"
(St Martin's Griffin, 2011)

"THE LUCKY ONES"
first published in "DEAD WATER"
(Hersham Horror, 2014)

"OSTRICH"
first published in "GREEN AND PLEASANT LAND"
(Black Shuck Books, 2016)

"GRANDMA KELLY"
first published in "666: THE NUMBER OF THE BEAST"
(Point, 2006)

"NOLAN HIGGS IS OUT OF HIS DEPTH"
first published in "THE BLACK ROOM MANUSCRIPTS VOLUME 3"
(Sinister Horror Company, 2018)

"ALMOST FOREVER"
first published in "THE MAMMOTH BOOK OF BODY HORROR"
(Mammoth Books, 2012)

"EVERYTHING AND NOTHING"
first published in 2010 by Infected Books

"THE DEAL"
"WE WERE SO YOUNG ONCE"
"AWAY WITH THE FAIRIES"
"THE LAST BIG THING"
first published in 2019 by Infected Books

THE LAST BIG THING

CONTENTS

BIG MAN

Big Man was written for **The Monster's Corner** collection – stories told from the perspective of the character who's usually the villain. That's a theme which has fascinated me for a long time, and it's something that's central to the **Hater** series: one person's terrorist might be someone else's freedom fighter. It's all down to perspective.

I was given carte blanche to pick any monster from any era, and I settled on a radioactive freak from a 1950's creature feature. I'm a sucker for a good (or bad) B movie, and **The Amazing Colossal Man** has always been one of my favourites. I always wondered what was going through the title character's mind as he caused all that devastation? Was he really trying to destroy the world, or was he just misunderstood?

It was like something out of one of those old black and white B movies he used to watch avidly when he was a kid: the army spread out in a wide arc across the land to defend the city, lying in wait for "it" to attack. Major Hawkins used to love those flicks. Although the reality looked almost the same and the last few days certainly seemed to have followed a similar script, it *felt* completely different. This, he reminded himself, was real. This was war.

It wasn't the Cold War US of the movies, it was mid-winter and he was positioned south-west of a rain-soaked Birmingham, almost slap bang in the centre of the United Kingdom. But the differences didn't end there. He wasn't an actor playing the part of a square-jawed hero, he was a trained soldier who had a job to do. And he was no rank-and-file trooper either. Today he was the highest-ranking officer out in the field or, to put it another way, the highest-ranking officer whose neck was on the line. His superiors were notably absent, watching the situation unfold on TV screens from the safety of bunker-bound leather chairs.

Roger Corman, Samuel Z Arkoff and the others had actually got a lot right in their quaint old movies. *The Amazing Colossal Man, War of the Colossal Beast, Attack of the 50 Foot Woman...* their monsters' stories always followed a familiar path: an unexpected and unintentional genesis, the wanton death and destruction which inevitably followed, the brief and fruitless search for a solution... but there was another facet to this story which the movies always glossed over. Many people had died, crushed by the beast in his fits of unstoppable rage. Property had been destroyed, millions of pounds worth of damage caused already, perhaps even billions.

Today they weren't about to face a stop-motion puppet or a stunt man in a rubber suit, this was a genuine, bona fide *creature*: a foul aberration which had once been human but which was now anything but; a hideous, deformed monstrosity which, unless it could be stopped, would keep growing and keep killing. The pressure on Hawkins' shoulders was intense. The implications were utterly terrifying.

Glen Chambers – the poor bastard at the very centre of this unbelievable chain of events – had, until a few days ago, been an anonymous nobody: a father of one, known only to his family, his handful of friends and his work colleagues. Hawkins could have passed him in the street a hundred times before and not given him a second glance. But now he had to forget that this monster had once been a man, and instead focus on the carnage the creature was responsible for. No one could be expected to remain sane through the torturous ordeal Chambers had endured, and it could even be argued that he was as innocent as any of his victims, but the undisputable fact remained: regardless of intent or blame, the beast had to be stopped at all costs.

Major Hawkins had first become involved after the initial attack at the clinic. The people there had done what they could to help Chambers, keeping him sedated and under observation while they searched for a way to reverse the effects of the accident and stop his body growing and distorting. And how had he repaid their kindness and concern? By killing more than thirty innocent people in a wild frenzy and reducing the entire facility to rubble. And then the cowardly bastard had gone into hiding until there were no longer any buildings big enough for him to hide inside.

The attack on Shrewsbury had ratcheted up the seriousness of the situation to another level, the sheer amount of damage and the number of needless deaths making it clear that destroying the freak quickly was of the upmost importance. This was a threat the likes of which had never been experienced before. Countless men, women and children had been needlessly massacred, their bodies crushed. The streets of the quaint market town had been filled with rubble and blood.

The Chambers creature had attacked without provocation, decimating Shrewsbury's historic buildings and killing hundreds of innocent bystanders. And when little remained of the place, it moved on and the destruction and bloodshed continued. They'd tracked the beast halfway across the country, following the trail of devastation left in its wake. The foul monstrosity had spared nothing and no one. Even livestock grazing in farmers' fields hadn't escaped. Hundreds of dismembered animal corpses lay scattered for miles around, many half-eaten.

But what was it doing now?

The creature, for all its incredible (and still increasing) size, had somehow managed to disappear. They knew it was close, but its exact location remained a mystery for now. There was no need to hunt it out; Hawkins was certain it would run out of places to hide and would have no option but to reveal itself eventually, and when it did his troops would be ready. They'd be resorting to Corman/Arkoff tactics to try and kill the creature: hitting it with everything they'd got, and firing until they'd either run out of missiles or the monster had been blown to hell and back. And then, if the dust settled and the hideous thing still managed to crawl out of the smoke and haze unscathed, they'd have to call in the big boys. A nuclear strike was an absolute last resort, but Hawkins knew the powers-that-be would sanction it if they had to (after all, it was less of a big deal from where they were sitting in their bunkers). Tens of thousands would die, maybe hundreds of thousands, but if the creature couldn't be stopped, what was the alternative? No one would be safe anywhere. In less than a week Glen Chambers had gone from a faceless nobody to being the greatest single threat to the survival of the human race. A hate-fuelled destroyer.

Major Hawkins distracted himself from worst-case-scenario thoughts of having to use battlefield nuclear weapons by recalling other B movie clichés, trying to find an alternative solution to the crisis. He almost laughed out loud when he considered the ridiculous and yet faintly possible notion that this thing might do a "King Kong" on him and head for higher ground. Imagine that, he thought, his mind swapping bi-planes and the Empire State Building for a squadron of Harrier jet fighters and the Blackpool tower...

'Sir!'

'What is it, McIver?' Hawkins asked quickly, concerned the young officer had caught him daydreaming.

'We've found it.'

The thing which had been Glen Chambers crouched in the shadows of the cave, shivering with cold, sobbing to himself as he hid from the rest of the world. He hurt, every stretched nerve and elongated muscle in his body aching with the pain of his ongoing mutation. He'd squashed his huge, still growing bulk into a space which was becoming tighter by the hour and he knew it wouldn't be long before he'd have to move. It was inevitable, but he wanted to stay here for as long as he was able. There had been helicopters flying around just now. They probably already knew where he was.

Earlier, just before he'd found this cave, he'd stopped to drink from a lake and had caught sight of his reflection in the water. What he'd seen staring back at him had been both heart-breaking and terrifying. In the movies, giants like him were just perfectly scaled up versions of normal people. Not him. Since the accident every part of his body had been constantly increasing in mass, but at wildly different rates. His skull was swollen and heavy now, almost the size of a small car, one eye twice the size of the other, bigger than a dinner plate. Clumps of hair had fallen out while other strands had grown lank and long and tough as wire. Glen had punched the water to make his grotesque reflection disappear, then had held up his fist and stared at it in disbelief; a distended, tumorous mass with a thumb twice the length of any of his fingers. And his skin! He hated more than anything what was happening to his skin. Its pigmentation remained, but it had become thick and coarse, almost elephantine, and the bulges of his massive body were now covered in sweat-filled folds and creases of flesh. The only thing, to his chagrin, which still seemed to function as it always had was his brain. It was ironic: physically he'd become something else entirely – unspeakably horrific – but inside he was still Glen. Horrifically deformed and impossibly sized, he now bore only the faintest physical similarity to the person he'd been just a few days ago and yet, emotionally, very little had changed. Same memories. Same attachments. Same pain.

Glen's vast stomach howled with hunger. He ate almost continually, but such was the speed of his rapid growth that his body was never completely satisfied. He reached down and with one hand picked up a sheep he'd killed, then bit it in half and forced himself to chew down, gagging on the bone and blood and wool in his mouth.

His arched back was beginning to press against the roof of the cave. Time to go before he became trapped. He crawled out into the afternoon rain and crouched there motionless. *I don't want to move*, he thought, *because when I move, people die. None of this is my fault, but I'm the one they'll blame.*

If there is a god, please let him bring an end to this nightmare.

Glen strode through the darkness on unsteady feet, feeling neither the cold nor the rain as he pushed on through the fields around the Malvern Hills. He'd spent a lot of time here before, good times before the bad with his ex-wife Della and her father, and being here again was unexpectedly painful. His stomach screamed for more food and he caught a bolting horse between his hands, snapping its neck with a flick of the wrist, then biting down and taking a chunk out of its muscled body. He hated the destruction he continued to cause, but what else could he do? And it was only going to get worse.

The effort of lifting his bulk and keeping moving was increasing and, for a while, he stopped and sat on the ground and rested against the side of British Camp, the largest of the hills, relieved that, for a short time at least, he wasn't the largest thing visible. The size of the hill allowed him to feel temporarily small and insignificant again.

Why had this happened to him?

Much as he'd tried to forget, he still vividly remembered every detail of the accident – the piercing light and those screaming, high-pitched radiation alarm sirens, then the disorientation when he'd first woken up in the clinic. It was like he'd been trapped in one of those old Quatermass movies his dad used to watch. But in those films the guy being quarantined had always been a hero – an astronaut or genius scientist – not anyone like him. He just cleaned the damn labs, for Christ's sake. He wasn't one of the scientists, he just worked for them.

They'd kept him pumped full of drugs for a time, trying to suppress the metamorphosis, studying him from a distance through windows and from behind one-way mirrors, none of them daring get too close. But there had come a time when the medicines and anaesthetics no longer had any effect and then the pain had been unbearable. He realized he'd outgrown the hospital bed and had crushed it under his massively increased weight. He was more than twice his normal size already, filling the room, and he'd become claustrophobic and had panicked. He wanted to ask to see his son, Ash, but his mouth suddenly didn't work the way it used to and words were hard to form. He tried to get up but there wasn't enough room to stand, and when he tried to open the window blinds and look out he instead punched his clumsy hand through the glass. The people behind the mirrors started screaming at him to stop and lie still, but that just made him even more afraid. He shoved at an outside wall until it collapsed, then scrambled out through the hole he'd made. He stood there in the early morning light, completely naked, almost four metres tall, and he fell when he first tried to run on legs of suddenly unequal length. They blocked his way with trucks, and he thought they were going to hurt him. He'd only wanted to move them out of his way but he'd overreacted and had killed several of the security men, not yet appreciating the disproportionate strength of his distended frame, popping their skulls like bubble-wrap.

He'd taken shelter in a derelict warehouse for a while as it was the only place he'd found large enough to hide inside. He lay on the floor, coiled around the inside of the building, and for a time he sat and listened to a homeless guy who, out of his mind with drink and drugs, had thought Glen was a hallucination. Now Glen leaned back against the hillside, crushing trees like twigs behind him, and remembered their one-sided conversation (he'd only been able to listen, not speak). Like the blind man in that old Frankenstein film, the drunk hadn't judged him or run from him in fear, but by the morning he was dead, crushed by Glen, who'd doubled in size in his sleep. Woken by the sounds of the warehouse being surrounded, he'd destroyed the building trying to escape and had literally stepped over the small military force which had been posted there to flush him out and recapture him. In the confusion of gunfire and brick-dust he stumbled away towards the town of Shrewsbury, another place he'd known well, avoiding the roads and following the meandering route of the River Severn across the land.

Christ, he bitterly regretted reaching that beautiful, historic place, and his swollen, racing heart sank when he remembered what had happened there. Still not used to his inordinate rate of growth (would he ever get used to it?) and the constantly changing dimensions of his disfigured body, he'd stumbled about like a drunk, every massive footstep causing more and more damage. He'd crashed into ancient buildings, demolishing them as he'd tried to avoid cars and pedestrians, unintentionally obliterating the places he'd known and loved with Della and Ash. He'd killed innocent people too as he tried to get away from the town to avoid causing more devastation, and their screams of terror had hurt more than anything else. He'd never intended for any of this to happen, but the final straw had been when he'd lifted his foot to step over what remained of a partially demolished row of houses and had seen a child's pram squashed flat on the pavement where he'd been standing. Had he killed the baby? He didn't wait to find out. Instead he loped off as quickly as he was able, his ears ringing with the sounds of mayhem he'd caused.

In the shadows of the hills, Glen lifted his heavy head towards the early evening sky and sobbed, the noise filling the air like thunder. *With every hour I am becoming less a man and more a monster*, he thought to himself. *I may not have long. If I'm going to do this, I have to do it now.*

They'd assumed he'd try and come back to this place eventually, that he'd want Della and the rest of her family to suffer as he had. It was the ideal location from which an attack could be launched on the creature – out in the middle of nowhere, away from centres of population – and a squadron of Hawkins' men had been deployed to take the monster out. They took up arms as the aberration's vast, lumbering shape appeared on the darkening horizon, still recognizably that of a man, but only just. Orders were screamed down the chain of command and a barrage of gunfire was launched as it approached. Bullets and mortars just bounced off its scaly skin, barely having any impact at all. Incensed, the creature destroyed many of its attackers and marched on, leaving the dead and dying scattered across the land.

And then, as the last rays of evening sunlight trickled across the world below him, it found what it had been looking for: Della's father's house. The beast strode towards the isolated building, ignoring the last few scurrying, ant-like men and women attacking and retreating under its feet. It swung a massive, clumsy hand at the waist-high roof of the house, brushing the slates, joists and supports away with a casual disregard, peering in through the dust and early evening gloom. And when it saw that the top floor was empty, it simply ripped that away too, taking the building apart layer by layer, kneeling on the roadside (crushing another eight men) and looking down into the building like it was a petulant child tearing apart a doll's house, looking for a lost toy.

They weren't there. The house was empty.

Disconsolate, Glen stood up and kicked what was

11

left of the building away, watching the debris scatter for more than a mile.

Way below him, a final few soldiers regrouped and launched another attack. They were the very least of his concerns now; irritating and unfortunate, nothing more. In temper he bent down and swept them away with a single swipe of his arm, then turned and marched onwards, immediately regretting their deaths but knowing he'd had no choice.

This was all Della's fault. If it hadn't been for her he'd never have been in this desperate position. Did she even realize that? Did she know she was to blame? Surely she must have had some inkling? If it hadn't been for them splitting up and making him sell the house, this would never have happened. If she'd just talked to him sooner, let him know how she was feeling, let him know how unhappy she was... She said he should have guessed, that she'd tried to tell him enough times, but what did she think he was, a bloody psychic?

It was Della's fault it had all gone wrong, and jumping into bed with her bloody therapist had been the final nail in the coffin, the full-stop at the end of the very last sentence of their relationship. But Glen accepted it had been his own bloody foolish pride which had subsequently exacerbated the situation. He'd wanted to do everything he possibly could to support his son, but when Cresswell earned more money in a month than he did in a year, he realized he'd made a rod for his own back. His pig-headed solution was to work harder and harder, to the point where money became his focus, not Ash. It wasn't Glen's fault he hadn't been blessed with the brains Anthony Cresswell had, or that he hadn't been fortunate enough to share the same privileged, silver spoon upbringing as the man who'd taken his place in Della's bed. Ash didn't even like him, he knew that for a fact. *He told me himself.*

Glen had been desperate to prove his worth and not let his son down, and that was why he'd agreed to take part in the trial (that and an undeniable desire to bulk himself up and become physically more of a man than he ever had been before – he'd certainly achieved that now). It was perfectly safe and legal, they'd told him as he signed the consent forms, a controlled trial of a new muscle-building compound for athletes. All the top performers will be using it this time next year, they'd said: twice the effect, a quarter the cost, completely undetectable and absolutely no risk... Maybe they'd been right about that, because he'd been taking it for a while and other than the weight gain and a little occasional morning nausea, there hadn't been any noticeable side-effects. It had almost certainly been the radiation from the accident which had caused the change – either that or a combination of the two. But even the accident had been Della's fault in part. If she hadn't got the courts involved and been so anal about the times he was supposed to pick Ash up and drop him back, then he wouldn't have been rushing to get his work finished on time, and he wouldn't have left the safety off when he was supposed to—

A sudden, piercing whoosh and a sharp stabbing pain interrupted his thoughts as a mortar wedged itself in a fold of leathery skin halfway down his bare back, then detonated. Glen howled with pain, his rumbling screams filling the air for miles around, shattering windows and causing panic.

Concentrate, he ordered himself, standing up as straight as he could and stretching back over his shoulder with an elongated arm, flicking away the remains of the missile with overgrown nails. Several more explosions echoed around his head – blasts which would have killed him before but which were now almost insignificant. He spiralled around, sweeping more military personel out of the way with one arm as if he was clearing them off a table, then he moved forward into the brief pocket of space and marched on. *What do I do now?* He tried to remember what happened next in the movies. Was this the point where they'd drop a nuke or something equally final on him? Try and gas him, perhaps? Should he just give up now or maybe head out into the sea and disappear like Godzilla? He wished an even bigger monster would appear on the horizon: his own Mothra or King Ghidorah, perhaps. He could fight them and defeat them and save the world and let Ash see that his daddy wasn't a freakish, evil creature now, that he was just misunderstood. He tried to imagine the fatherly monologue that fucker Cresswell might deliver to Ash tonight: 'Your father was once a good man, but good people sometimes turn bad, and he had to be destroyed...'

In the distance up ahead now lay the city of Birmingham – a grey scar covered in thousands of twinkling lights, buried deep in the midst of oceans of green – and he began to walk towards it, breaking into a lolloping, sloping run as he gradually picked up speed, his heart thumping too fast.

Home. I have to try and get home.

The city, he quickly decided, was his safest option – perhaps his only remaining option. Surrounded by millions of people, the military wouldn't dare risk using weapons of mass destruction on him there, and those same people would become hostages by default. His presence alone would be enough of a threat to force the authorities to do what he wanted.

The beast tore across the land, leaving a trail of deep, dinosaur-sized footsteps. In its shadow people scattered in fear, running for cover but knowing that nowhere was safe anymore. Distances which took them hours to cover could be cleared in minutes by the towering grotesque which loomed over all of them. And as it neared Birmingham and the density of the population around it increased, so did the level of carnage the creature caused. Knowing that the city was clearly a target, the authorities did everything they could to evacuate the panicking masses but getting away was impossible. In no time at all every major road was gridlocked, and the monster simply kicked its way through the unmoving traffic without a flicker of concern. It destroyed a reservoir in a fit of rage, stamping on a dam and flooding a heavily populated residential area. A hospital was demolished when the beast tripped and fell, hundreds of patients and staff killed in a heartbeat. Scores of schools, homes and other buildings were obliterated; untold numbers of people wiped out by the remorseless, blood-crazed behemoth.

They had managed to clear a section of the city centre but only partially. There were still people around, some fleeing in terror, others unaware of the approaching threat, just heading home from work. In a last-ditch attempt to divert the creature, Major Hawkins launched an aerial attack.

The first fighter planes raced towards their target and fired, their munitions barely even registering on the monster's calloused skin. More through luck than judgement, it flashed an enormous hand at one of the planes and caught its wing with the tips of its longest two fingers, sending it into a sudden, spiralling free fall from which it would never recover. The pilot ejected – too small for the behemoth to see or care about – and as his parachute opened, he drifted down behind the horrific man-monster, studying the stretches and folds and impossible angles of the abomination as he fell from the sky.

Several other jets met with a similar fate, as did a tank which was unwittingly crushed under the monster's foot like an empty can of drink. It continued towards the centre of the city, marching between massive office-blocks, at eye-level with their high roofs, knocking one of them over like it was made of Lego. How many people were still in there, Hawkins wondered from a distance. How many more are going to die?

An iconic shopping centre was destroyed in seconds, rubble raining down over the suburbs, severed electrical connections and small explosions lighting up the scene like camera flashes. A historic cathedral which had proudly stood for hundreds of years was wiped out in the blink of an eye. The destruction was apparently without end.

Hawkins readied himself to make the call he'd been dreading and consign the monster, the city and hundreds of thousands of people to a white-hot, nuclear fate. His mouth dry and his pulse racing, he watched the beast in the distance. Hawkins's soldiers stood their ground, nervously waiting for orders to engage despite knowing how ineffective their weapons would be. Some turned and ran, desperate to get away before either the aberration attacked them or they were wiped out by whatever godawful weapons the powers-that-be were forced to resort to using.

Hawkins paused when the creature's ex-wife burst into his command truck and demanded to speak to him. She argued the scientists and generals had failed to come up with anything useful, so he should hear her out before he did anything he'd regret. Goddammit, he thought as he listened to her, this was like the final scenes of one of those bloody B movies he couldn't get out of his head. 'Let me see him,' she'd pleaded. 'Maybe he'll still listen to me? Please just let me try.'

What harm could it do when so much had already been lost? It had to be worth a try. The intensity of the aberration's attacks was increasing, more lives being lost with every second. Hawkins options had reduced to zero.

Glen didn't know which way to turn. Where do I go now? He was still deep in the heart of the city and, to his horror, had levelled much of it. If he bent down and squinted into the confusion in the ruined streets below he could see the full extent of the damage he'd caused. He'd taken out a loan for a car six months ago so he could see Ash, and it had taken every spare penny he'd had. Today he'd destroyed thousands of vehicles – all of them belonging to someone like him. He'd demolished homes like the one he'd once shared with Della and Ash. And worst of all were the bodies. He hadn't wanted to hurt anyone. How would he have felt if this had happened to someone else and Ash had been killed in the fallout? Glen lifted his head and roared with pain, the volume of his pitiful cry shattering the last few remaining windows and causing more badly damaged buildings to collapse.

Let this be over.
My body hurts.
Please let this stop.

Surrounded by soldiers, Della walked through the parkland. Cresswell chased after her, dragging Ash behind him. The kid's tears were audible even over the sounds of fighting.

'You can't do this,' Cresswell protested. 'This is madness. Della, listen to me!'

'No, Anthony, *you* listen to *me*,' she said, turning back to face him. 'If there's anything of Glen left inside that thing, then I need to talk to him.'

'I won't let you.'

'You can't stop me.'

She turned and walked on, her armed guard forming a protective bubble around her, leading her out towards the expanse of grassland they were trying to direct the creature towards. She could see his outline in the distance now, a huge black shadow towering over the tombstone ruins of the city. High overhead a phalanx of helicopters flew out towards the monster in formation, each of them focusing a searchlight on the ground below. She waited nervously for them to return, wrapping her arms around herself to keep out the cold.

It happened with surprising speed and ease. The creature seemed to be distracted by the helicopters, and it immediately moved towards them, perhaps realizing that, as they hadn't attacked, their intentions were peaceful. Della's heart began to thump in time with its massive footsteps as it neared, and she caught her breath when it seemed to lose its footing for a moment. It lashed out and swatted one of the choppers like it was a nuisance fly, knocking it into its nearest neighbour and sending both of them spiralling to the ground in a ball-shaped mass of metal and swollen flame. How many people died just then, she wondered? How many more died when the wreckage hit the ground? How many people has Glen killed?

The aberration lumbered ever closer, clearly in view now, illuminated by the remaining helicopters which soared higher until they were beyond its massive reach. Della looked up at it in disbelief, stunned by its size and also by the fact that despite the huge level of deformation, she could still clearly see that it was Glen. Its enormous frame was grossly misshapen, but there was something about the shape of its mouth and the way it held its head that she recognized; the jaw line that both he and Ash had, the colour of those eyes...

When the creature saw the soldiers around its feet, it leaned down and roared. Della thought it sounded like a cry for help rather than an attacking scream, but the military clearly thought otherwise. One of the troopers nearest to her raised his rifle, and the monster picked him up between two enormous fingers and tossed him away. She watched the body fly through the air and hit a tree, then cringed when she heard a sharp cracking sound which was either the tree trunk or the soldier's bones. The monster roared again, this time with such force that she was blown off her feet. Another soldier rushed to help her up. She got to her feet and shook him off, then ran out towards the behemoth.

'Glen!' she yelled. 'Glen, it's me, Della.'

The aberration went to swipe her out of the way but stopped. It crouched precariously, lowered is huge head and stared at her. Then, after a pause of a few seconds which felt like forever, it crashed down onto its backside, the force of impact like an earthquake. Della's armed guard held back, more out of fear than anything else.

'I just want to know why, Glen,' Della said, still walking closer, not sure whether the thing could hear or understand her. 'All those people killed, and for what? I know you must have been scared, in pain even, but why...?'

The monster stared at her, eyes squinting, trying to focus, massive pupils dilating and constricting. Then it lifted its head to the skies and roared louder than ever.

A single figure ran through the trees. Cresswell raced towards Della and grabbed her. 'Come with me,' he said, trying to drag her away. 'That's not Glen any more. Damn thing can't understand you. Stay here and it'll kill you. You've got Ash and me to think about and —'

He stopped talking when he realized the gigantic creature was looking straight at him, glowering down. He backed away, cowering in fear, but there was no escape. A single massive hand wrapped around him and tightened, its grip so strong that every scrap of oxygen was forced from his body. The monster lifted him up and held its arm back as if it was about to throw the doctor into the distance.

'Dad! Dad, don't!'

Glen stopped.

Had he imagined Ash's voice? He pulled his distended arm back again, ready to hurl Cresswell out of his life forever. Out of all of their lives...

'No Dad, please.'

Glen looked down and saw his son standing in front of him, and suddenly nothing else mattered. He stretched out and dropped Cresswell more than half a kilometre away, far enough away not to have to think about him, then carefully moved Della and the remaining soldiers out of the way too.

Ash stood in front of his dad, completely alone and looking impossibly small.

'*Hello, big man,*' Glen wanted to say but couldn't. '*I'm sorry, Ash, I didn't mean for any of this to happen. I didn't want anyone to get hurt.*'

'You okay, Dad?'

'*Not really,*' he didn't say as he gently picked his son up and held him up to his face. Ash sat down cross-legged on the palm of his father's hand.

'I've been really worried about you.'

'*Me too, Ash.*'

'They've been saying all kinds of things about you,' Ash said, pausing to choose his next words carefully. Glen's heart seemed to pause too. 'But I don't believe them. I mean, I know you *are* a monster now, anyone can see that, but I know you didn't want to be one. I don't think you wanted to hurt any of them. I kept trying to tell the man that you didn't mean for any of it to happen. I told him to try and imagine how you must be feeling. You're big and strong and everything, but I bet you're scared.'

'*I am.*'

'I said they should leave you alone. I said they should find you somewhere safe to rest, maybe build you the biggest house in the world, something like that, then let the doctors work out how they're going to get you back to normal again.'

'*I don't think that's going to happen, sunshine. I think it's too late now.*'

'I miss you, Dad. I've been really scared.'

'*I've missed you too.*'

'They said you were coming back here to kill everyone, and I told them that was rubbish. I said you were coming to see me. Was I right, Dad?'

'*You were right, son. I just wanted to see you again. Just one last time...*'

Glen Chambers sat in the park with his son in his hand and he listened to Ash talking until his massively engorged, broken heart could no longer keep him alive.

THE DEAL

I have no idea where this horrible, seedy little story came from. Every now and then you get a germ of an idea that implants itself into your brain and won't go anywhere until it's finished. That's what happened with **The Deal**. It started as a *what if*, and became something I didn't expect at all.

I used to give this story away to prospective new readers. With hindsight, it probably put a lot of people off!

I must be out of my mind. I never thought it would come to this. I mean, I knew I was in trouble, that I had to do *something*, but this is like something out of one of those shitty made-for-TV crime movies. I'm seven floors up in an otherwise empty high-rise that'll be rubble less than a month from now, and I don't know what the hell I'm doing here.

The waiting is endless. All this space and silence gives me too much time to think.

This isn't fair. It's not my fault, it's just how I am. It's all about perspective, that's what I keep telling myself. What turns one person on might repulse another. You can't choose your kink, but by God I wish you could. Maybe then I'd have found something that wasn't such a taboo, something that wasn't so likely to get me locked up. If she hadn't found out what I like then I wouldn't be in this fucking mess right now, she wouldn't have any hold over me and I could have just kicked her out. And what pisses me off most of all is the fact that she's been sleeping her way through the male population of the city for the last few years and no one gives a damn. *She's* the one who cheated on *me*.

I've done nothing. I don't hurt anyone. I keep myself to myself. I just look at pictures.

I tell myself I'm a frigging idiot and I should get out of this place before it's too late, but I'm out of time. He's here. I hear footsteps right behind me.

I smell him before I see him.

I go to turn around, but he reaches out a hand lightning fast and grabs the back of my neck, stopping me from moving. 'Don't look at me,' he hisses. 'Don't you fucking look at me. You don't need to see who I am. Understand?'

I whimper. *I fucking whimper.* A fifty-two-year-old man whimpering like a fucking baby. It's pathetic, but I do what he says. I don't argue and I don't turn around.

Why am I putting myself through this?

I should have just walked away when she found out, should have thrown in the towel and admitted defeat. I could have gone to Thailand or somewhere like that... could have disappeared. But now it's too late because he's here and contact has been made. I try to look at his reflection in the cracked window but he's directly behind me and I see nothing. He knows exactly what he's doing. I can smell him, hear him, feel him, but I can't bloody see him.

And Jesus Christ, he smells so bad. It's a grubby, unwashed stench: booze and bad breath and frequent whiffs of worse things... he makes me want to heave. I swallow down bile and try to compose myself. 'I'm sorry, I didn't think, I just—'

'I don't want your apologies,' he says, his mouth against my ear, 'I just want you to do exactly what I say. Follow my rules and I'll do your job for you, screw up and you're on your own. It's that simple.'

'I understand.'

'You'd better. The fact we're having this conversation at all tells me you're already in a shit-load of trouble. Pissing me off is only going to make things far worse.'

I keep telling myself to stay calm, but all I want to do is turn and run from this vile bastard and not look back. I'll go to the house, grab some things then disappear into the night like I should have when she first found out. But I know I can't. It's too late now. He won't let me. He's a killer. A *hitman*. Christ, it even sounds stupid, like something out of a third-rate crime novel. Is this really worth the risk? Does Moira deserve to die? That's debatable, but she's backed me into a corner and taken away all my other options. If she tells anyone what she knows about the things I like to do, my life's as good as over.

I've heard what they do to people like me in prison.

'So who is it?' he asks.

'My wife.'

'You don't say. Now there's a surprise. Been cheating on you, has she?'

'Pretty much constantly for the last ten years, but that's not the problem.'

'I didn't think it would be. So why get in touch with me now? Tell me the full story.'

'Why do you need to know?'

'Because I need to be sure you're serious. I need to know you're as desperate as you seem. This is a risk for both of us. I need to know you've got as much at stake as I have, as much to lose.'

'Believe me, I have. She... she knows things about me.'

'What kind of things?'

'Things I've done.'

'Business deals?'

'No, more personal than that. The kind of things I like...'

It's hard talking about this stuff – about my acquired tastes – even when I'm on my own in the house, chatting online with like-minded people. Tonight, though, it's nigh on impossible. When I don't immediately give him an answer, he starts taking random pot-shots. 'I'm guessing it's either kids or animals,' he says wearily. 'It's usually one or the other. Sometimes both.'

'Both?'

'Don't sound so righteous. You're in no position to judge.'

'She's got evidence...' I start to explain, telling him as little as possible, neither confirming or denying.

'And if that evidence was to come out...'

'I'd be screwed.'

'Job gone, house gone, wife gone, cash gone, freedom

gone. Straight to the slammer for you, you dirty little pervert.'

'That's about it.'

'So why haven't you just done a runner?'

'What, and leave her with everything? Do you have any idea what I'm worth?'

'I do, actually. I knew money would come into this somewhere, it usually does. It's the root of all evil, you know.'

'Is that right?'

He just laughs, and finally relaxes his grip on the back of my neck. 'Okay, okay... I get the picture. I know where you're coming from. Perversion's in the eye of the beholder, I say. One man's meat is another man's murder, and all that bullshit.'

'Exactly.'

'Well, friend,' he says, his sudden unexpected and unwelcome familiarity making my skin crawl, 'you're in good company. We're both in the same boat, to a certain extent. If people knew how I get my thrills they wouldn't be too happy.'

'And why's that?'

'Doesn't take a genius to work it out, does it? Let's just say I enjoy my work. Probably a little more than I should do.'

Shit, is he into necrophilia? Will he want to have sex with Moira after he's killed her? I almost laugh out loud at the prospect of that. Good luck to him. Who am I to judge? For all I know, my particular quirks might still rank higher up the deviance league table than his. Is screwing a corpse more socially acceptable than —

'Okay,' he says, derailing my bizarre train of thought, 'here's the deal.' The tone of his voice has changed again. This is deadly serious. He means business. 'Fact is I get off on killing. Can't tell you why or how it started, but that's how it is. There's something about doing someone in that drives me fucking wild. This is more of a hobby than a job for me, so I'm more than happy to help you out with your little problem. Now I've made a few enquiries and I know a fair bit about you and your situation and, even more importantly, I know you know nothing about me. I know you can afford my fee and I know you wouldn't be here unless you didn't have any other option, so all you need to do is agree to my terms and we'll get the ball rolling.'

'Your terms?' I ask, my throat dry and my voice barely audible. 'I thought I was just supposed to pay you in cash. I didn't know there were terms and conditions.'

'There are always terms and conditions,' he says, then he pauses ominously. 'Bit embarrassing, really,' he explains, sounding sheepish now, like I've caught him playing with himself. 'I have superstitions. I'm a little bit OCD, I think.'

'Superstitions?'

'Just a couple. Nothing too weird in the overall scheme of things.'

'Go on.'

'I only kill when I'm specifically asked to.'

'Okay.'

'And I only kill in pairs.'

All I hear is his second point. 'You only kill in pairs?'

Alarm bells are ringing again. Fucker's going to kill me too once he's got rid of Moira. I try to make a run for it but he anticipates and, anyway, he's far faster and far stronger than me. He shoves me up against the dirty glass and now I can't move.

'It's really not what you're thinking. I don't like odd numbers. If you ask me to do a job, you have to ask me to kill two people.'

'But there's no one else I want dead.'

29

'You don't have to name them, you prick, just tell me to do it. Look, I'm sorry, but this is just how it is. Some people can't stop messing with light switches or washing their hands, others won't step on the cracks in the pavement. Me, I get freaked out when I've killed an odd number of people. It's two or none, that's the rule.'

'You're talking about me, aren't you? Makes sense – take me out and there's less chance of anyone linking back to you. Forget it. Deal's off. This is bullshit. I should have—'

'Calm down and take it easy, sunshine,' he says, leaning up against me, his face too close for comfort, suffocating me with his halitosis. 'I've really got to come up with a better way of selling this to clients,' he mumbles to himself. 'Look, it won't be you, right? I'll find the second victim for myself, I just need your permission to kill them, okay?'

'My permission?'

'Just tell me I can do it,' he yells, getting frustrated. His sudden anger makes my bladder weaken. 'All you need to know is it'll be someone you don't know. Someone you've never had any connection with. Someone who doesn't mean anything to you...'

'But I don't understand.'

He shoves me against the window again, my face pressed so hard against the cold glass I think it's going to give.

'It turns me on, okay? We all have our little quirks, don't we? Some littler than others, if you know what I'm saying. Well this is mine. You want one killing, but you have to order me to do two. Buy one, get one free. There'll be no repercussions for you, I swear. You won't know anything about it. Your only link to the killing will be me, and believe me, I'm not about to go public. I've got as much to lose as you have, probably more.'

He eases off, releases the pressure, steps away.

'I don't know about this...'

'You still married?' he asks.

'Just about.'

'Is she insured? You still paying the premiums? I'll make it look like an accident. You could come out of this with a profit.'

'Everyone's a winner.'

'Everyone but your missus,' he says ominously. Then he becomes quiet. Too quiet. 'Oh, and I forgot to say, I only kill on Mondays, that okay?'

'What? You're taking the piss...'

'You got me!' he laughs, filling this ruin of a place with his foul noise. 'Just kidding. Look, pal, I know this is a big deal for you. I expect you've never been involved in anything like this before and chances are you won't ever be again. Your life must be a real fucking mess because when people call for me, I know they've hit absolute rock bottom. I understand. I get it, I really do. Been there, done that, got the T-shirt. I know what you're going through, so I'm gonna make this easy on you. I'm leaving now. If you want, you can do the same and you'll never hear from me again. But if you decide you do want my help, come back to this place before the weekend and leave me a sign.'

'What kind of sign?'

'I don't know, use your imagination. Write something on the walls. Leave the cash here, too.'

I'm in a no-win situation. My options feel like they're reducing by the second. I can either trust this sick bastard – and I've never felt like trusting anyone *less* – or I can hope Moira keeps her mouth shut, but we both know that's not going to happen. Which is the lesser of these two evils? I stare out into the night through the grubby window and try to make sense of the chaotic thoughts filling my head.

'Okay,' I tell him. 'I'll be back before the weekend.'

He doesn't answer. I turn around to look for him but the sly fucker's already long gone, disappeared into the darkness.

Fuck it, I need a drink. I stop at a bar on the way home, trying to work out what the hell I should do. I could always just disappear, I tell myself again for about the hundredth time tonight. Maybe I could fake my own death? Neither option is definite enough. There's always a chance I'll be found, and I don't want to spend the rest of my days constantly looking over my shoulder. I've been doing enough of that as it is.

I want Moira dead. That much is certain. I don't trust her and I can't pay her off. I need her gone.

There are too many people in this bar. It's packed and I find myself looking from face to face to face, staring at each of them, hoping I won't see anyone I recognise or that anyone recognises me. I don't, of course, and that makes me feel a little better. I've never been here before, probably won't come here again, and for a few precious minutes I'm anonymous; innocent and free. I'm right in the middle of everything that's happening but strangely disconnected from it all.

See that woman on her own over there? Who is she? Why's she here? Why's she on her own? Is she waiting for someone? Has she been stood up? Does she live alone? Is there anyone waiting for her at home tonight? If she never made it back, would anyone notice? Is she the one the hitman's going to kill if I ask him to do the job? Should I even give a shit? If she knew what got me into the mess I'm in, she'd be disgusted, but who's to say any of the other fuckers in here are any better? Who knows what goes on behind closed doors. There are tattooed freaks in here, others who look like alcoholics and addicts. In this bar there could be rapists, gang bosses, traffickers, perverts who make me look like an angel... in comparison to this lot, I'm not hurting anyone.

All I do is look at pictures on a screen.

The bitch has got me by the balls. She's turfed me out of the house now and she says she's going to the police. I know she'll do it soon if I don't take control of the situation. I'll give her her due, sometimes Moira's business sense is almost as good as mine. She's biding her time, waiting for the right moment to strike and make the optimum profit. She's doing everything to maximise the damage and get the most out of me she can before my inevitable fall from grace.

I need to stop this.

I need to take action.

I went back to the ruined high-rise this afternoon, straight from the solicitor's office. The bitch really got to me today, really got under my skin. I made myself do it while I was still angry, before I'd had a chance to calm down and talk myself out of it. I climbed the stairs back up to the seventh floor, left the cash where he told me, then spray painted a message on the wall that no fucker could miss.

Nothing.

Two weeks waiting. Two weeks of silence from him and non-stop grief from her.

I'd managed to convince myself that I'd been fucked over again, either that the hitman was someone Moira had paid to set me up, or that the meeting had never happened in the first place. Had it just been a deluded, drink-fuelled fantasy? I was on the verge of giving in when everything changed.

I was starting to think I should just pay her off and damn the consequences. I'd agree to the divorce and all her terms and if she still went to the police, I'd decided I'd go kicking and screaming. I'd tell them she knew everything. I'd tell them she helped me feed my various unsavoury habits and implicate her somehow. But all that's academic now, because everything changed today.

He's done it. *She's dead.*

A police officer knocked on the door an hour or so ago, and if I hadn't been so numb with panic I'd have probably tried to make a run for it. I thought he'd come for me, that she'd told them everything, but I could tell from the way he approached me – submissive body language, voice low – that wasn't the reason he was here. He asked if he could have a word, that he was sorry but he had some terrible news, and when he asked me to sit down it was all I could do not to jump up and punch the air. I knew what was coming next. The hardest part was pretending I gave a shit. I just sat there, head bowed, looking down at the carpet, biting my lip to stop myself grinning.

'How?' was the only question I could ask.

'The investigation's still on-going,' he explained, running through the usual disclaimers, 'but on the face of it, it looks like it was a tragic accident. It's going to take a while to piece things together, but it seems her car got stuck on a level crossing. There was no one else about. Seems your wife was trying to get it moved when the train hit. If it's any consolation, she died instantly...'

That was no consolation at all, actually. I wanted her to suffer. It was a struggle to hide my emotions. I could have kissed the police officer (but that's really not my thing).

In the two months since Moira died I've experienced every emotion imaginable. Relief, guilt, paranoia, unadulterated joy, loneliness, regret, sorrow... even now, almost eight weeks on, and the way I feel about her continues to change virtually by the hour. We had some good times before the bad. I miss the woman I originally fell in love with, but we both changed. I know what I had done to her was wrong, but she didn't leave me with any choice. She could have just walked away – I'd have seen her okay, truly I would – but she took away all my other options and left me with only one. Now she's gone the constant fear and uncertainty I've been struggling with for months has finally lifted, but I don't feel good about what I did.

The coroner's verdict was that her death was accidental. Credit where credit's due, my "friend" knew exactly what he was doing. He covered his tracks impeccably and left nothing to chance. But then again, that's something else we have in common. When your personal tastes aren't socially acceptable, you do whatever needs doing to be discrete and keep things hidden. Who knows, if I'd been as thorough as him in the first place, maybe I'd have avoided all this mess?

There's no evidence of the hitman left at all now. Even the derelict flats where I met him have gone, demolished along with every trace of our meeting and agreement. I'm glad. If I never see him again it'll be too soon.

But the guilt's still there. I have to keep reminding myself what Moira could have done. She'd had the power to destroy me on every level with just a few words whispered to the wrong people. I tell myself daily that I did what I had to do and that, in her own way, she was every bit as bad as me (albeit in a far more socially acceptable way). She fucked scores of men in my bed and showered them with my money. My liaisons, on the other hand, were all virtual. And I just paid for access to the pictures and videos I wanted, I didn't even take them, didn't meet anyone.

I need to get over this and accept, once and for all, that she got what she deserved.

It's odd, though, I'm actually beginning to feel more remorse over the hitman's other killing now, the one I was forced to sanction. Some days I feel the guilt growing inside me like a cancer. I keep telling myself that nobody's perfect, and chances are whoever he killed was as flawed as me in one way or another, maybe even more so. In this sordid, shitty little world we live in, you're hard pushed to find anyone who is completely, genuinely, one hundred per cent pure. We're all as bad as each other. Our so-called society breeds deviance and corruption like a disease, encourages it even. For fuck's sake, you can get whatever filth you like pumped directly into your home via the 'net. Kids in their bedrooms can get hold of worse stuff than I've watched with just a few clicks of the mouse.

In public I'm playing the grieving ex-husband, and I'll continue to do so until people stop watching me, until they stop checking I'm okay and asking how I'm coping. They mean well, but I could do without their offers of support. When I need a shoulder to cry on, I'll pay for one.

It's late. I light a cigarette and slump back in my seat. A perfect evening draws to a close: some 'me' time in front of the computer with a few drinks and no interruptions. I sink into the chair and relax. My eyelids are getting heavy.

There's a sudden sharp stinging pain in the side of my neck. I go to slap the bug or whatever it is away but I can't. My arms are heavy and I can't feel my hands. Can't even move them now. I try to get up but I can't move. Whole body frozen. What the fuck...?

I smell him before I see him.

It's the same foul reek I remember from before, filling my nostrils, and I know it's him. His stench is indescribable but also instantly recognisable. I manage to move my head slightly but it locks mid-turn like rusted machinery. I can see him moving out of the corner of my eye. He takes a couple of steps forward until he's in full view and he grins at me. It's the first time I've seen him properly and I physically can't look away. There's no doubt it's him. And weirdly, the thing I feel most of all is disappointment. He's so *ordinary*, so unexpectedly unimportant-looking. He's no different to me. You'd struggle to pick either of us out in a crowd. My head droops down slightly and I can't lift it back up. I'm left staring at his crotch. Sick bastard has a hard-on.

'Good evening,' he says. 'How are you? It's been a while.'

I try to talk but my mouth has seized. Some sound comes out. Single words at a time. 'What... doing...?'

'What am I doing here? Do you really have to ask? I'm finishing a job.'

'But...'

'Haven't you worked it out yet?' he continues, slipping his hand down the front of his trousers and starting to feel himself up. 'I was very careful to explain it all at the outset. Remember what I told you?'

He crouches down so we're at eye level. Wish I could look away but my eyes won't move. Can't even blink now.

'You... said...' I start to say, every word an effort, having to work hard to make any noise.

'I'll remind you,' he says, catching my cigarette as it falls from my frozen fingers. He takes a long drag, his hard cock gripped tight with his other hand. He pauses for a second and stops wanking, almost losing control. 'You'll have to excuse me, I fucking love this.'

'Why... here...?'

'I told you I only kill in twos, and I said I only kill when someone asks me to do it. It's a bit weird, I know, but that's just how I roll. You should know better than most, my friend, you can't control what gets you horny!'

I suck in more air, forcing my jaw to move again, managing to spit out a few more words. 'You... said... not... me...'

'And that's exactly right,' he says. He grins as he leans closer, my cigarette between his teeth. He knocks my drink off the table next to the chair and onto my lap with his free hand. The whiskey soaks my clothes, but I can't feel it. The bottle rolls off the table and hits the floor. 'I killed your wife and some other loser, just like you asked.'

'Then... why... you... here...?'

'Oh, I'm on another job now,' he says, as he lets the cigarette fall from his lips. He grins and rocks back on his heels. I see wisps of smoke, then the flicker of the first few blue flames, almost invisible. He pulls my head up, then steps back as the fire takes hold. He's watching me as he's jerking off, face screwed up with concentration. 'The guy who asked me to do this job was a lot like you, actually. Desperate, self-obsessed, completely broken. You're someone else's murder number two now, my friend. He didn't know you. Didn't know anything about you. You mean nothing to him, and he means nothing to you. Sound familiar? Don't worry, though, I'll get to him eventually. That's the deal.'

THE LUCKY ONES

I remember taking the kids on holiday to Wales one summer. We'd spent a long, idyllic sunny day on the beach: blue sky, hot sun, beautiful countryside. Then we drove a few miles down the coast and reached Port Talbot, site of the one of the biggest steelworks in the world. The contrast between the landscape we'd driven through and the industrial works we found was vivid and startling, and that set me thinking... what if the steelworks was all that was left? What if the factory – which, perched on the shore, looks to all intents and purposes like an oily, self-contained city in itself – outlasted everything else? I was approached to write a story for a collection called **Dead Water**, and I immediately thought back to my trip to Port Talbot. So the location was set, and a lesson from an operations management course I'd been on years earlier (honest!) helped me with the world building. From all this came the story of **The Lucky Ones** – a group of people left behind after the end of everything.

Villiam is one of the lucky ones. He knows this, because his mother tells him so, several times every day. One of the old men told him too, that time he dared to question. The old man hit him across the face, bloodied his nose. 'You're safe, you're warm, you're alive,' he shouted at William when they caught him trying to get away. 'Things don't get better than that anymore.'

But William's not so sure.

The factory is home. It's a man-made island; a mass of concrete walls and metal pipework, surrounded by water on all sides. The acidic seawater is devoid of all life. Toxic. Poison. It isolates them from everything else, leaves them vulnerable and exposed.

This place used to be an immense steel production facility, connected to the mainland by road and rail. Not anymore. Not for a long time. All connections to the land have been permanently severed.

The factory itself used to be many times this size, once employing more people than are probably left alive in total now. Now the last vestiges of industrial activity are confined to one end of the complex, with the remains of the isolated population eating, sleeping, learning and living alongside the furnace, the chimneys, the exhaust fumes and noise.

The decline began when war broke out, so long ago that the reasons for the fighting have been all but forgotten. Our brave men and women are still out there, though, risking their lives on foreign, polluted shores, battling to preserve the freedom of those who keep the factory fires burning. William's most recent letter from his father, received only last week, said his division had secured an important tactical advantage in the preceding days, and that the end of the fighting would almost certainly soon be in sight.

It's a funny old beast, this place; a safe and reassuring home, yet with all the restrictions and inflexibility of a prison. William's teacher used to always use the word *symbiotic* to describe it. *The factory needs its people, and the people need their factory,* she used to say, and she was right. *You can't have one without the other.* For years the people have kept the furnaces lit and stoked, and in return the factory has kept them warm and dry, safe from what the rest of the world has become.

But William is still not convinced, no matter what they tell him. He longs to be like his father. He wants to fight alongside his old dad in the trenches and on those muddy, contaminated, battlefields so very far from here. He's worried that at this rate the war might be over before he gets called up. He has no photographs of Father, just a memory which gets a little less defined each day, almost a memory of a memory now. He longs to see him again. William thinks if he was out there fighting too then maybe, just maybe, the war might end a little sooner and both he and Father could come home to the factory together. The cabin he shares with Mother is coffin-tight, but he'd willingly give up the little space he has to be able to share it with Dad once more. Father's letters from the frontline are regular, but it's just not the same, is it?

The old men tell them very little. They frequently disappear off across the oily sea on their boats, vanishing into the acrid smog, then return again days later, bringing back with them enough food and water for the people, and enough fuel and metal for the factory. There's never any real news. *Our soldiers are making great gains,* is usually the limit of their grudging, moribund updates. *All we can do is keep doing what we're doing. Keep producing the weapons casings. Our loved ones won't thank us if the bullets run dry mid-battle, will they?*

William is feeling particularly frustrated this morning.

Today the grease and oil and the heat and the smell of the factory are getting to him more than usual. It doesn't help that Frank, the lad he's working with, won't shut up. Frank's mother has gone to fight, called up unexpectedly last month, and he's almost gloating. 'I'm so proud of her, Will,' he says. 'Can't wait 'til she writes. Hey, maybe she'll be stationed with your dad. Imagine that, eh? You and me working next to each other here, and our parents fighting together overseas.'

'Yeah, just imagine it,' William says, sounding as dejected as he feels.

'What's the matter, Will?'

How much does he tell him? It's tempting to let rip, to get it all off his chest, but he knows Frank doesn't deserve it. He wouldn't understand. More importantly, he also knows that Frank will go running straight to one of the old men and tell, and that's a boat-load of hassle Will could well do without. But William can't just sit there in silence and keep it all bottled up much longer. He remembers Father talking to him once when he was little. He'd been getting angry about something stupid, and Dad had told him he had to let it out, not keep it in. *Imagine if the factory didn't have chimneys*, Dad had said. *All those fumes building up inside with nowhere to go...*

'Don't you ever wonder what it would be like to be somewhere else?'

'All the time,' Frank answers quickly. 'I hope to find out when I'm called up. That's unless the war ends before then, of course.' He pauses, then asks 'Why?'

'I'm just missing my dad, I think.'

'How long's he been away?'

'Eight years.'

'Mother's only just gone. Can't wait to hear from her.'

'Wouldn't you rather she was still here?'

'I'd like to see her, if that's what you mean. She never

43

said goodbye. But if she can help win us our freedom, then that has to be for the best, doesn't it?'

'Do you think things will be any different when the war's won?'

Frank doesn't answer this time. He pretends he can't hear over the mechanical clatter.

William knows there's no point prolonging the conversation any further. Frank just doesn't get it. None of the others do. Part of him wishes he could be like them and just accept everything without question, but it's hard and getting harder. When he goes to class, William likes to look at the history books. He sees pictures of cavemen and Romans and the Victorians, and he can't help thinking how, back then, things always seemed to be getting better as the years rolled by, how everything steadily improved, how people learned more and experimented more and achieved more... So why aren't things getting any better anymore? He's going to be seventeen in a few weeks' time. He can remember being seven, before Dad went off to fight, and everything was exactly the same back then: the same jobs, the same places, the same faces, albeit less wrinkled and tired.

William tried to get away once, that time the old men caught him. He tried to hide on one of their boats when he was just a kid, but they found him and they beat him for his troubles. 'You'll have your chance,' the oldest of them told him. 'Don't wish these years away.'

Easy to say, not so easy to do when you're up to your elbows in sweat and grease for eight hours a day, six days a week.

There's one positive thing about today, and that's that when you work hard like this, the time goes fast. It's not long before William's home again. He spends a little time talking with Mother when she gets back from her work, then they go down to eat together. The food is simple and bland but it does the trick. Stomachs full, they go home via the small library and take out one of their favourite books each. They spend the evening in their quarters together, both lost in the pages.

Another morning, another shift.

Frank's on a day off today, and William thinks that's a good thing, because the other kid's sunny disposition has been doing his bloody head in all week. William puts on his ear protectors and the safety goggles which slip, then starts his machine. *Thump – thump - thump...* it's easy to get lost in the rhythmic pounding of the old contraption, turning thin-rolled sheets of metal into casings for the bullets and shells our men and women will fire at the enemy. He watches the casings drop into the crate and wonders how far each of them will travel. How many thousands of miles will the ammunition he makes be sent before it's used? Who might his bullets kill? Might he have already milled the shell which takes out the leader of the opposition and brings the enemy to its knees?

Despite all the noise and the heat and the pressure, you can tell straight away when things aren't right. Everything is so routine, so precise, so regimented, that the unexpected silence when something falls out of line is somehow louder than the forge or the rolling machines, or even the heaviest press on the shop floor. And William knows something big has just happened not far away.

The uneasy quiet spreads. It's like the wind has gusted the sound out of this cavernous place.

Then, the chaos.

Lights flash and klaxons blare. An accident, it has to be, either that or a machine failure. A risk to production is as serious as a risk to health around here. William stops his machine and takes a step back into the shadows, trying to work out what's going on. A hiss of high-pressure steam both deafens and blinds him temporarily, and when the rest of the shift is ordered out, he misses the signal. He's wrong-footed and confused and he remains exactly where he is, crouched down small in the dark, invisible and overlooked.

Incidents like this happen regularly. Not every day regularly, but often enough. It's become a well-rehearsed routine, and the place is cleared in a matter of minutes. The old men in the control room kill the alarms and seal the doors, and William realises he's trapped where he shouldn't be. And that feels good.

He creeps forward, still sticking to the shadows, hiding in plain sight. And now he can better see what's happened. A broken tool, it looks like. Something has snapped or severed and has flown off a machine like a bullet. It's hit John Champion. William can see the metal bit sticking up out of his chest, and he can also see that he's not moving. *Blimey... John Champion's dead. The place won't be the same without him,* William thinks. *He's been here forever.*

William definitely shouldn't be here now, but he doesn't think he'll be able to get away without being seen and getting into serious trouble for not following procedures. His mind starts to race. With just John Champion's corpse for company, he starts to wonder if this might be the lucky break he's been waiting for. In the factory, when a door shuts like this, you don't see what's happening until the old men open it again. But he's on the wrong side of the closed door today. Without even trying, he's been given a chance to break free from the shackles of his daily routine. Even if it's only for a few minutes, even if he only gets to see one or two things he hasn't seen before, it's got to be worth taking that chance, hasn't it?

Maybe not.

Nothing happens, and his excitement turns to boredom.

No one's going to miss him. His shift's over now, and Mother's is just beginning at her station elsewhere. He could stay here all night and she wouldn't even know he hadn't been home. But as minutes turn to hours, even the seconds start to drag. He inches ever closer to dead John Champion. His injury is horrible. William has to swallow bile. The broken bit has ripped a diagonal gash down the poor bugger's front, leaving everything open and on view. William remembers his biology classes and tries to work out what's what inside of Champion, but it's all red and brown and mushy and slimy and he can't make anything out. It makes him wonder if the stuff they showed him in those biology books in class was right.

It might be an hour later, maybe as long as two, but the factory door finally opens again, wide enough for a couple of the old men to enter. They're pushing a stretcher on a trolley between them and they barely speak, only to curse each other when one pushes too hard or the other snags a wheel. They stop a short distance from where William is crouched, next to dead John Champion. They talk in voices too low for William to be able to make out. Something distracts them momentarily – the broken machine, it looks like – and almost before William realises what he's doing, he's already done it. He crawls across the grated factory floor on his hands and knees and gets underneath the gurney, hidden from view by an oily-smelling sheet.

William hears grunts and groans of effort as the two old men pick up John Champion's body and lay it on the stretcher. They start to push the trolley away. 'True what they say,' he hears one of them tell the other, 'dead men weigh twice as much as them what's still breathing.' And it's all William can do not to laugh out loud.

The stretcher is wheeled down corridors William doesn't recognise. He can't see much, but he knows from the direction they've taken that they're heading into a part of the factory he hasn't been to before. It's exciting and frightening in equal measure. William thinks he should maybe get off the trolley before it's too late, but the thought of the beating he'll get from the old men keeps him where he is. Besides, when is he going to get another chance like this to explore? *In for a penny, in for a pound*, he remembers his dad saying once. He wasn't sure what it meant at the time, but he thinks he gets it now.

They leave the stretcher in a large, echoing space. When the old voices fade, William risks peeking out. He definitely doesn't know this place. It's like the shop floor where he works, but without any machines. That's not to say it's empty, though. There are crates and crates and more crates. They must be full of the munitions the people have made.

William's left here for hours. Cramp in his legs forces him to move eventually. He walks around, trying to get the feeling back, but doesn't dare touch anything. He hears someone coming, and so looks for somewhere to hide. Underneath the trolley is too open and prone. Instead he gets into one of the crates that's still half-empty, covering himself in bullet casings. He's scared. The familiar smell of the metal helps him stay calm.

And as the old men return, William knows he's done something here which will prove to either be the best thing ever, or equally possibly, the gravest miscalculation he'll ever make. Whatever happens, his choice has been made. *Your die has been cast*, was another of Father's sayings which rattles around his head.

He doesn't need to see to know what's happening

now.

All of the crates – including the one he's hiding in – are being moved. Wheeled down a steep ramp.

A heavy door slides open, and suddenly everything changes. William immediately feels it, and he smells and tastes it too. He's outside. First time in years. It hurts his chest. And he knows the only reason they could be wheeling these crates down this particular ramp is to load them onto one of the boats.

And he knows he's escaped the factory.

And he knows it's too late to turn back.

For the first time in his life, the ground beneath his feet isn't solid. The boat rocks, deadly water lapping the hull just inches from where he's hiding.

But William's not scared now, not nervous. He feels *alive!*

He lies still for as long as he can, but his back and legs hurt. There are no voices here, just machine noise, and he gets up and looks around. He's in a sealed hold (he thinks that's what this part of a boat is called) and there are a series of small, grubby portholes on either side. Strange to have windows in a cargo hold, he thinks. Maybe this boat carried people once? Imagine that.

He presses his face up against the glass to look outside. It's not like when he looks out of the factory windows: here everything is that much closer, that much more dangerous. The dead water is like an oily sludge. Sometimes the boat seems to struggle through it as if it's fighting back. Sometimes it's black and viscous, like the gunk he wipes off his machine at the end of his shift. The water has a sweet, distinctive stench... catch a whiff of it and you're okay, but breathe in too deeply and you'll feel it burn. William can't take his eyes off it. From the factory windows the water always looked opaque, but down here he can see that it's not. It was a trick of the light. The polluted ocean is full of stuff... from dust-like grains of silt to other unrecognisable pieces of debris, larger lumps of who-knows-what. *A few seconds in that filthy mire*, he thinks, *and you've had it.*

He hasn't thought about it until now, but William wonders where the ship is going. He's always assumed there are other factories, other places, but it's not something people talk about. Will this journey last days or weeks? And now he's starting to worry and feel nervous again, because he hasn't thought this through. He doesn't have any food or anything to drink. If the boat sails for anything longer than a day or so then when they open the hold they'll find that John Champion isn't the only corpse they're carrying.

William sits in a corner and waits, because waiting is all he can do. He chews his nails nervously. The boat bobs up and down in the murk, and it's a totally alien movement which churns the emptiness of his stomach, making him want to throw up the little he's eaten today. He breathes in deeply, slowly... but not too deeply or slowly because between the rancid water and dead John Champion's body, it stinks in here.

A sudden change of direction.

The boat turns right – *is that starboard or port?* – and William lurches with it. A case of bullet shells is upended, its contents spilling everywhere. William resists the instinctive temptation to clean up. *Remember, you're not supposed to be here.* It's just that looking out for resources, protecting every last scrap of everything... that's second nature back home.

William scrambles across the hold to look outside. *Wow.* He's never seen anything like this before. He can see another factory like his out there, but this one is on land! He's only ever seen pictures of dry land before, but he's seeing it with his own eyes and it seems to go on and on and on forever... He knows he should hide again but he wants to keep looking. This place is as fascinating as it is frightening. It must be the place where they put the explosives in the bullets and shells, then where they ship them out from to the troops on the frontline. *Is this where the soldiers leave from? Did Father pass through here all those years ago?* And then the thought strikes him, *I might be able to join the fighting!*

It's difficult to comprehend just how much things have changed in the last few hours, how much his world has changed. When he woke up and went to work it felt like just any other shift, but *everything* is different now. He's on the verge of something huge here, he knows it, the beginning of a great adventure. A life filled with action, excitement and reward, not just grease and grime and machine parts. Maybe, just maybe, he'll find out where Father's been stationed and he'll be able to get himself sent there too? Imagine that! He knows his mother will be upset and worried initially, but a letter home will help. He'll write to her as soon as he's able. Goodness, imagine the pride Mother would feel if she received a letter from him *and* Father? He wishes he could be there to see her face when she opened that!

The boat lurches again, in the opposite direction this time, then it stops. It turns a tight circle in a stagnant harbour, then he hears the engine noise change as it's thrown into reverse. William pushes his face hard against another grubby porthole, and he catches a glimpse of another ramp behind the boat before it disappears from view. This must be it. They must have arrived. Strange, he always thought it would have taken much longer to get anywhere. William hides himself away in the half-empty crate again, his heart thumping with excitement.

But one thought strikes him while he's waiting... why has this been so easy? He hopes security will be tighter when they disembark (he thinks that's the right term). What if he was one of the enemy? The damage he could do just doesn't bear thinking about.

The crate he's in is transferred from the ship to the shore and soon William risks getting out again. This must be the largest room he's ever seen. There are many crates and boxes, separated out into many different areas. And through large windows he can see into other parts of the complex. Whatever, wherever this place is, it appears endless.

William is light on his feet. He's light full-stop. That's a good thing because it helps him move around without being seen. And there's plenty he wants to see while he's here. He decides he should take his time and have a good look around before he makes his next move. The old men are usually away for a couple of days at a time, so he knows he doesn't have to rush into anything and reveal himself too quickly. William's a sensible boy, a *clever* boy Mother says. He knows what he's doing.

None of the doors here are locked.

Maybe that's just to make it easier for the old men? They've got enough to worry about, without having to mess around with bunches of keys. This place will have good defences, William's certain of that. In fact, there are probably garrisons of soldiers surrounding them right now, protecting these vital supplies from enemy attack.

William follows a long corridor, not knowing where it's going to take him. He can hear the familiar, reassuring thump of machinery and he heads straight for it. But where he expects to see metal being milled and fire, smoke and sparks, instead he finds a remarkably different process. There's water here: thick, black water being sucked in from outside. There's more pipework than he's ever seen before, like some kind of impossible musical instrument. He hides behind the largest inlet and watches an old man and woman tend to the machines. All those years on the shop-floor have given him a good understanding of how things work. Back home, the untreated metal goes in one end and the finished bullet and shell casings come out the other. Here, the dirty sea water enters one pipe and, somehow, cleaner water comes out the other end. *This must be where our drinking water comes from*, he thinks. And he's right, because some of the water is being decanted into the familiar looking barrels he's grown up with, soon to be loaded onto the boat and taken back to the factory. But not all the water is being shipped out. Some of it is being transported elsewhere and, when no one's looking, he follows these pipes into another part of the building.

Not for the first time today, William can't believe what he's seeing.

He's inside still, but he's outside too. How can this be? It's an entire room made of glass; a vast, echoing place. There's nowhere to hide here, so he can't risk going any further, but he so wishes he could. There are things in this place he's only ever read about in books... rectangles of yellow grass and sheep. Sheep! *So this is where we get our wool from... maybe there are cows providing milk too?* He'd heard a rumour that the precious tallow they use in the factory when they're cutting screw threads came from real sheep, but he never honestly believed it, not until now. He backs out of the glass room, but he makes a mental note to come back here later. If he's going to be stuck here for a few days, then this is where he'd like to spend most of his time.

He can't go any further forward this way, so William heads back towards the boat. His eyes are more accustomed to the light levels now, and this time he sees another exit, a set of double-doors he missed before. He wastes no time in going through them. He's really excited now, keen to explore. What other wonders does this incredible place hold? If the things he finds on this side of the complex match those on the other, then he thinks he might try and stay here forever. Maybe, once they've calmed down (because he knows they'll be furious with him), he might be able to persuade the old men and women to move more people here from the factory? They could come here on day trips, or maybe even holidays? A few shifts here would do most folks the power of good.

This room is colder than the others. Much colder. There's harsh, electric light, the likes of which he only sees in the communal parts of his factory home: the kitchens, the mess hall, the school. And right in the middle of the room, under the brightest light he's ever seen, is the stretcher trolley John Champion's body was transported here on. The dead man is still on it, covered with a sheet, a box of his belongings laid at his feet. William's about to go and check it really is John Champion, when another door is opened and two old men and an old woman appear. They're wearing heavy aprons like the cooks wear back home. William presses himself back against the wall, knowing he can't leave this room until they do, and he watches.

And William soon wishes he was anywhere but here.

After they've taken off his clothes and his wedding ring, they slit the veins in John Champion's neck, and drain his blood into plastic cartons. They skin him. They remove his internal organs – they still don't look like they did in his school books, but this time William knows exactly what's what, particularly when they unspool John Champion's intestines and slop them into a metal bucket. They take out his teeth and remove some of his bones. They shave off and collect his hair. One old man uses a step up and then, with one knee resting on John Champion's throat, he saws the top of his head open and scoops out his brain. The inescapable sights, smells and sounds combine and William feels like he's going to faint, but somehow he manages to keep himself upright.

In less than an hour John Champion has all but ceased to exist: his component parts now divided between various vats and tubs. Blood soaked and weary, the old people cart everything away.

Now William's mood has changed. His optimism has disappeared and has been replaced by anger, borderline rage. What is this? What's the meaning of this foul behaviour? He follows the old people around the complex, their decrepit bodies and dulled senses no match for his youthful speed and agility. They barely even realise he's there, perhaps stopping momentarily when they think they hear something, then continuing on their way, convinced they haven't.

William watches them grind down John Champion's bones and teeth. He sees them hang out his skin to dry. He watches them do things to the blood and turn it into some kind of powder. He watches them clean and repair his clothes, making them like new. Everything useful is packed up in crates. From his head to his toes, John Champion has been recycled.

This is horrible. William is incensed and he goes deeper into the complex. When he finds who's in charge here, he's going to demand answers. And when he gets home, he decides, he's going to tell everyone about the sick butchery which goes on here and the other secrets he's uncovered.

He stops at a different window when he hears another mechanical noise. He looks through a window, scared for a second that it's the boat leaving, but it's not. It's a boat with wheels, driving across the poisoned land outside. In the history books they called it a truck, and it's loaded up with all kinds of rubbish. There are tracks worn in the yellow-brown dirt, indicating that this journey has been made countless times before. He sees the truck stop and two old men get out and start unloading. These poor buggers look exhausted. Beaten. They're wearing masks and goggles, and one of them stops and takes off his mask and coughs hard until he's sick.

William keeps going. At the end of this corridor is a lone door marked 'Communications' and he thinks this must be it, this must be where those responsible are based. He bursts through, ready to have his say, but there's no one here. All that's in this room are two electric typewriter machines. They're working themselves: tap, tap, tapping on the end of big spools of paper without anyone sitting at their keyboards. A blade cuts the paper and a folding machine hides the words. William picks a finished letter out of the wire basket it drops into. He knows this is going to be important. Orders from headquarters, perhaps? Requisition requests from the front line?

"HELLO TO ALL AT HOME.

THINGS ARE GOING WELL OUT HERE. WE'RE MAKING GREAT GAINS. WITH LUCK ON OUR SIDE THE ENEMY WILL SOON BE DEFEATED AND WE'LL ALL BE HOME.

WITH ALL MY LOVE AS ALWAYS, FATHER."

William looks at letter after letter. The familiarity of them hits him like a punch in the face. There's some variety, of course, some letters coming from Mother, some bearing slightly different news, but William knows without doubt that every letter he ever received from his father originated from this room.

Numb with shock, he continues to walk. He finds himself in another area, this one much more like the factory he calls home. There are familiar smells in here, comforting noises, heat, metal and machines. He instinctively follows the process flow but wonders if he's looking at it wrong because it doesn't make sense. The casings he and the others make are being melted down. Then the metal is being formed into sheets, bars and rods before being cooled. They're the exact same sheets, bars and rods they use to make the casings in the factory back home. Someone must have made a mistake here, because this process is pointless. They're just undoing all the hard work William, his mother, and all the other people do. Even worse, without bullets and shells there can be no war. How can Father be fighting if he doesn't have anything to fight with?

The pieces start to fall into place.

William works it out.

Broken, he traipses back to the boat. His brief adventure is over and he doesn't want to be here anymore. He doesn't know where else to go but home, what else to do. He skulks through the shadows and waits while old people load the hold for the trip back to the factory. Food, fresh water, clothing, fuel, metal.

When there's no one else around, William makes his move. But he's not been so smart this time. One of the old men is still here, and he's just as fast as the stowaway. He grabs William's arm tight and won't let go. The old man is stronger than he looks. 'What the bloody hell are you doing here?'

William doesn't answer. He can't find the words. The old man glares at him. Unexpectedly, his expression softens. He can see the pain in William's face. 'I thought...' William tries to say before he starts to sob uncontrollably.

'I was like you once,' the old man says. William looks up at him, tears rolling down. 'I was always asking questions, never happy with what I had, always wanting more. Sound familiar?'

William nods and wipes his eyes, feeling seven again, not seventeen. 'I just wanted...'

'To fight? To escape?'

'Yeah...'

'I'm sorry, son, I really am. Just go home. Tell yourself you never came here. I'll make a deal with you, you don't tell anyone what you've seen, and I won't tell anyone I found you. Okay?'

'Okay.'

The old man lets William go and pushes him towards the back of the boat. 'We'll be heading home in the morning. Stay here for now. I'll find you something to eat.'

William watches him go, then calls him back. The old man looks annoyed. He glances from side to side, concerned someone might hear. 'But the war...?' William asks. 'My father...?'

'We've all got to have something to believe in, haven't we? Otherwise there'd be no point to any of this. There was a war once, but I don't know what happened, none of us do. That's not the point, though.'

'But all our work, all for nothing...?'

'You reckon? No, son, it's not for nothing. It keeps people holding on and gives them something to believe in. Now do me a favour, get back in the hold and keep your mouth shut. Otherwise you'll get both of us into strife, understand?'

'I understand,' William says, and for the first time he does.

Next morning they make the return trip back across the dead water. William's relieved to see home appear on the black horizon. He likes the way the ocean laps around the factory on all sides, isolating it... protecting it. The old man looks out for William and gets him safely back inside. Mother's fast asleep, exhausted. William changes and gets ready for work. His shift is due to start soon.

He walks onto the shop floor, feeling old before his years. Frank is already hard at work, but he stops when he sees William. He has a huge grin on his face. 'Look at this, Will,' he says, fishing a folded piece of paper out from his back pocket. 'It's from Mother. It arrived this morning.'

"HELLO TO ALL AT HOME.

THINGS ARE GOING WELL OUT HERE. WE'RE MAKING GREAT GAINS. WITH LUCK ON OUR SIDE THE ENEMY WILL SOON BE DEFEATED AND WE'LL ALL BE HOME.

WITH ALL MY LOVE AS ALWAYS, MOTHER."

Elsewhere in the factory, William knows other letters are being delivered. John Champion's children will hear from their father soon. It'll be a relief for them to know he's made it to the front line. They'll be proud to hear he's fighting for them, keeping them safe.

William starts up his machine and focuses on his work, drowning in the *thump – thump – thump*.

William is one of the lucky ones. He knows this, because he's seen it for himself.

OSTRICH

Remember **Tales of the Unexpected? Alfred Hitchcock Presents?** I know I missed the mark when I was asked to write a story about this green and pleasant land I call home, but I couldn't help myself. I focused on people more than places, and instinctively started thinking about those TV shows of old and how the twist in tale often involved looking under the prim and proper surface of life in parts of the UK and revealing what lies beneath. We English can be frustratingly polite much of the time, and it often causes more problems than we'd like to admit. I frequently curse myself for not immediately saying what I'm actually thinking and for allowing true feelings to go unsaid, because whilst that might avoid an uncomfortable conversation in the short-term, it'll often just be delaying the inevitable. One way or another, the truth will out. **Ostrich** takes that to the extreme.

We had such a beautiful home.

I can still remember that buzz of excitement on the day we got the keys and the place was finally ours. I was pregnant with Sophie, so Norman did all the heavy lifting while I sat there with my feet propped up and my big belly sticking out, telling him and the removal men what went where. So many years ago now but he's never let me forget it!

Twenty-six years we'd been there, and I still loved the place. We stretched ourselves to buy it and it took a long time to get back on our feet and get everything just as we wanted it, but it was worth all that effort in the end.

I was the envy of my friends. Jacqui was always telling me how she wished her house was the size of ours. I met Jacqui in the playground when Sophie started school and we immediately connected. We had a lot in common and remained friends long after our kids lost touch. Though she, Phil and the kids seemed happy enough with their lot, I always thought it was a shame they were so boxed-in when we had all that space going spare. It wasn't anyone's fault, just the way things work out sometimes. Phil owned his own business but he got himself into trouble when the stock market crashed (or something like that... I can't remember exactly what happened). It was just after the last of their kids left home. Shame, really. When Jacqui should have been taking it easy and enjoying herself, she ended up back at work instead. Poor love. Norman didn't want me having to work like that.

I always said I wanted two children, maybe even three, but Norm decided we should stick with one. That meant we always had plenty of room. Sophie had a playroom as well as her bedroom, and we still had a spare bedroom in case anyone came to stay. Not that people stopped over regularly, mind. Mum stayed with us on a couple of occasions before she passed, but I reckon I could count on one hand the number of times Norm's folks visited. It didn't seem to bother him. *Funny buggers,* he used to call them. I always got on with them okay, but he was more cautious. There was a big falling out in the family before he and I got together, but to this day I don't know exactly what happened. He didn't like to talk about it, and it upset him if I asked.

Sophie never came back after university, and that left the two of us rattling around. I left her bedroom as it was in case she ever needed it, but she'd always been an independent girl. She has a good job now and is in a relationship and I couldn't be happier for her.

I didn't used to see Sophie as much as I'd have liked. She was more than an hour and a half's drive away, and her place was a pig to get to by bus or train. There were no direct routes and I used to hate having to change at stations. I always got so het up and flustered if I had to get off one train then go and find another.

I should have made more of an effort and driven over there more often. Truth is, I never liked driving Norm's car. We sold my Mini when he was between jobs and cash was tight and we never replaced it. He didn't think there was much point, and I tended to agree. We had one car between us, what was the point of having another? It would have just sat in the garage most of the time. We usually went out together and he put me on his insurance for emergencies so I could drive it if I ever needed to. Truth be told, I never fancied the idea of driving any of Norm's cars. Too big. He always had huge, powerful cars – Land Rovers and the like. I missed my little Mini. I used to love zipping around town in it.

I worked hard and kept the house nice, but the garden was Norman's domain. The front and back lawns were like putting greens. Absolutely perfect. At the height of the summer he'd be out there with the mower three or four times a week, sometimes even daily. He liked to get it looking just right. The stripes were always perfectly measured and dead straight, and the grass was the lushest green you could imagine. It was when the weather turned particularly hot and dry that you could really see how much care he put into his lawns. I used to notice it most when I was walking back from the shops. The neighbours' lawns would all be dried-out and yellowed around the edges, parched-looking, but ours would still be deep, deep green. Sometimes I'd see the neighbours looking, and occasionally one of them would pluck up the courage to ask Norm how he kept it looking so nice. 'It takes a little effort and commitment,' he'd casually tell them, making it sound like it actually took no effort at all.

I'll be honest, though, Norman did obsess over his grass. I remember him hitting the roof one time when I wanted to go away for a week but he didn't want to leave the garden. I'd booked it all up as an anniversary surprise, but I hadn't thought it through. We usually managed a couple of long weekends away each year, but rarely anything longer. I didn't mind cancelling, though. It would have been a shame for all his hard work to have been undone just because I wanted a few days in the sun. We toyed with the idea of going out of season, but as he pointed out, it didn't make a lot of sense. 'Might as well just stay at home and save the money,' he'd say if I mentioned it. It did become a bind, though, him not wanting to go anywhere. It stopped me seeing as much of Sophie as I'd have liked.

Despite everything, I had to remember Norm's feelings. It was easy for me. I wasn't the one with the high-pressured job who worked long hours. He said if he could do without a fancy holiday abroad, then so could I. It was difficult to argue with that.

From time to time I did find myself running out of things to do, though. I toyed with the idea of going back to work after Sophie went off to uni just to keep myself busy, but I didn't know what kind of job I'd be able to do. Norm was dead against the idea from the outset. He said I didn't need to work (which was true) and that because I'd been out of the job marketplace for so long, I'd have struggled to find anything worthwhile (which was also true). He said he didn't want me stacking shelves or sitting on a till somewhere but, you know, I think I would have been happy with that. Norm thought the neighbours would have got the wrong impression. He didn't want them thinking we were hard up or anything like that. He used to regularly remind me how lucky I was. He said 'do you want to end up like your friend Jacqui?' She always looked worn out and stressed, like she had a million and one things to do and no time to do them.

For what it was worth, Jacqui said herself that she thought I was mad to even consider working if I didn't have to. She said I should have joined a club, but hobbies have never really been my thing. I used to like badminton but I hadn't played for donkey's years. I collected teapots (unusual, I know) but that was hardly the most social of interests, and I'd long run out of space for them anyway.

I've always loved clothes shopping. That was a real weakness of mine. I could never resist a bargain. I used to get such a buzz picking up a new dress then trying to find an occasion to wear it. Norman used to say I wasted his money, but I'd just tell him it wouldn't be wasted if he took me out more often. He always promised he would, but he was under such a lot of pressure at work and when we made plans, nine times out of ten we had to change them. Half the outfits in my wardrobe I'd probably worn only once or twice, if at all. Such a shame. It was usually only family dos I got dressed up for. I'd go over the top when I had the chance, even though it didn't always go down well. Norm said I showed him up when I'd turn up at his brother's house in a fancy new frock when him and everyone else were wearing jeans.

He had a point, I suppose.

My immediate family was my real hobby. Between keeping the house nice and looking after Norman and Sophie, I always seemed to have more than enough on my plate.

Like I said, we had such a beautiful home. If I close my eyes and think back, I can still remember every little detail of every room. I remember the smells and the way it sounded; the creaks and pops at night when the heating switched off, and the rustle, rattle and clunk when the postman would deliver our mail and it dropped on the mat. I used to get a bit obsessive looking after the place I'll admit, but I was no worse than Norman with his bloody lawns.

I've always been a tidy person, but I did start taking things to the extreme. I'd spend ages dusting and cleaning and arranging and rearranging. I used to like my teapot collection to look nice, so I'd leave a few of them out on show on the sideboard. I regularly changed them and moved them around, but I always had the big yellow one Mum left me out on display. It meant a lot, that teapot. Mum inherited it from her mother, and it reminded me of when I was growing up.

I did like everything to be just right, though. I used to line up the handles and spouts of the teapots so they were all pointing the same way. Norm used to take the mickey out of me something rotten. He used to joke I'd got that obsessive compulsive disorder thing. He might have had a point. I hadn't realised how obsessive I'd become until I put the TV on one lunchtime, then started fussing with my collection. By the time I sat down to watch the box, the one o'clock news had finished and *Doctors* was halfway through. I'd spent more than three quarters of an hour trying to get everything just right.

Looking back now I realise I'd let things get out of perspective. It's hard to see when you're in the middle of it. You often don't realise until someone else points it out, do you?

It was my friend Mandy who first made me aware. She called around one day and we were having a good old natter about something or nothing. I made us both a sandwich, and it was only when she pointed out that I'd just thrown out half a perfectly good loaf of bread that I realised something was wrong. It was going out of date the next day, but I'd got it into my head that I shouldn't let food get anywhere near its "best before" date. I realised I'd been throwing milk out when it still had a good couple of days shelf-life, and I'd got into the habit of doing the same with meat and vegetables too. Mandy asked me what was going on and she was like a dog with a bone, refusing to let go. I remember feeling really uncomfortable, because it's not nice when someone's putting you on the spot like that, is it? But Mandy and I had been close friends for a long time, and if there was anyone I trusted to be brutally honest with me, it was her.

She was asking me all kinds of questions about cooking and cleaning and whether or not I was happy, and then she asked me what Norman thought of it all and the question floored me. 'I don't tell him,' I remember answering. 'He'd be cross if he knew I was wasting money.'

'But it's because of him you do it, isn't it?'

I remember struggling to answer that. I was stammering and umming and ahhing, and then the penny dropped. You see, one time a couple of months before,

I'd made Norm a sandwich and hadn't realised the loaf had started to turn. There was a little bit of blue mould on one of the slices. I couldn't see it, but he could sure taste it. You'd have thought I'd tried to poison him, the fuss he made. He gave me such a hard time. He was justified, mind. It couldn't have been nice.

So Mandy started asking if everything was all right between me and Norm which, of course, it was. I did tell her he'd started staying at the office later and later, and the things she said and the way she was looking at me got me thinking. She called me an ostrich because she said I had my head buried in the sand. I didn't agree. Mandy had divorced her husband years earlier, and she came across as being bitter. She said it was obvious Norm was having an affair, because this was how it started with her Peter, and that I needed to do something about it sooner rather than later. Much as I didn't want to believe her, the more I thought about what she'd said, the more convinced I became that she was right.

Mandy really fired me up. So much so that, a couple of days later, I found myself sitting in the middle of town waiting for him. *Watching* him. I put on a dress I'd bought a couple of weeks ago that he hadn't seen before and that I felt good in and I set myself up in the coffee shop opposite. It was the perfect location. Norman's office was directly across the road and the seat in the coffee shop I chose was so good I could see right inside and watch him at his desk. All afternoon there were women coming over to see him and ask him questions about this, that and the other, and every time I saw someone new I was thinking *is it you? Are you the one? Are you the hussy trying to tear my marriage apart?*

Norman never left the office before six (or so he told me), and as the clock crept past the hour I started to feel more and more nervous. I knew that any minute I'd see her.

What if she's younger than me?
What if I know her?
Was she at last year's Christmas party?
What if she's better dressed?
What if she's prettier?

You think all these pointless thoughts when you're nervous, don't you?

The clock was ticking and more and more people were leaving the office for the night. The light had started to fade and the electric lights coming from inside the office just made things even worse. It was as if someone was shining a spotlight on Norm so I could see his every move, and it felt like they were doing it to make me suffer. I didn't know what I'd done wrong. Had he strayed because I hadn't been paying him enough attention? Was the house not clean enough? Was it because I'd tried to poison him with that bloody sandwich?

It got to almost half-six and my mind was running overtime. Why was she late? What kind of games was she playing? Sounds crazy now, but I actually found myself getting angry thinking about this phantom woman messing Norman about. Ridiculous, I know.

And then, around about seven o'clock, he packed up his stuff and left.

Luckily I managed to jump on a bus before him, and on the way home I realised something that made me feel a thousand times worse than I already did. Norman wasn't having an affair after all. He just didn't want to come home.

I felt like such a failure. What kind of a wife was I? I decided two things that night. First, that I'd try harder to keep Norm happy. Second, that I wouldn't ever speak to Mandy again.

*

A week later was my birthday.

I was still feeling awful, so I resolved to make the day as enjoyable for Norman as I hoped it would be for me. We went out to dinner that night – the first time we'd been out as a couple in ages – and we had a lovely time. We went to one of his favourite pubs (we always got a good meal there – *stick with what you know* was one of Norman's mottos) and it was super. Just like the old times.

He spoiled me rotten. Flowers, chocolates, and a new vacuum because I was always moaning about the old one. It was top of the range. Practically lifted the carpets from the floorboards, it did!

Things turned a little sour soon after.

It was a Saturday afternoon, I remember it clearly. Norm had been working in the garden all morning, and I'd taken the opportunity to run my new vacuum around and do a spot of tidying up. Dinner was almost ready. I always tried to time it carefully because I knew he didn't like to lose his rhythm when he was working on the lawn. If I knocked him off his stride and the stripes weren't quite right, it would take him twice as long to correct and the dinner would be ruined.

I'd just finished mopping the floor when he came in. I told him his food was ready and he asked if he had time for a shower first. I told him he didn't but he went up anyway, telling me that whenever I said it was five minutes to dinner, it was always closer to ten, and this time he actually was right. It took me an age to clean up all the grass clippings he'd managed to walk into the house.

We'd barely started eating when the phone rang. He went out to the hall to answer it, and I knew straightaway who he was talking to. I couldn't make out what was being said, but I could tell from the way Norman was speaking that it was our little girl on the line. I also sensed that something wasn't right.

'Who was it, love?' I asked, just to be sure.

He ate a few more mouthfuls of food before answering.

'Sophie.'

'And is she okay?'

More food. More chewing.

'She's fine.'

I didn't want to push him too hard because he and Sophie often didn't see eye to eye and he'd have just said I was nagging at him, but I knew something was up. Sophie didn't often phone the house. She usually texted.

'What did she phone for?' I asked, keeping my voice as light and airy as I could.

He seemed reluctant, but he eventually answered. 'Her friend's been in an accident.'

'Oh no. Which friend?'

Norman spat out his answer. '*That* friend.'

Now I should say at this point that Sophie's gay. It's not my cup of tea and it's not what I'd have chosen for her, but she's happy and Kerry, her girlfriend, is lovely. She's nine years older than Sophie and very sporty and not particularly feminine, but we've always got on and Sophie thinks the world of her.

'Poor Kerry. Is she all right?'

'She's in hospital. Got knocked off her bike, apparently.'

'Is she badly hurt?'

'A couple of broken bones. Nothing too serious.'

'It sounds pretty serious to me. We should go and see her.'

Norman put down his knife and fork and looked across the table at me. 'When, exactly?'

'I don't know... one evening perhaps?'

'Visiting hours would be over by the time we get

there.'

'Next weekend, then?'

'I was thinking about going into the office next Saturday morning.'

'But you never go into the office on Saturdays.'

'I've got a deadline coming up.'

'When were you going to tell me?'

'I'd forgotten about it. Do I have to ask permission now?'

'No, I'm just saying it would be nice if you'd mentioned it, that's all.'

'I told you, I'd forgotten.'

'What about tomorrow, then?'

'Too short notice.'

'Well if you're going into work next Saturday, can I borrow the car?'

'Seriously? You haven't driven since you got rid of the Mini.'

'I'll be okay...'

'I don't have time to take you for a test drive or anything like that, not this week.'

'I'll catch the bus, then. Or the train.'

'Ease up on the questions, for Christ's sake, it's like being interrogated by the police. I've told you everything I know. I'll find a way of getting you there if that's what you really want.'

I called Sophie back later. It turned out to be more serious than we'd first thought, that Kerry had almost died in the accident. Norm booked me a ticket and I caught the train to see them the following Tuesday. I stayed overnight, but I'd have happily stopped longer if he'd booked me an open return (he said he'd wanted to be sure I got a seat on the way back). Sophie gave me such an ear-bending when I was about to leave. She said her dad was a bully, and that he sulked if he didn't get his own way. I stuck up for him like I always did.

A couple of days later I took a telephone call which shook me to the core. It was Jacqui. Her Phil had died. It was very sudden. Apparently he'd been at work and had dropped dead from a massive heart attack in the middle of a meeting. He knew nothing about it, so that was something, I guess, but my heart went out to Jacqui. It makes you count your blessings when you hear about something like that happening, doesn't it?

The funeral was a week later.

My Norman always got on quite well with Phil, so he took the afternoon off and we were able to pay our respects. It was a lovely service. The crematorium was almost full. Oak Hill's quite a big crem, so you're doing pretty well if you manage to fill anything more than the first four rows. Loads of people turned out to say goodbye to Phil.

Poor old Jacqui was in such a state afterwards. We didn't go back to her house for the wake because Norm wanted to get away, but I managed to grab a few minutes with her before we left. Poor love could barely hold herself upright. She looked exhausted. Her face looked hollow, like she hadn't slept for a month. I remember it clear as day. She looked up at me, tears rolling down her face, and she said 'how am I going to cope without him?'

It played on my mind for days afterwards. Made me think about what I'd do if I didn't have Norman.

Anyway, she clearly coped all right, because next time I saw her she was a different woman. It was a week or so later, and we passed each other outside the shops. I didn't recognise her at first. I had to do a double-take. She looked radiant. She'd had her hair done and she was wearing a lovely outfit. I'd always thought she was a little too thin, but she looked just right. She looked *alive*. She was grinning from ear to ear, so much so that it made me wonder if Phil's death hadn't pushed her over the edge.

I asked how she was doing and she said 'really good, thanks Sue.' And then she paused and pulled me closer like she didn't want to be heard. 'I feel guilty saying this, but I'm really happy.'

Happy? I couldn't understand it. She and Phil had been inseparable like me and Norm. She could see that I was confused.

'I loved Phil more than anything,' she told me, 'and I miss him every minute of every day and I think I always will. I expect I'll probably crash at some point soon, but...'

'But what?'

'But right now I'm enjoying my freedom. I'm my own boss for the first time in almost thirty years. I watch what I want to watch on TV, I eat what I like when I like, I go out when I feel like it... I know Phil wouldn't have wanted me to mope around feeling sorry for myself, so I'm not. Honestly, Sue, it's given me a whole new lease of life.'

I didn't say anything, of course, but I thought she'd completely lost her marbles.

That night I was sitting with Norman watching TV. It was his favourite programme (you know the one... that BBC sitcom about the Muslim councillor from Birmingham). He was howling with laughter, but for some reason I just couldn't see the funny side. I felt awful guilty, but I couldn't help thinking about how I'd be if Norman died. Worse than that, I found myself thinking about killing him. It sounds silly and wrong when I say it out loud like that, but I sat there on the sofa watching him watching telly, and I tried to work out how I could kill him and not get caught.

I remembered watching an old black and white horror programme when I was a little girl. I don't remember all the ins and outs of the story, but the gist of it was that a woman got rid of her husband by clubbing him around the head with a frozen leg of lamb, which she then cooked and served to the police officers who'd come around to the house to investigate hubby's disappearance. I remember thinking *it's a shame lamb's so expensive at the moment,* and I made a mental note to have a look next time I went to Waitrose (and I'm not even joking).

I thought about poisoning him. It wouldn't have been difficult to slip something into his food – he usually wolfed down his dinner so quick it barely had time to touch the sides – but I knew I'd never be able to cope with the police questioning. I know Mandy called me an ostrich that time, but there's a world of difference between shoving your head in the sand to avoid saying what you think and lying intentionally. I could never have done it.

I thought about sabotaging the brakes of his car but, if I'm honest, I wouldn't have known where to start. I could have put petrol in at a push and maybe put air in the tyres, but anything else was beyond me and it would have aroused more than a little suspicion if I'd started asking Norman questions about mechanics all of a sudden.

How about a trap? What if I left the gas on? How about if I slipped something in his drink and left him to drown in the bath? The possibilities were endless...

Of course, it didn't take me long to realise how silly I was being. I felt guilty as sin the next day. What a horrible bitch I was for thinking such things about the man who doted over me. The house, Sophie... if it hadn't been for Norman I wouldn't have had any of it.

He came home late from work again next day, but that was good because it gave me time to spruce up the house and cook a special meal. I made his favourite – beef stroganoff – and he ate every scrap. We dozed together in front of the telly, and this time I managed to keep my thoughts in check and stay focused on the screen.

The weekend began like any other.

I had loads to do, and I spent Saturday morning working around the house while Norman groomed his perfect lawns. I finished just after midday and started cooking dinner, and while I was waiting for the vegetables to boil, I telephoned Sophie. It had been a few days since we'd spoken and I wanted to know how Kerry was getting on.

I couldn't get an answer. Strange.

I carried on with my jobs and tried calling their flat a couple more times. Still nothing. I couldn't get an answer on their mobiles, either. It wasn't like Sophie, and I was concerned. I had a horrible, sickly, nervous feeling in the pit of my stomach that something was very wrong.

When Norman came back in from the garden, he could tell that I was upset. I told him what had happened and how worried I was, but he didn't seem surprised. 'Well you won't get through to her,' he said, sounding almost aggressive.

'Why not?'

'Because she's not at home.'

Norman walked deeper into the house, leaving a trail of grassy footprints on the recently mopped kitchen lino and the hall carpet.

I followed him into the lounge. He was already in front of the TV, grubby shoes still on and grass stains everywhere.

'What's going on, Norman? What's happened?'

'Her friend's taken a turn for the worse.'

'What?'

'One of those hospital superbugs. MRSA, or something like that.'

'We've got to go and see her.'

'Why? It's not Sophie that's sick.'

I just looked at him. 'How can you say that? We're talking about Sophie's partner here.'

'I knew you'd be like this,' he grumbled. 'That's why I didn't say anything. We'll go and see her tonight.' And he turned up the TV to let me know in no uncertain terms that the conversation was finished.

I felt myself tensing up. I wanted to scream and shout at him, but I couldn't do it. I just shoved my head into the sand as I always did, automatically switching to full-on ostrich mode.

I went back to the kitchen to check on dinner, picking up bits of grass from the carpet as I did. Then I stopped and checked myself, because something was niggling at me. My legs felt like jelly, but I knew I had to ask him and I stormed back to the lounge. 'How did you know?'

'Huh?'

'About Kerry... how did you know she was ill again?'

His eyes never left the screen.

'Sophie phoned.'

At that point I probably should have shut up and gone back to the kitchen, but I didn't. I walked over to the sideboard and started checking the spouts of my teapots were in line, my hands shaking with anger and nerves.

The words were stuck in my throat, but I made myself ask.

'When did she call?'

'Last night,' he answered casually.

I couldn't believe what I was hearing.

'Last night? Why didn't you tell me?'

'Because I knew this would happen. I was tired last night and I wanted to get the lawns cut this morning. I knew you'd go over the top like this.'

'Over the top? Would you even have said anything if

I hadn't asked?'

'Listen, love, I don't have the energy for this right now. It's been a tough week at work. You don't know what it's like, sitting here all day every day with your feet up.'

I'd got the bit between my teeth now.

'No, *you* don't know what it's like. I only sit here all day every day because you won't let me do anything else.'

I'd said it without thinking, without realising, and I waited nervously for his reaction. I thought he was going to explode, but he didn't. He just smiled at me and shook his head.

'You have a very funny view of things sometimes, Susan.'

'I'm going to see Sophie,' I told him. 'Are you going to take me?'

'Later. I've got to finish the lawns first.'

'Fine. Just drop me at the station, then. I'll get the train.'

'Did you not hear me? I've got to finish the garden first. I won't get another chance. It's going to rain the evening.'

'I'll go without you then,' I said, and I meant it.

Norman just laughed. 'You're not going anywhere. You can't do anything without me, love. You're bloody useless.' And he kicked off his shoes and stretched out on the chair.

I had a moment of sudden clarity. It all made sense.

'Mandy was right,' I said. 'And Jacqui, too.'

'What are you on about now?'

'It's all my fault.'

'Have you completely lost your mind?'

'I let you do this.'

'Let me do what?'

'I let you control me.'

In a single sudden move, I picked up mother's yellow teapot and smashed it over Norman's head. He yelled out in agony.

'Sorry, love,' I instinctively said as he got up and lumbered towards me, blood running down his face.

'You stupid bitch... what did you do that for? Jesus. Get me something to stop the bleeding.'

'Get it yourself.'

I felt awful, but I knew what I had to do next.

He walked towards me but clipped the corner of the coffee table and fell forward. He was on his knees in the middle of the room, one hand on the table and the other on the top of his head, trying to stem the blood flow. It was dripping everywhere, all over the carpet. I wasn't bothered.

In for a penny, in for a pound.

I picked up the biggest crockery shard I could find and stabbed him in the back. And again. And again. And again. And again. And again...

I sliced him to ribbons then left him for dead in the middle of the lounge and went and had my lunch.

There wasn't much left to do outside, actually. He'd finished the front lawn, and there was just a bit of edging to do in the back. It didn't take long at all. I didn't make as neat a job of it as Norman, but it didn't matter.

That afternoon I drove to see Sophie and Kerry. Driving wasn't so bad. A bit nerve-racking at first, but I started to enjoy it after a few miles. Norm's big car had some welly, that's for sure.

I had a lovely time, all things considered. Sophie asked where her dad was, and I told her I'd left him in front of the TV, which was as close to the truth as I wanted to get. Kerry's condition had stabilized, and Sophie and I had several cups of tea and a long overdue catch-up while she was sleeping.

I was tired when I got home, and the enormity of what I'd done hit me as hard as I'd hit Norm with the teapot. I sat perched on the edge of the sofa and I sobbed and I sobbed and I sobbed.

I think it was relief more than anything. Just nerves and shock. Because then I stopped.

I poured myself a sherry to calm my nerves and slowly started to relax. It was almost eleven o'clock, the time we usually went up to bed, but I stayed downstairs instead. I watched a godawful film on TV – a soppy romcom Norman would have hated – and had another sherry. By the time I went up I was half-cut and completely exhausted. I left the washing up from dinner to soak (it would still be there in the morning, I thought), and I left my dirty clothes in a pile on the bedroom floor. He hated it when I did that.

I felt nervous. Terrified. But also strangely calm and relaxed. It was odd having the whole bed to myself. I slept like a log.

Next morning I made a half-hearted attempt to cover my tracks, but the grassy footprints and the massive bloodstain were a dead giveaway (pardon the pun). I got as far as dragging Norman's body out into the back garden because I had some stupid idea that I might be able to bury him. I knew I'd done a terrible thing, but there was no going back now. Funny thing was, I wouldn't have wanted to go back even if I could. The luxury of not having to constantly consider someone else all the time was blissful. I felt free. It felt good.

I tried digging a hole in the middle of the lawn, but I didn't get far. It was too much like hard work and after about an hour of trying, all I'd managed to dig was a hole about twelve inches square and the same deep. Anyway, Norman's body had gone all stiff and inflexible with rigor mortis, stuck in the same kneeling position in which he'd died. *Stiff and inflexible*, I remember thinking, *no change there then.*

I shoved his head in the hole and filled it in. There he was, right in the middle of his showpiece lawn: head down in the dirt, backside sticking up into the air.

'Now who's the ostrich?' I said to him.

I was going to phone the police, honestly I was, but Clive and Miriam from next-door got there before me. I'd have liked a little more time on my own first, but it didn't really matter.

And that's how I ended up in this place.

Any regrets?

They've said I'll never leave here but that's okay. I honestly don't mind. Most (not all) of the people in the unit are lovely and I enjoy keeping my little room tidy. I've got a few things of my own to remind me of home, and I don't have to cook or think about anyone else. I'm free. Unrestricted. Uninhibited. I can relax and be myself for the first time since... well, since I met Norman, actually.

I've got some good friends here and my own TV I don't have to share so I can watch my programmes when I like. Sophie and Kerry try to drop in and see me every couple of weeks.

Everything's so much easier now.

Life is good.

GRANDMA KELLY

Forgive the sudden change in tone here, because **Grandma Kelly** was originally written for inclusion in a young adult horror anthology. It was my first serious short story commission after the **Autumn** books had taken off, and I was asked to write a zombie story for teenagers. I was inspired to give **Autumn** away for free online by **Marillion**, one of my favourite bands, and one of the first bands to fully embrace the collective power of their fans and the Internet (you should check them out – they're not the band you might remember).

By way of a weird little tribute, I named the characters and places in this story after the band members. I wrote and told them what I'd done, but I must have scared them off. They never wrote back...

I must be stupid. I knew it was going to happen. All I needed to do was make that one catch and the game would have been safe. The ball seemed to hang in the sky over my head forever and I think I'd already decided I was going to drop it. I kept staring up and I could feel everyone else watching me. I blew it. I made a mistake. I stretched up for the ball instead of waiting for it to come down. I felt it hit the tips of my fingers and bounce away. That was eleven o'clock this morning. No one's talked to me since. Plenty of people have been talking about me though. I overheard Connie Franks moaning about "that idiot Amy" outside the upper school toilets between classes. I'm not an idiot, I just get it wrong sometimes.

I guess everyone has days like this – long, difficult days where everything seems to go wrong and you can't do anything right. At lunchtime I upset Millie Trewavas – the last person still talking to me – and this afternoon I found out I'd made a huge mistake with my Literature assignment. I copied the question down wrong last week and I've answered it all wrong. It has to be in tomorrow. I'll be up all night re-writing it.

It's been raining hard like this for hours now and the streets are flooded. It was dry and bright this morning. I didn't even bring a coat. I've had to tuck my notes inside my jacket to try and keep them dry. I'm really going to need them tonight. If I don't start work on my assignment as soon as I get back I've had it.

And that's just *perfect*.

Some stupid car driver has just gone racing past me, straight through a huge puddle of rainwater which stretches from the gutter to the white line in the middle of the road. It sent a wave of dirty, cold water crashing down over me. Now I'm soaked through and I can feel the water dripping and dribbling down my neck. My notes are soaked too. By the time I get home all I'll have left is a soggy, inky mess. I'll never be able to make any sense of it.

It's almost five o'clock already. The bus is late tonight. What should I do? Do I wait here or start walking? Maybe Mum, Dad or Kevin will come and pick me up? Who am I kidding? They'll probably all be at home now, warm and dry, sat with their feet up in front of the TV and their cars parked on the drive. I bet they haven't even noticed I'm not back yet.

I really don't like this stretch of road. Moseley Street, I think it's called. It's long, straight and steep and it's very dark tonight. The houses are all along one side of the road and there are just a few street lamps dotted along the way. I always seem to be on my own when I'm walking up here. Most of the other kids who go to Rothery College live closer to the centre of town and they go the opposite way home. I'd phone Dad and ask him to come and pick me up but my phone's out of charge. I should have charged it earlier but I've been chasing my tail all day and I didn't give it a second thought...

What was that?!

Someone just crashed into me and knocked me flying. I'm on my knees in a puddle before I know what's happened and now I've dropped my notes. My papers are blowing all over the place. Quick, I have to make sure I don't lose them... Wait, someone's helping. I can't make out who it is. I scramble back to my feet and the light from the nearest lamppost is just strong enough for me to see that it's a lady, older than me but about my height. She's got a handful of my notes. She thrusts them at me and I take them from her.

'Sorry,' she mumbles. 'I'm so sorry...'

Something's not right here. She looks about as old as my mum and she's only wearing a dress and a cardigan. It's freezing cold and pouring down with rain and she's not even wearing a coat! Her face is ghostly white and behind her glasses her eyes are wide, dark and frightened.

'Are you okay...?' I start to ask, but before I can finish my question she's gone. She pushes past and disappears into the darkness.

I keep walking. If I wasn't so tired I'd try and run up the hill but I'm cold and I'm wet and I don't think I could manage...

'Where did you come from?' I shout suddenly. Another woman has just appeared in front of me and my heart's in my mouth. She really scared me, just appearing like that. What is it with the people on this street? At least this one didn't knock me over. There must be something wrong with her, though. She's really old and like the other lady I just saw she's not dressed to be outside. All she's wearing is a thin white nightdress and she's drenched. She doesn't even have anything on her feet.

'Are you lost?' I ask because I don't know what else to say. 'Do you live here? Were you with that other lady?'

She doesn't answer. In fact, she doesn't do anything. She just stands there right in front of me, perfectly still. I wave my hand in front of her face but she doesn't react. I don't even know if she can see me. Her eyes aren't moving.

What am I supposed to do now? I can't just leave her out here to freeze, can I? I look up and down Moseley Street but all I can see is darkness in every direction. Wait a second, the front door of the nearest house is open. It's blowing open and closed in the wind and I can see a light on inside. I'll take this lady back indoors. Even if it's not her house someone in there might know who she belongs to.

'I'm going to get you inside,' I tell her. 'We'll get you into the warm and out of this rain.'

Still no response. I glance around again, hoping I'll see someone who can help, but there's no one. I don't seem to have any choice so I take hold of the old lady's limp hand. She feels icy cold. She should be shivering and shaking (I am) but she isn't moving at all. I pull her towards me and her feet slowly start to shuffle in my direction. Walking backwards so that I can watch her I lead her through the garden gate towards the front door of the house.

'Hello,' I shout as we reach the door. 'Hello, is anyone here?'

Nothing.

'Is this your place?' I ask her, even though I know I won't get an answer. 'Do you live here?'

The rain is still clattering down all around us. Even if this isn't her house I'm going to get her inside. I pull her through the door. It's not much warmer in here but it's dry and quiet and we're finally out of the howling wind. I push the door closed behind me and just listen. The house is silent.

'Hello,' I shout again. My voice echoes around the walls. 'Hello!'

The old lady stands behind me in the middle of the hallway, still not moving. Rainwater is dripping off her body and splashing down onto the bare wooden floorboards. I take a couple of steps further into the house, leaving her where she is for now. On a little round table next to an old-fashioned telephone is a pile of unopened letters. I pick them up and look at the name and address.

'Mrs Kelly?' I ask. 'Are you Mrs Kelly?'

She lifts up her head and looks at me. My heart starts to beat faster again. At the mention of her name she's finally starting to react. Now she's staring right at me and the expression on her face is changing. She looks confused... now she looks hurt... now she looks angry. I'm getting scared.

'Look,' I start to say, backing away from her, 'I'll just leave, okay? I'll get out of your way and let you get on with...'

I don't get to finish my sentence. She starts to run at me and I'm so surprised it takes me a couple of seconds to react. Considering the fact that she must be numb with cold and about eighty years old, Mrs Kelly moves with frightening speed. I want to get to the front door but she's blocking my way and I can only go deeper into the house. Suddenly she leaps at me – flying through the air like an attacking animal – and I put my hands up to defend myself. I shove her to the left and manage to bundle her through an open door into a pitch-black room. I quickly reach into the darkness and grab hold of the door handle and pull it shut. There's no lock. She's got hold of the other side of the handle and she's trying to yank it open. There's a high-backed chair across the hall. I stretch and just about manage to reach it with my fingertips. I drag it over and wedge it under the handle before taking a couple of nervous steps away.

This is crazy. I have to get out of here. I have to get out right now and get back home and tell Mum and Dad about... Wait, what was that? A heavy thump comes from inside the room. The door clatters and rattles in its frame. After another couple of seconds it happens again. Then again and then again. The old lady must be throwing herself against it! She's trying to break out! What's wrong with her?

None of this is making any sense. I try the phone but it's dead. I should just walk out of here right now but my conscience is stopping me. What would happen to Mrs Kelly if I did? I can't just leave her, much as I want to. Who knows what damage she'll do to herself? Feeling scared and uneasy I walk past the room where Mrs Kelly is trapped (she's still hammering against the door) and then go into the next room and switch on the light. It's a cold and empty living room. There's hardly anything in here other than a few sticks of old furniture. It looks like it's being cleared out. There's a space where a TV used to be and the bookcase and shelves are empty. The kitchen at the end of the hallway is the same, although the light's already on in there. There's no food in the cupboards. Everything looks really old-fashioned and out-dated.

There's a bad smell at this end of the house. It's so bad that I get distracted by it and it's only the banging from the old lady in the room down the hall that makes me remember what's happening. The stench is like stale vomit, and it seems to be coming from a glass that's been left on the draining board. It's a long, tall glass which is filled with something dark, black and sticky, like that horrible strong beer that Dad drinks but a thousand times worse. I pick it up and I can't resist sniffing it. God, I think I'm going to be sick... Before I throw up I tip the stuff down the sink and watch it slowly seep down the plughole like thick molasses.

The noise has stopped.

She's finally gone quiet. Has she worn herself out, or has she realised that she can't escape? Maybe she's hurt herself? I don't want to but I make myself go back to the door and listen. It sounds awfully quiet in there. Perhaps I should have a look inside?

'Mrs Kelly,' I whisper. 'Mrs Kelly, are you all right?'

She throws herself at the other side of the door again and the sudden noise makes me trip back with surprise. I end up on the floor on my backside and I look up as she starts banging and thumping again, a hundred times louder than before.

'Stop it!' I shout. 'Just stop!'

There's a moment's pause before the loudest thump

of all. Mrs Kelly hits the door with such force that one of the wooden panels near the top begins to crack. I hear the muffled pad, pad, pad of her quick footsteps inside the room and then another massive, clattering, splintering bang. I crawl away from the door as I hear her footsteps again. This time her head smashes right through the top of the door, sending sharp bits of wood flying across the hall. She reaches her arm down through the hole and starts yanking at the chair that's keeping her trapped. What's going on? A few minutes ago she could hardly walk, now she's smashing down wooden doors?!

Mrs Kelly is hanging out of what's left of the door now, swinging and slashing her arms through the air furiously, stopping me getting to the front of the house. Maybe there's another way out? As I start to move back towards the living room she manages to shift the chair and free herself. Now she's running down the hallway towards me. She's moving faster than I am! I dive into the living room and slam the door shut. Almost immediately I can feel her hammering on the other side. I drag a dusty old sofa across the room and manage to push it hard against the door. Then I shove a table and a chair behind it and drag the empty bookcase into the gap so that there's a line of furniture running right across the room. She won't get in here now. Problem is, how do I get out?

Bang, bang, bang!

What was that? Jumping with fright and surprise I spin around to see another ghostly-white face pressed against the window just behind me. I scream so loud it hurts my throat. The figure at the window thumps its hand against the glass again and suddenly I feel like I'm trapped in some bad horror film surrounded by zombies. But I can't be, can I?

It's the other lady I saw out on the street. I didn't recognise her at first. Her wet, windswept hair is plastered across her face and she's shouting at me to let her in. She hammers on the window again. What do I do? Will she be like Mrs Kelly or will she be worse? I don't have any choice. At least if the window's open I can try and get out.

I reach out and flick up the clasp. I push the window open then move back across the room. It's hard to keep calm with Mrs Kelly smashing against the door on one side of me and this lady climbing in on the other. She drags herself headfirst through the window and ends up in a heap on the threadbare carpet. She stands up and reaches back outside. She heaves a heavy shopping bag into the room and pulls the window to.

'I'm Sheila Hogarth,' she says, breathing heavily and dripping with rain, 'and I'm really, really sorry.'

'Sorry?' I mumble, surprised. 'Why are you sorry?'

'Because all of this is my fault. I didn't think it would happen so soon. I thought I'd be able to stop it before it got this bad.'

Mrs Kelly slams against the door again and startles us both. I feel more scared and confused than ever and jumping through the open window seems like my best option. I start to shuffle slowly along the wall, trying to keep as far away from Mrs Hogarth as I can.

'Why is it your fault?' I ask her. 'And who is that outside?'

'That used to be Jemima Kelly,' she answers, sniffing back tears. 'It used to be my grandma. I don't know what it is now.'

'What do you mean "it"? Why's she trying to kill me?'

Mrs Hogarth sighs and leans against the nearest wall.

'I got it wrong. I made a mistake and I'm sorry.'

I can't get my head around any of this. I'm next to the window now but I stop before going outside.

'Would you please tell me what's going on? I'm cold and I'm wet and I need to get home. I've got an assignment to write tonight and... and I'm frightened.'

Mrs Hogarth takes another step towards me and I take another step away. The door at the other end of the room rattles and clatters again, distracting us both. She looks back at me then clears her throat and finally starts to explain.

'Grandma died on Monday,' she says quietly.

'So why is she still here? It's Thursday. Shouldn't someone have taken her away by now? And anyway, how can she be dead? She's out there, banging on the door!'

It sounds even more crazy when I say it out loud. This can't be happening. Mrs Hogarth starts to walk towards the door. It's beginning to give way under the pressure of Mrs Kelly's constant battering.

'Have you ever lost anyone close?' she asks me. She's crying.

'My uncle died last September.'

'When he'd gone, did you start to think about all the things you wish you'd said to him but never did?'

'Dad did. He still says he should have made more of an effort to see him. Why? What's this got to do with anything?'

'If your Dad had a chance to see your uncle one last time, would he have taken it?'

'Of course he would.'

'That's what I did. See, I know how to get that chance. Well I thought I did...'

'What are you talking about?'

'Grandma's sister, Aunty Peggy, she told me what to do. She lives just round the corner. I saw her after Grandma died and she told me.'

'Told you what?' I ask her. Mrs Kelly's hand smashes

through the door and I move towards the window again.

'She showed me how to make up a solution...'

'A solution?' I interrupt. 'What do you mean? A medicine or something like that?' I stop and think for a second. 'Are you talking about a potion?'

She turns around and frowns at me.

'Don't say potion,' she scowls, 'that sounds ridiculous.'

'Nothing sounds ridiculous when there's a dead old lady banging at the door.' I tell her.

'Call it what you like,' she sighs. 'Whatever it is, you administer it to the body and it sort of calls the spirit back for a while.'

Sounds crazy.

'So what went wrong?' I ask.

Now she looks almost embarrassed.

'Bit silly really,' she says, looking down at the floor and shuffling her feet like a little kid who's getting told off in class. 'I mixed it up wrong. I've never been that good with numbers. I put too much of one thing in and not enough of another. I got confused with grams and ounces.'

'What happened?'

'I called Aunty Peggy,' she begins, stopping for a moment as Mrs Kelly's bony fist smashes through a second door panel, 'she told me that the solution attracts the spirit back to the body...'

'And if the solution's not right?'

'She said a spirit would still find its way back...'

'But?'

'But it wouldn't necessarily be the right spirit. I realised what I'd done as soon as I'd given it to her. I'm so sorry, it's bad enough that I have to clear this mess up. I didn't mean for anyone else to get involved.'

I'm having trouble believing this.

'So who's inside your grandma's body now?'

'Don't know. Could be anyone. Thing is, Aunty Peggy says it doesn't matter. She says the wrong spirit in the wrong body is bad news whatever. Doesn't matter who or what it is.'

Can any of this be true? The fact is there's a crazy old woman pounding on the door who, just a few minutes ago, could hardly move. A few more minutes and she'll be inside. We have to do something.

'Aunty Peggy told me how to fix it,' Mrs Hogarth says suddenly. She bends down and starts looking through her shopping bag. 'She said if I don't act quickly, Grandma will get stronger and stronger. The longer we leave it, the worse it will get.'

She stands up and holds a drinks flask up in front of her.

'What's that?'

'Another solution,' she answers. 'It'll put a stop to this.'

'How?'

She shrugs her shoulders and starts to open the flask. The room is suddenly filled with a horrible stench, worse than the one in the kitchen. My stomach starts to turn somersaults and I have to concentrate to stop myself from being sick. I look up and see that Mrs Kelly has smashed her head and shoulders right through the top of the door now. She's reaching down, trying to move the sofa.

'We have to get her to drink it,' Mrs Hogarth says.

'How are we supposed to do that?'

She shrugs her shoulders again.

'We'll just have to let her in and hold her down.'

'She's your Grandma,' I tell her, thinking about how strong and unpredictable the dead old woman has become. 'You can hold her.'

'We can't do it yet,' she whispers secretively. 'We have

to finish the solution first. Aunty Peggy says it needs to be tuned to the person who died.'

'Tuned? How?'

'You have to add a bit of body to it.'

That's it. I can't take any more of this. I start to climb out the window.

'Please,' Mrs Hogarth wails, 'please don't go... I need your help.'

'And I need to get out of here,' I mumble, one leg already outside.

'Please!' she cries, and I stop and look back at her. She looks helpless and terrified. What happens if I don't help? How strong will Mrs Kelly become? 'I'm not talking about cutting off a finger or an arm or a leg,' she sobs, 'just a little bit of her. Some hair or skin...'

I just want to go home, but I know I can't leave her.

'So how are we going to do this?' I ask as I climb back inside.

'Easy really. We cut her nails.' Mrs Hogarth grabs a pair of scissors from her bag. It's like she had this all planned. 'You hold her arm still and I'll cut her nails.'

I can't believe I'm doing this. I run across the room and grab hold of one of Mrs Kelly's bare, spindly arms. She's so strong! She almost picks me off my feet and it's all I can do to keep my balance and hold on to her. Mrs Hogarth manages to prise her vicious fingers apart and then makes a few nervous snips with the scissors. Mrs Kelly smashes me back against the wall, knocking all the wind out of my body, but still I keep hold of her. Mrs Hogarth drops down and combs the carpet by my feet for the tiny, boomerang-shaped nail clippings.

'Have you got enough?' I scream as Mrs Kelly throws me forward and gets ready to hurl me back again.

'Think so,' Mrs Hogarth replies, dropping the nails into the flask and doing up the lid and shaking it like a barman making a cocktail. 'Hope so,' she adds under her breath.

Mrs Kelly is starting to get really, really mad. I let go of her arm and manage to duck out of the way as her hands swipe at me. I watch as she steps back and gets ready to throw herself forward again. I run for cover as she smashes through the door with more strength than ever. Splinters of wood fly around the room in every direction as she breaks through and crashes down onto the sofa. She turns towards me and I'm terrified. I can't move. Her face is twisted with anger and hate and thick strings of sticky dribble are dripping from her yellow teeth and running down her chin.

'Grab her!' Mrs Hogarth screams as Mrs Kelly lunges for me, springing up from the sofa and flying through the air. She wraps her arms around me and I fall backwards, cracking my head on the floor. I look up into her cold, black eyes. I try to free myself but I can't. She's too strong.

'Roll over,' Mrs Hogarth shouts. 'When I tell you, try and roll over onto your front.'

'I can't,' I wail, trying not to cry. Mrs Kelly's face is close to mine now. I can feel her spit dripping onto me.

'Yes, you can,' she hisses. 'Do it!'

Last chance. I can't get this wrong. For a split-second I think about my dropped catch this morning. I have to concentrate this time. I can't let myself mess this up, everything depends on what I do now. Grunting with effort I bring my knees up to my chest and lift the frail frame of the old lady up into the air. She might be strong but she's still light. I push her up as high as I can and then roll over to my right. I can feel Mrs Hogarth helping, shoving Mrs Kelly's shoulders down. A sudden rush of movement and we've done it. Now Mrs Kelly's the one lying on the carpet and I'm on top looking down.

'Move your head!'

I do as I'm told and I tilt my head away as Mrs Hogarth pours the horrific, sticky, foul-smelling liquid into Mrs Kelly's open mouth. She keeps pouring – far more than she needs to – until the old lady's mouth is full and the gross stuff is trickling down the sides of her wrinkled face. She grips me even tighter and I can feel her fingers digging into my skin. I scream as she grips tighter and tighter and tighter until... she lets go. Her bony hands loosen and I push myself away. I roll away and crawl into the furthest corner of the room.

Mrs Kelly is finally still.

'Is that it?' I whisper.

'Think so,' Mrs Hogarth replies, standing over the body of her grandma.

But it isn't. The fingers on the body's right hand start to twitch. Now its whole hand is moving, and now it's spread to both of its arms and its legs. Now the whole of what used to be Mrs Kelly is shaking and twitching so badly that it's almost lifting itself off the ground. Is she going to attack us again? It gets worse and worse and worse and then... it stops. Dead Mrs Kelly is motionless. I'm too scared to move. Mrs Hogarth waits for a second then shuffles forward and prods her dead grandmother's shoulder. She doesn't react. She shoves her again, this time a little harder. Still nothing. Now she's shaking her and shaking her. Nothing.

'Sorry, Grandma,' she says quietly as she lifts up the body and holds her tight.

I didn't say anything to anyone else about what had happened once I got home last night. In fact, by the time I'd got changed, eaten and started work on my assignment, I was having trouble believing any of it had happened myself. The assignment took almost all night to finish and by the time it was finally done everything that had happened with Mrs Kelly and Mrs Hogarth had faded away to little more than a bad dream.

This morning I'm more concerned with college than dead grandmothers. I'm dreading class today. Another day of being called a loser by my so-called friends. I might have lost the game yesterday, but they didn't see what I did last night, did they? If I hadn't helped Mrs Hogarth who knows what might have happened? They'll never know how I—

Mum bursts into my room. 'Get up!'

'What's the matter?'

'Just do as you're told and get up,' she yells. She sounds scared. 'Get dressed and pack a bag. We're leaving.'

'Why?' I shout after her but she's already gone. I get up and run to the door. 'Mum? Mum, what's wrong?'

She's halfway down the stairs. She stops and looks back at me. She looks terrified.

'Crazy people,' she explains, wiping frightened tears from her eyes. 'Town's full of crazy people. Your dad's gone to work. I need him to come home but I can't get hold of him...'

I go downstairs and stand in front of the TV. I can't believe what I'm seeing. The middle of town is like a war-zone. There are massive crowds of people running around, fighting with each other and tearing the place apart. They're all acting like Mrs Kelly last night. But how could that be? They'd have needed to drink the solution, wouldn't they? How could they have...?

I sit down on the edge of the sofa and hold my head in my hands. It was me, wasn't it? I feel like I did when I lost the game yesterday, but a hundred times worse and a thousand times more frightened. I did this. How could I have been so stupid? I wasn't thinking. Three-quarters

of a glass of solution poured down the sink and the end
of the world has begun.

I have to find Mrs Hogarth...

WE WERE SO YOUNG ONCE

This story was written specifically for this collection. A friend of one my daughters lost her mother to cancer at an early age. She was a wonderful person, a true free spirit, and her debilitating illness and untimely death was a devastatingly cruel blow. She was relentlessly positive and upbeat, and left a huge impression on everyone she met. I remember our two families meeting up to form a single unruly tribe, then setting out from home and walking cross-country for mile after mile. We'd stop at a pub we all knew well – the midway point of our hike – for lunch. By road it was barely any distance, but on foot it was a different matter. We walked through the crumbled ruins of an ancient abbey, negotiated herds of cows, and followed the route of a long dried-up canal: all things we'd have missed in the car. Those days were typical of the approach to life of our late friend, and that approach was one of the influences behind this story. Shortly after her mum died, my daughter's friend posted a picture on Facebook of her family as kids. The caption read simply, we were so young once.

Other than the old man in the bed, the room was empty. No monitors. No noise. Nothing but the wait. He drifted in and out of sleep, hovering on the blurred and increasingly ill-defined borderline between conscious and unconscious. The soft hiss as the door opened woke him briefly, then recognition helped bring him around fully. He was pleased to see a friendly face, not another one of the medical team, here to prod and poke and check him incessantly.

'Hello, Joshua. How are you feeling today?'

Joshua blinked into the light and smiled faintly. He tried to sit himself up but couldn't. Karl helped him and did what he could to hide the surprise on his face. The other man was light as a feather.

'That's something of a redundant question,' Joshua wheezed, his voice full of air. 'I'm very tired all the time, and that surprises me because all I seem to do now is sleep.'

Karl took off his hat, coat and gloves and checked his hair in the mirror. He fetched a chair and carried it across the sparsely furnished room. He sat near to the head of the bed and angled his position carefully so Joshua could look at him with minimum effort. 'You're right, of course,' he said. 'What did I expect you to say? It's one of those silly, instinctive questions. You walk into a hospital room and you feel duty bound to ask the patient how they are.'

'We've all done it. Remember when Aunt Hilda told us about Ernest's cancer?'

'And your response was *you're joking!*'

'I know. Awkward, wasn't it?'

'You didn't mean anything by it.'

'I was struggling to take it in.'

'But Hilda took exception.'

'She certainly did. Anyway, I'm not taking exception.

I'm fine as it happens, all things considered. Actually looking forward to the rest.'

Karl turned towards the window. He pretended to scratch the side of his nose but instead wiped away a tear, hoping the old man in the bed hadn't noticed.

He had.

'There's no need for that,' Joshua told him, his voice little more than a whisper. 'Don't be sad. It's natural. We can't go on forever. Built-in obsolescence, wasn't that what they used to call it?'

'Yes, for cars and computers and mobile phones, but not people.' The expression on Karl's face changed. 'You've always been a stubborn bugger, Josh. I just wish you'd listened and met me halfway.'

'There is no halfway. You know how I feel about this. How I've always felt.'

'How many times have we had this conversation?'

'Far too many. Only once more though, I think.'

A pause, both of them waiting for the other to speak. Karl reached for his jacket and took a screen from the pocket. 'Here, look at this. I found it the other day.'

He flicked through images until he found the one he wanted, then held the screen so that Joshua could see. A grassy field. A summer's day. All the family together. Joshua squinted to focus, allowing memory to fill in those details he couldn't quite make out.

'Would you look at that.'

'Do you remember that day?'

'I do, I do... goodness, we were so young once.'

Karl turned off the screen and lay it on the bed. He hesitated before speaking again. Should he bother? Was there any point them having this discussion – this *argument* – again? As usual, his frustration got the better of him. He just couldn't help himself.

'It didn't have to be like this, Joshua.'

'I wanted it this way.'

'I know, and I also know that if we had another fifty years or more to keep debating it, I still wouldn't understand why you've made the choices you have.'

'You don't need to understand. We're all different. I don't want you to understand or agree, I just want you to accept.'

'But it's such a waste. So bloody pointless.'

'You think? That's where we'll have to agree to disagree. My life has been far from pointless.'

'I know... wrong choice of words, perhaps, but you could have had treatments. There were procedures. You don't have to die yet.'

'We all die eventually.'

'Yes, but why now?'

'I was worried I'd get bored waiting.'

'That's no answer.'

'Well that's my answer.'

Exasperated, Karl rested his hand on the bed. Joshua slowly lifted a tired, trembling hand from under the covers to meet it.

'What are you looking at?'

'Which finger was it?' Joshua asked.

Karl turned his hand over and showed him his right index finger. 'This one.'

'Nasty break, that was. You went the most peculiar shade of green.'

'It was your fault.'

'And you've never let me forget it.'

'I've never known pain like it before or since. That was the last time I went without immediate anaesthetisation. I've had worse procedures since then, far more invasive, but the pain's always been closely managed. The agony when I broke that finger was incredible.'

'I still maintain I was hammering in the right place. It

was your hand in the wrong place that was the problem.'

Karl laughed. He raised his hand and studied it intently. 'It took a lot of work to put right, this finger of mine. They talked about amputation when it first happened, remember? Imagine that! Thank goodness Rashid introduced me to Dr Steele. I've lost track of the number of times I've been under Steele's knife since then. He's one of the very best.'

'There's no doubting his skill.'

'This finger shows how far we've come in the last fifty years.' Karl admired his perfectly reconstructed digit. 'It was a pretty standard bone repair and tidy-up originally, but it was never completely straight once it had healed. By the time we got around to looking at it again, the tech was far more advanced. Steele replaced the bone down to the knuckle with alloy, if you remember, then he restored and recoloured the skin, removed the imperfections. He did such an excellent job that I had him do a complete clean-up of both hands in the end. I'd had a pronounced lump and groove from where I used to hold a pen at school, back before it was all touchscreens and the like.'

'I remember.'

'It wasn't anything much, didn't cause me any problems, but it was ugly and I couldn't stand it. Steele removed it and levelled it for me. He went on to do a lot of work on the veins after that, tied them up nicely. And he's balanced the age discolouration since then too. Dealt with all the blemishes and moles.'

'Movie star hands,' Joshua said.

'I wouldn't go that far. Anyway, as you know, it all went from there. I'm in tip-top condition now, all things considered. Healthy body, healthy mind, and all that.'

'Shouldn't it be healthy mind, healthy body?'

'Should it? Whatever.'

Karl was so preoccupied with his reconstructed digit that it took him a while to realise how intently Joshua was now admiring his own right hand. When he noticed Karl was watching, he held it up and turned it around to show him. Palm facing outward, he asked 'remember that?'

Karl winced at the vicious-looking scar which zig-zagged across the old man's palm. 'I've lost count of the number of times I tried to get you to have that put right. You've always worn that scar like a badge of honour.'

'Yes, because that's exactly what it is. I earned it. And anyway, it healed all right in the end, didn't it?'

'Only just. It was touch and go.'

'Remember when I did it?'

'How could I forget? We were climbing in Ecuador.'

Joshua shook his head. 'No, I was climbing.'

'We both got to the top.'

'Yes, but you used that gyro-platform-thingy.'

'The view was the same for both of us, though. Pretty incredible, as I recall.'

'Yes, but it wasn't all about the view, was it? You're still missing the point, all these years later. For me it was about the excitement of the climb, about living on the edge. You're right, it bloody hurt when I caught my hand, but I don't remember the pain, I just remember the adrenalin rush of the climb and the sense of achievement when I'd finished.'

'And I remember the panic in the camp when they heard you were injured.'

'It was just a cut, nothing serious.'

'Serious enough for you to use the platform to get down off the mountain.'

'It looked far worse than it was.'

'It got infected.'

'And it healed.'

'After you'd spent more than a week in bed burning up. You delayed our return home. Cost me a business deal.'

'And got you another one, as I recall. You met Maureen Wilmington while you were out there looking after me, didn't you? You've certainly benefitted from your association with the Wilmington Institute since then.'

'That's beside the point.'

'I think it's exactly the point.'

Joshua began to cough. Karl fetched him a glass of water and held it to his lips.

'I'm tiring you out,' Karl said.

'Not a problem. Nothing left to save my energy for except these few moments.' He lifted a trembling hand and brushed fine wisps of white hair from his left temple. 'This was always my favourite scar,' he said, and when he smiled the ends of the scar disappeared into the wrinkles around the corner of his eye. 'Remember it?'

'How could I forget?'

'If I hadn't done it I never would have met her.'

'And if I had a credit for every time I'd heard this story...'

'Then you'd have enough to pay for another lifetime of surgeries.'

'With change to spare.'

'You've spent so much over the years.'

'The family never went without.'

'True.'

'And you've spent more than your fair share too.'

'I have. I've spent my money on doing things, going places. I spent my money on living.'

'And I spent my money on not dying. Different sides of the same coin.'

'Hardly.'

'Let's not argue again. Not now.'

'Agreed. You'd win today for once. Too tired.'

Karl laughed and shook his head. 'You were telling me about your favourite scar.'

'Like you say, it's nothing you haven't heard a hundred times before.'

'Once more, then.'

'I came off my bike in the scrub, remember? Hit my head on a rock and smashed up my ankle.'

'I remember.'

'You'd got my recovery all paid for and planned out.'

'I remember that, too.'

'And I refused your recommendation. You said they could have replaced my broken bones with something stronger, but I didn't want to do it. There's something about the fragility. Keeps a man's ego in check.'

'But your ankle broke several more times afterwards. You could have avoided that.'

'Maybe. Perhaps I'm just a sucker for punishment.'

'Or perhaps you fell in love with your physiotherapist? Victoria was a lovely girl. She brought out the best in you.'

'We had almost twenty years together. Just a blink of an eye for you, but twenty of the best years for me.'

'Just so sad that she—'

'Don't. You see, you always do this and there's no need. You miss the point. There was nothing you or me or any of your team of incredible doctors and surgeons could have done about it. Wrong place, wrong time. Pilot error. I console myself with the thought that she knew nothing about it other than maybe a second or two of confusion when the plane began to break up. She phoned me before take-off and she was so happy, so looking forward to getting home. She'd been to one of her favourite parts of the world and she had a head full of memories.'

'So sad, though. Even after all these years...'

'Don't you sometimes wish you could end your time like that, though? In a way I'm envious of her. I should have been on that flight too. Now look at me – a tired old man, running out of life, just sitting here waiting to breathe his last.'

Joshua slumped back in the bed, exhausted by all the talking. Karl stood up and began to pace the room, his inevitable frustration beginning to show. It always did.

'I just wish you'd—'

'Stop, please.'

'But—'

'It's a bit late if you're planning on lecturing me again. I doubt even the incredible Dr Steele could do anything for me now.'

'You're wrong. It's not too late. Steele could help you keep going for a while longer.'

'And what would that achieve? Another few days in this comfortable cell?'

'It's not a cell.'

'It might as well be.'

'But if only you'd let them try. You could have a few more years still. It's incredible the things they can do now.'

'I don't doubt it.'

'I know your lungs are shot. There are new artificial lungs now that are self-powering. Never get tired. Steele was telling me about a new type of implant that will regulate the heartbeat for a hundred years or longer.'

'And? Would I still be me? I've never liked the prospect of being part-man, part-machine.'

'So bloody overdramatic. I've lost track of the number of procedures I've had, and I'm still me, aren't I?'

'And to think it all started with a broken finger. You've got a lot to thank me for.'

Karl didn't react. 'There's nothing they can't do these days.'

'Other than prevent death.'

'And that will never change, but we can at least defer it now. Look at me – my hips, shoulders, knees, wrists, ankles and elbows will outlast the rest of me. My hair is as thick and strong as it was when I was in my twenties. My hearing has actually improved with age and, thanks to the implants, so has my sight. My skin is strong, my gut is healthy, my muscles are good.'

'You are a fine figure of a man,' Joshua said from his bed, paying the price for his sarcastic tone as a chuckle became a laugh, became a wheeze and then a full-blown coughing fit. Karl passed him his water and he drank a little. Once composed, he continued. 'You put me to shame, I know. My hair – the few strands remaining – is thin and white. My eyes have long lost their focus, and if there was any more noise in this room, I'm sure I'd struggle to make out your voice. I've barely got out of this bed for weeks and I likely won't leave this room again unless it's on a gurney. I haven't stood by myself for several months. My bones are brittle. They'd snap like twigs if I fell.'

Karl became emotional again, barely able to look at the man in the bed. He looked so small. 'You infuriate me. You're stubborn and you're selfish.'

'Selfish? Because I refused to wrap myself in cotton wool? Because I've lived? I done things you could only dream of. I've seen more sights in more places than you can imagine.'

'And as a result you look every day of your age and more,' he said. 'I look thirty years younger and will likely go on for decades more yet.'

'Doing what, though? Do you feel the same as you did thirty years ago?'

'Yes,' Karl replied without hesitation. 'Better, actually.'

'Then I'd suggest you've just been treading water all these years, not living.'

'Bullshit.'

'Help me up.'

'What?'

'Help me out of bed.'

'After what you've just being saying about your bones?'

'Yes! Live a little, eh?'

'It's too dangerous.'

'What's the worst that could happen? I'll most likely have expired by the end of this week or next. I don't think it's too much of a risk.'

Against his better judgement, Karl obliged.

Joshua's bedclothes weighed more than the man. To Karl he felt empty. Paper-light. He took his time, slowly shuffling Joshua around until his legs hung over the bed, then edging him forward until his outstretched toes made contact and his milky-white feet slid into long-unused slippers.

With a strong, supportive hand under Joshua's left arm, Karl helped him stand upright. 'I've got you,' he said, and he had, for he was easily supporting the other man's insignificant frame. 'You okay?'

Joshua nodded. 'Light-headed. Give me a second.'

Karl gripped tighter, but not too tight. Enough to keep the other man safe, but not so hard as to bruise his parchment skin or damage his brittle bones. Joshua wavered, as if being blown by the wind, but after several more seconds he was ready to take a step.

They walked together to the window.

'Open it,' Joshua said.

'It's cold out there,' Karl warned. 'You'll catch your

death.' Joshua just looked at him, then leant against the wall and gazed out over the gardens which stretched out behind the hospice. The sun was warm on his face. As requested, Karl opened the window and Joshua drank up the freshness of the breeze.

'You've had it wrong all these years,' he said to Karl.

'No one's perfect. I've had double the years of most men.'

'Twice as wrong, then. All that time you've wasted in surgery and in recovery. All the times you held back for fear of getting your hands dirty or a hair falling out of place.'

'Stop mocking me. I've done plenty. I've travelled. If Victoria had travelled less, maybe she'd still be here to-day?'

'Maybe, but Christ, how dull life would have been if we hadn't taken chances and risks. All those things we'd have missed. The places we'd never have seen.'

'Did you not hear me? I've travelled too.'

'You have, yes. Over the years you've shown me an incalculable number of images and clips you've taken from various aircraft and viewing platforms. You've only ever got as close to the rest of the world as your telephoto lens allows. You've barely touched or tasted. Your experiences have been sanitized and streamlined. You've seen only the tourist-friendly version of the countries you've visited. The edited highlights.'

'You're wrong.'

'You know I'm not. You've lived your life through a touchscreen. You'll always deny it, but if you're honest with yourself, you know I'm telling the truth. So what if I injured myself along the way and wore my body out – I lived! You... you've covered yourself in bubble-wrap and tissue paper and have only experienced – truly experienced – a fraction of things you could have.'

Karl's shoulders slumped. 'You're right, of course,' he admitted. 'Living for this long has come at a price, both financially and emotionally.'

'So many people in your life have come and gone.'

'True. But losing you... that will be the bitterest pill of all to have to swallow.'

Karl put his arm around the shoulder of the frail figure next to him and helped him to sit down on the window seat. He kneeled in front of him, listening to the old man's laboured breathing, watching the over-pronounced rise and fall of his chest. He looked at Joshua's shaking hands. Liver spots and broken, blackened veins. Yellowed nails. White hairs.

'Don't be sad,' Joshua said. 'This is what I want. I have no regrets.'

Karl nodded, and wiped away more tears. 'I know.'

'I've lived the life I wanted to lead.'

'I know that, too.'

'Then stop crying.'

'But how can I when you're going to die? No man should have to bury his own child.'

NOLAN HIGGS IS OUT OF HIS DEPTH

We're back in Wales again, and back looking at the impact of industry on the Welsh people and landscape. I grew up in the 1980s with clear memories (but a desperately limited understanding) of the decline of the mining industry. As I learnt more, I was struck by the enormity of the impact the closure of the pits had on the towns and villages around them, how mining had been the very lifeblood of these communities.

After watching Xavier Gen's phenomenal 2007 movie **Frontiére(s)** where the characters use tunnels to escape a family of cannibalistic neo-Nazis, I had an idea for a crime caper gone wrong. I substituted the the abandoned pits of South Wales for the claustrophobic farm tunnels of the film, and sent desperate unemployed ex-miner Nolan Higgs back underground for one last shift.

Nolan Higgs tightly grips the steering wheel of the silver Ford Sierra. Hands clammy. Pulse racing. Everything hinges on this job and he's not going to bugger it up this time. He's planned this meticulously, down to the last inch. No fluffs, no mistakes, no screw ups and no trouble. Not like last time (or the time before that). Today, Nolan's in charge. They don't know it yet, but he's the one calling the shots.

It's not the job itself that's making him nervous, it's what comes afterwards. They won't be expecting it. People have underestimated Nolan for too long now. All of them do it, even Marina, but he's going to show them. Today, his and Marina's lives are going to change for the better, forever. Goodbye to a life of petty pilfering. Goodbye to their dingy council flat on the outskirts of Llanelli. Hello to... well, he's not entirely sure what just yet. *The world is your lobster, Nolan,* as half-pissed Uncle Trevor always tells him when they've been out on the lash.

Marina hadn't been happy when he'd told her, though. 'We've been down this road too many times before. I don't know how much more I can take.'

'It'll be different this time, lover,' he told her.

'Yeah, but you said that last time, didn't you? And the time before that an' all.'

'I know, but I mean it. I've changed, love, honest I have. This is my last job, I swear.'

'I just want a normal life, Nolan. One where you're not looking over your shoulder all the time. One where the police aren't knocking on the door every couple of days. I want a decent house, a garden big enough for the dogs. I want to settle down and have kids. I want satellite TV, Nolan.'

'You'll have all that and more.'

'We haven't even had a TV since you missed the payments and Radio Rentals took it back.'

'I know. I'm sorry. I'll sort it out, I promise.'

'You said that last time too.'

Nolan knows he's let Marina down more times than he can remember, but he's not going to let the same thing happen today. Last time he was out of his depth and he got caught out. He was their patsy, their fool, and he didn't cotton on until it was too late. He's learnt a lot in the time he's been away. That last fella he was bunked up in his cell with during his last stretch, Barry Bevan, he taught him a few things and put him right about others. Made him look at things in a whole new light, did Barry. He was a scrawny little runt of a bloke with the face of a rat and all the airs and graces of one too, but he knew what he was talking about. He was a lifer. He'd been inside for a long stretch for armed robbery and GBH, with little prospect of getting out in the foreseeable. 'It's my job to pass on what I've learnt,' he told Nolan. 'But do it better than me, lad, and don't get caught!'

'Trouble with you, Nolan Higgs,' Marina says, 'is you don't know when to quit. You don't realise you're in over your head until it's too late, and it's everyone else that pays the price.'

Not this time. This is different. I've got a whole new outlook on life now, a new perspective.

But for now Nolan needs to focus on the job at hand. Engine running. Eyes fixed on the back of the warehouse across the way. Ready to put his foot down and disappear the second it all kicks off.

Everyone knew Jason and Boyce from the estate. And if they didn't actually know them, then they knew of their reputations. Proper legends, they were. The bad boys of Camarthenshire. So when their associate Gary Coleman had looked Nolan up in the clink a few weeks before he'd been due for release, it had been something of an ego boost for him. Roping him in on a job and promising a cut... well that just legitimised Nolan's gangster credentials. Barry had shared his enthusiasm. 'That's great, Nolan. A job like that'll help you move up the ranks, give you the confidence to start branching out on your own, know what I mean?'

Nolan had known exactly what Barry had meant. Their lives had followed relatively similar paths until now: both of them working at the (now shut down) Aberfoil pit before realising their dubious talents would better serve them elsewhere. Barry had robbed on the side and had been doing all right for himself, thank you very much, until a bit of business with an ex-mate had turned nasty and he'd been sent down. Nolan's career change from reluctant miner to full-time thief had been more as a result of Mrs Thatcher's decision to close Aberfoil than anything. 'The old witch did you a favour, boy,' Barry regularly told him when they chatted after lights out. And Barry was right.

It was like having your own personal tutor locked in the cell with you, twenty hours a day. If Nolan was too harsh on himself, Barry would put him straight. When he beat himself up because he'd let Marina down and was inside again, Barry made him see the bright side. 'You need setbacks like this to be able to get yourself on the right track and straightened out. You know what you done wrong, Nolan, and you know what you need to do different next time. Those boys you're getting involved with, they're proper nasty bastards they are, and they think you're a loser. You know what, son? Let them think it. You know you're better than that, and so do I. You can use their prejudices to your advantage.'

And that's exactly what Nolan's doing today.

*

We're off.

The sound of shooting coming from inside the warehouse is unmistakable. Two muffled cracks in quick succession from the sawn-off barrels of Boyce's shotgun. Just a kneecapping, they'd said, just enough to slow up the nightwatchman, nothing more serious than that. Using firearms always ups the ante in this game, but Nolan's not worried. He's not intending on hanging around.

He switches off the radio (It was Starship's *Nothing's Gonna Stop Us Now* – shame, he bloody loves that song, he's decided it's him and Marina's new theme tune) and focuses, feeling cool as a bloody cucumber.

Here they come.

Their timing is spot on. Just like they'd told him it would be.

Jason, Boyce and Gary Coleman come running out of the warehouse all balaclava'd up, each carrying a massive sports holdall full of cash. Nolan runs around to the back of the car and pops open the boot. He's back behind the wheel before they've made it across the street. He waits for three thumps as the bags are chucked inside, then the clunk and slam and the boot is shut.

Jason goes for the passenger door, but it's locked. All the doors are locked. No one's getting in. Boyce hammers on Nolan's window and shouts 'open this fucking door,' but Nolan doesn't. Instead he puts his foot down and drives away like bloody hell.

He watches the three of them in the rear-view mirror for as long as he's able. Spitting feathers, they are, but that's no real surprise given the circumstances. He's pulled the rug out from under their feet. That'll teach them to underestimate Nolan Higgs. The police will be round the warehouse in no time, and Boyce, Jason and Coleman will be banged up and sent down before tea.

*

'It's a bloody easy job, man,' Coleman had told him. The two of them had been on washing detail, loading and unloading endless shitty grey sheets into and out of industrial-sized washing machines. The air had reeked of bleach, burning the insides of Nolan's nose and giving him the sniffs. 'There's three bookies and two video shops. Dewi Rees has his managers drop the weekend takings at his warehouse late Sunday night or early Monday morning. Boyce knows a guy who knows a guy who says there's hardly any security cover at that time, because despite being rolling in cash, Dewi's also a tight bastard and he reckons no one would ever think he'd be dumb enough to stash that much loot on site like that. All the blokes he's got working for him think they're the only ones dropping off. He gives them all different times and different routes, so no one but Dewi knows exactly how much is there. He picks it all up himself from the warehouse at nine o'clock Monday morning, regular as clockwork, usually with a couple of heavies in tow. Thing is, night shift in the warehouse finishes at four, and the early shift don't come in until five. Gives us an hour to get in and clear him out.'

Nolan knew you'd have to either be extremely confident or really bloody stupid to want to do over Dewi Rees. 'There's gotta be more to it than that?'

'No, man, I swear,' Coleman had told him. 'Boyce has checked it all out. Mental, ain't it? Thing is, no one would ever think Dewi would be daft enough to cut corners, same as no one would think anyone would risk doing bloody Dewi Rees over. So you in or what?'

Later, when Nolan had talked (in general, non-specific terms and without naming names) about what was being planned, Barry Bevan had told him exactly why it sounded like such a good idea. 'You see, Nolan, I told you. Mind games.'

'Yeah, I understand that...'

'I don't know if you do, son. This is the perfect opportunity for you to get one over on them. They're using you because they think they can, and that gives you the upper hand. They think you look up to them, that you're scared of them—'

'And they're right.'

'—so you need to play your own mind games too. Let them think you're dumb, but act smart. Stay one step ahead of them.'

This morning, Nolan reckons he's nearer five steps ahead. More of Barry's invaluable pearls of wisdom rattle around his head as he drives sedately through the streets of Camarthen, keeping to thirty in built-up areas, not taking any chances. *It's not about trying to get away fast, it's about driving so as you don't attract any unwanted attention. Go slow. Take your time. Not looking suspicious is far better than driving like a bat out of hell.*

But it's bloody hard, man, knowing you've got three of Llanelli's finest criminals and, very soon, half the South Wales police force on your tail.

Nolan Higgs is a wanted man now, and it feels amazing. He's the criminal's criminal. The man who screwed over the men who screwed over *the* man.

Keep some of the details to yourself, Barry had told him, *don't tell no one.* That was why he'd used the black gaffer tape to change the car's plates, altering a 'F' to look like an 'E' and one of the 'C's to look like a 'G'. He'd acquired the car for the job according to Boyce's spec, and had made the alterations before driving it to the lock up, before anyone else had clapped eyes on it. As far as they were concerned, the Sierra had always been B398 GEG. He'd stripped the tape when they'd gone into the warehouse, and now it's plain old B398 GFC again. That'll wrong-foot the pigs, he thinks.

First stop.

Scrubland.

No buildings, no roads, no reason for anyone else to be here.

Add in a couple of extra steps they won't be expecting.

Extra step one. A second car.

He'd bought this old knacker for peanuts the last time he got out of nick. It was a beaten-up old wreck that had taken him all this time to get match-fit again. A beige Austin Maestro. The kind of motor he'd usually have been too embarrassed to be caught driving. Something his Granddad Fred (God rest his soul) would have loved. That was another tip Barry had given him. *You don't want to be driving anything too flash or too fancy, Nolan. A get-away car should blend in. They'll be expecting you to be driving something fast and smart-looking. You need to get yourself something that looks like a heap but won't let you down.*

Extra step two. Back to where we started.

It had taken Barry a considerable length of time to persuade Nolan as to the benefits of this particular nugget of wisdom. *Go back to where you started,* he'd said. *The last place they'll be looking for you is right under their noses.*

So that's exactly what he's done, even to the point of driving down several of the roads around the vicinity of the warehouse. It's hard not putting his foot down when he sees the police swarming all around the place, though. No sign of Boyce and the boys here. All gone. And there's a distinct lack of activity, despite the police numbers. All the signs are pointing to it being over.

Bloody hell, man. Was it really that easy?

When are all those bloody cynics and naysayers going to shut up and start trusting him? Nolan knows what he's doing. Of course, he's never going to be able to confront them and tell them all that he was right and they were wrong, because he's going to disappear and none of them will ever hear from him again. Good job, too, because if Jason or Boyce or Dewi bloody Rees ever get wind and manage to track him down, he'll be a dead man.

But they won't.

They'll never find him.

Make like a magician and disappear.

That had been Barry's last piece of advice. The two of them had been sitting in the cell watching *Blockbusters* on Barry's black and white portable when he'd just dropped it casually into conversation. Barry told him how to do it, and told him where, too. Aberfoil. The closed-down colliery. Somewhere Nolan knew well.

Make it look like you've gone, lad. Let them think you've had a change of heart or lost the will to live or something. Let them think you've done yourself in.

Nolan came out here a few days ago and checked the place out. It was just like he remembered, except more overgrown and dishevelled. Sad, like. Last time he was here the pit had been filled with noise and activity, like a force of nature. Now it was just an empty shell. Same as all the other pits round these parts.

Nolan parks the Maestro at the top of the slope down to the lake. Deep as anything, that man-made pool. One of those places where you tend to lose two or three local kids every time there's a hot spell in the summer. The water's dark as oil and cold as you like. Nolan thinks there's probably all kinds of nastiness down at the bottom of this massive murky lake.

Good job he's not going anywhere near it, then.

He takes the bags of money out of the boot, along with the mining equipment he also brought here with him. Some was his own, the rest of it belonged to his old dad.

If there's one thing the folks round here aren't short of, it's spare mining gear. Then he gets back in the car and reverses it right up to the very edge of the slope. Then a little further back still. When he gets out – taking his time, careful as anything – it's like that film with Michael Caine that's on ITV every bloody Christmas. The one that finishes with the bus balancing on the side of the mountain. Except today it's a Maestro on a slag heap.

Back on solid ground again and he gives the front of the car a hefty shove, strong enough to send it rolling backwards towards the water. It's an underwhelming ending. Nolan was expecting noise and splashes and all kinds of crazy, but instead what he gets is the beige-coloured car sinking back into the depths like it's slipping into an ice-cold, muck-filled bath. That's good, though, he tells himself. If they trace him this far, he wants them to think he drowned. They'll waste days and weeks recovering the car, looking for the body and the bags. Plenty of time for him to disappear.

Just Nolan and three big bags of cash left now.

He puts on his overalls and his safety helmet and battery pack, then picks up the money. It weighs a ton, but it's his future Nolan's lugging around here, so he'll put up with the pain. A future for him and Marina in Alicante. He's got it all mapped out. Sun, sea and sex for the rest of their naturals. Goodbye to the Valleys, hello the Costa Blanca.

Time for the encore. The last piece of the performance. The real disappearing act.

Nolan trudges towards the mouth of the pit, boarded off but not impenetrable. It's eerie quiet, not a soul for miles. The atmosphere is foreboding and even Nolan, a man who almost exclusively focuses on the here and now, is overwhelmed by the lost history of this place. Thousands, maybe hundreds of thousands of men must have walked this path to disappear down below the surface to win the coal which powered the country until Mrs Thatcher tore the heart out of the industry. Four generations of his own family had worked here, with him being the last. *Oh well,* he thinks, *it's a shame about your jobs and all that, but that's not my problem.* Nolan reckons he's got more money in these bags than most of those blokes would have earned in a lifetime.

They'd hatched the plan between them in the cell one night after dark. *What about one of the ventilation shafts? Barry had said. Remember? One of them has a really gradual slope. It comes out about a mile and a half further down the valley.*

Nolan switches on his helmet lamp then checks his pockets for car keys. He's had so many sets of keys this morning that it's been difficult keeping track of them. The Sierra, the Maestro, and the blue Austin Metro he's left near the other end of the escape shaft. All present and correct.

Right. This is it.

It would be easy to get nervous at this stage, and Nolan thinks he might have bottled it by now if the stakes hadn't been so high.

The lift cage is useless, obviously, because there's been no power down here for months. He remembers the route, though, and uses the emergency ladders to work his way down, dropping the bags in front of him a level at a time. The main shaft is in good repair. It's dark and damp, but these places always are. It's just like he remembers, and he thinks that if someone flicked a switch somewhere, the old place would be up and running again in a heartbeat. The Tories called this progress, but none of the men who worked down here and lost their jobs would agree.

Lower and lower, deeper and deeper. A man could

lose his mind in a place like this. The older blokes liked to wind the new lads up when they first went below ground. He remembers when he was fresh meat, being scared shitless hearing stories about miners who'd taken a wrong turn and ended up lost in the maze of caverns and passages below the surface. Every pit had its legends; men who'd lost their way then lost their minds when the batteries powering their lamps had died. Because you never get used to the dark in a place like this. Your eyes don't adjust. It's enough to send even the sanest bloke round the twist.

Nolan wishes he hadn't started thinking about all that now, because it's playing on his mind. The harder he tries to think about something else, the harder it gets to ignore his fears. Remember that story about old John Thompson? They said he'd been gone for almost a week before they found him. Chewed his own hand off at the wrist, the legend went. It was all bullshit and bluster, Nolan knows that, but he can't deny it's making him feel very bloody scared on his own down here at the moment. He walks along an endless empty tunnel, hundreds of yards belowground, dragging the bags behind him, wishing he was on his way out.

He's so preoccupied that he almost misses the turn.

What was it Barry said? *Stay alert and don't let your mind wander.*

It's only by chance that he spots the T-junction, and it makes his legs go weak with nerves because he knows that if he'd missed it, he could have kept walking forever... down and down, deeper and deeper.

But he's okay.

The bags are getting bloody heavy, mind.

Before he enters the passage that's going to get him out of here, he stops for a well-earned breather. He sits on fifty grand cash in stacked up bags and opens a can of Tango he'd stashed away in the Maestro. He toasts his own success. *You showed them all, boy. You won!* He can't wait to get out of here now. He's got it all worked out: take the Metro to Neath and pick up Marina from her aunt's, then drive down to Dover and get on the ferry. *Don't matter how long it takes to get to Spain, lover,* he told her when they last spoke. *Once we're there we've got the rest of our lives...*

Pop downed, he crushes the can and throws it away. He belches, and the sound echoes endlessly around him. By the time the noise has finally faded away to nothing, he's back on his feet with the bags and is heading up into the ventilation shaft.

It's hard going. Barry said it would be. Nolan can't quite shake the nagging doubts from his mind. *Is this the right tunnel? Am I going the right way? Will the battery last? Will I last?* But he keeps going because today he's filled with a new-found inner confidence he didn't know he possessed. He's no longer resigned to playing second fiddle to minor cons and local gangsters. He's his own man. He took Marina to the pictures last week and they saw that gangster flick everyone's on about, *The Untouchables.* That's Nolan today, that is. *Un-bloody-touchable.*

The slope is very gradual but very definite, and the longer this shaft goes on, the more uncertain he feels. The walls are getting closer, that he knows for a fact because when he stops and stretches out his arms now, he can touch both sides of the passage. And he's having to stoop too. He thought it might just be because the bags are so heavy, but no, the roof of the shaft is definitely lower here. Barry said it was like this. He said it would be a squeeze towards the end. Nolan doesn't have a choice now, anyway. Apart from the fact he'd struggle to turn around or go down backwards, he's ditched the Maestro and the coppers might still be able to trace him here when they find the original getaway car abandoned. No, there's no option. He just has to keep going.

Oh, but that tiny chink of light right up there is the most beautiful thing he's ever seen.

It took him a few seconds to realise it was even there. Just a grey smudge of shadow to start with, a smear of *something* on the edge of the endless *nothing* his lamp light doesn't reach. Nolan's sweat-soaked and completely knackered, but seeing the light fills him with energy again. He can do this. *I'm going to do this!*

He reckons it'll be easier to push the bags than to pull them now. He needs his arms out front, not behind. He drags two of the sports bags through between his legs, then manages to swing the strap of the third over his shoulder so he can carry it while keeping his hands free for pushing the others ahead.

The slope of the shaft increases noticeably like Barry said it would. Almost there!

Whether it's the low ceiling or the weight of the bag on his back or the effort of pushing the other two while climbing upwards he's not sure, but with less than a hundred yards to go, Nolan has to get down on his knees. A little further still and he lowers himself onto his belly and crawls along. The ground feels more uneven when you're crawling like this. It's covered in debris. There's a greater risk of this happening nearer the surface (because there's more going on up top), and there's been a few very minor cave-ins. Barry said he thought this had happened here. It's nothing too serious, though. Nolan knows he wouldn't be able to see the way out if there was a problem, would he?

So close now.

That small rectangle of light has continued to increase in size, and if it wasn't for the two bags of money he's pushing in front of him obscuring his view, Nolan thinks he'd almost have a clear view of the outside world by now. He might even be able to see the Metro. The last stretch is always the hardest though, isn't it?

Here there's a particularly awkward fallen rock to negotiate. A large section of the roof has dropped, leaving him a ledge to climb over. Once he's done it, he reckons it'll be plain sailing. Nolan reaches between the bags with one outstretched hand and feels his way around. It's okay. From what he can tell, there's a drop of less than a foot. Plenty of room on the other side. It's a good job he's always been a skinny bugger, he thinks.

He edges further forward, pushing both of the bags until he feels them drop down. Then another few inches so he can check they've landed safely.

That's a relief. All present and correct.

Let's get out of here.

But Nolan can't move.

He's stuck.

The bag on his back is making it difficult to move, but there's no way back so he keeps trying to push through, inch by inch. Barry said it would be tight, but he never thought it would be as bad as this. The harder he tries, the more he's wedged in place. When Nolan can't move any further, he just about manages to get his left arm down by his side and, with much fumbling and stretching, is able to undo the clasp on the third bag's strap. That's a relief. He's got a little more freedom again now, some leverage. He holds onto the ledge with the outstretched tips of his right hand and pulls himself forward and upward.

Slow progress.

Even slower progress.

No progress at all now, actually.

Sun, sea and sex...

Nolan looks up (as best he can – his chin is dragging

on the ground and there's not enough room for him to fully lift his head), then grips the ledge again and tries to heave himself forward once more. When he can't get any purchase with his fingers, he pushes against the sides of the narrow passage with his feet.

He moves another inch or two, then comes to a complete stop.

Head now wedged over to one side, body trapped between the slope and the roof, one arm sticking out in front and the other locked behind. Heels against the ceiling, toes on the ground. Legs pressed tight together, unable to separate. Rock on all sides. No space whatsoever.

Can't go forwards, can't go backwards. Can't go anywhere.

Stuck.

Absolutely, completely, hopelessly, impossibly stuck.

'Help!'

Nolan screams until his throat is hoarse, but he knows there's no point, because no one knows he's down here and no one else is coming. No one comes round these parts anymore, not since the pit closed. That was why Barry told him to pick the place, after all.

'Somebody help me!' he yells again, but he already knows in his heart that no one will. And that terrifying, claustrophobic certainty makes him try to kick and push and scratch and shove even harder to get himself free. But the harder Nolan struggles, the worse it gets.

Nolan Higgs is trapped, and he's not going anywhere.

It's seven years and a month later when he's finally released. He was never a lifer, but Nolan never questioned that. He wasn't in for armed robbery and GBH either, just fiddling (both kids and books, as it happens). No matter now, though. All that's behind him.

The first thing he does after getting out is find himself

a car, and the first place he goes is the pit. More specifically, the ventilation shaft. He hopes he can remember everything he said after all this time, hopes it all worked out as he and Nolan planned.

It takes him an age to find the entrance to the shaft and to clear the overgrowth and undergrowth from it. Being a little bloke has its advantages, and he ties himself to the end of a long rope, ties the other end to the bumper of his car, then puts on his old hard hat, turns on the light and enters the tunnel. It doesn't take him long to reach the spot he remembers, the place where the roof fell in and made the shaft all but impossible to pass.

Seems like it worked just as he'd hoped. Better even.

Nolan Higgs' body is little more than a husk wrapped in scraps of cloth, part-preserved by the relatively ambient conditions underground. Fortunately the sports bags appear to have better stood the test of time. He takes the two that Nolan managed to push through the gap and looks inside. Bloody hell, he can't remember ever having seen so much cash, other than in the movies. There's more money here than he'll ever need. He doesn't think he'll have time enough left to spend it all, but he knows he'll have a bloody good go at trying.

Before he crawls back out to start the rest of his life with Nolan's hard-earned loot, Barry Bevan stops and looks back at his dead ex-cell mate. 'So trusting, Nolan, so bloody gullible. All that time I spent telling you how not to be bossed around by them, but you still went and did exactly what I told you. You were always destined to be a loser, lad. Always completely out of your depth.'

AWAY WITH THE FAIRIES

The last year of my mother-in-law Betty's life was pretty bloody miserable. She had cancer, and she came to live with us in Birmingham for most of that time until she went into hospital. She ended her days in a hospice, and it was the most remarkable place; desperately sad and yet always warm and welcoming. The staff there were incredible. Some of the other patients clearly knew they were there to die, whilst others had no idea at all, often arguing with the nurses to try and get released or simply making their own spur of the moment attempts at escape. Without having much direct interaction, we got to know many of the patients just by being around them. If you've ever spent time with someone as they approach the end of their life you might have felt the same strange mix of emotions as me: you don't want them to die, but equally you know it's probably the kindest thing for them. And in that peculiar period of time where the rest of the world carries on regardless while your life is put on pause and your relative's life fades away, emotions can run high. This story was written for this collection.

'**Y**ou really are heartless, Andrew, you know
that?'
'So you keep telling me, sis.'
'I just wish you'd show a little respect, that's all.'
'What, like he showed me?'
'He did a lot for us.'
'When? He was never there.'
'He worked long hours to support the family.'
'To support his drinking.'
'Give it a rest. Stop talking about him like he isn't
here.'
'But he's not here. Jesus, Jess, look at the state of him.'
Andrew waved his hand in front of his father's face. No
reaction. 'See? He's long gone. Away with the fairies.'

Jessica and Andrew sat either side of the bed, Dad between them, propped up with pillows. His face appeared
hollow, cheeks sunken now that his false teeth had been
consigned to a plastic beaker. His eyes looked ahead unblinking, looking through everything, staring at nothing.
Not a movement. Not a sound. Not a flicker. Sometimes
the hospice felt more like a morgue.

Jessica lowered her voice. 'The nurses were saying last
night how he can probably still hear everything we're
saying.'
'Shit. I hope not.'
'They said he's probably getting a lot of stimulation
from listening to us talking.'
'Arguing.'
'*Talking.*'
'Well he doesn't look very stimulated. I have to keep
checking he's still breathing.'
'Please, Andy, just try and be nice.'
'Nice? Nice? For fuck's sake, when was he ever nice
to me?'
'I know you two didn't get on—'

'And whose fault was that?'

'—but I wish you'd try and make an effort. Let bygones be bygones.'

Andrew crossed his arms defiantly and slumped back into the uncomfortable plastic chair. 'I'm wasting my time here.'

'Do it for Mum.'

'Ease up on the emotional blackmail, Jess. Give me one good reason why I should stay?'

'Because it's the right thing to do. Besides, you've not been here twenty minutes yet.'

He checked his watch. 'Seriously? Christ, feels like hours.'

'And you only ever come once a week. Twice at most.'

'I'm busy. I'm working.'

'Yeah, so am I, but I still manage to get here most nights.'

'I don't know why you bother. He doesn't even know you're here. Why d'you keep putting yourself through it?'

'Because he's my dad. You just don't get it, do you? I'm not here for me, I'm here for Dad.'

'Yeah, but chances are he'll never wake up.'

Jessica paused, on the verge of tears. She bit her lip, but then said it anyway. 'It's all about the odds with you, isn't it?'

'Oh, here we go...'

'I've said too much.'

'You have, but go on, you've started now. Might as well put the boot in.'

She paused again, then spoke. 'I wasn't going to bring it up. Not here.'

'You might as well. Dad's past caring. Anyway, it was him who first took me into the bookies. Hadn't set foot in a betting shop until he dragged me in before the match one Saturday.'

'I know, I remember. Mum gave him hell over it. Especially when...'

The words dried up.

'Go on, sis, don't hold back.'

She shook her head. 'You lost so much to gambling, Andy. The house, the kids, your marriage...'

'You don't have to tell me. I'm not proud.'

She lowered her voice again. Even in his current state, she didn't want Dad hearing her. 'I'm worried that when Dad's money comes through, you'll gamble it all away.'

Andrew shrugged. 'So what if I do? He won't care. He's no use for it now.'

'That's hardly the point. I just think—'

'*I don't want to die.*'

Jessica was interrupted mid-flow by the desperate, pleading voice of another patient in another bed in another bay elsewhere on the hospice wing.

'I don't want to die,' she said again.

'Jesus, here we go,' Andrew muttered, bracing himself.

'It's just Brenda next-door,' Jessica sighed. 'Have a little compassion, will you? These people are dying. They're here to see out their days peacefully.'

'Peaceful? That's the last thing this place is once she's fired them all up.'

'I don't want to die,' Brenda said again, a little louder this time. Then again. 'I don't want to die.' And again and again on an increasingly desperate-sounding loop.

Andrew looked over his shoulder at Raymond, the wizened, white-haired old gent in the bed diagonally opposite Dad's. Raymond had been sound asleep but had perked up and shuffled upright as soon as he'd heard Brenda's moaning. Andrew braced himself. 'Here it comes... Any second...'

He hadn't spent anywhere near as much time in the hospice as his sister, but he'd been around long enough to get used to the routine and he watched for Raymond's inevitable reaction. Unlike the majority of the patients in this wing of the hospice. Raymond was still communicative, yet his reality appeared to be several decades out of date. He'd been a teacher once, by all accounts, and on regular occasion when Brenda's recurring outbursts triggered him off, he still believed he was. 'Jennifer Billings, is that you?' he shouted to someone who wasn't there. 'What have I told you? You're never going to amount to anything if you're not prepared to put the effort in.'

'It's about time he eased up on poor old Jenny, don't you think?' Andrew laughed to himself. 'Don't know what she did to deserve all this abuse. Must have left an impression on the stupid old goat.'

The noise was mounting. The woman in the next-door room continued moaning, and Raymond continued to berate non-existent Jenny. True to form, their combined noise triggered the next one off. Enid belonged in a bed two bays farther down the corridor, but she was mobile and the only place she didn't go was where she was supposed to be. 'Help me, I'm sick,' she wailed, her voice higher in pitch than both the others, easily discernible. 'Somebody help me. I'm sick.'

'They're all sick,' Andrew grumbled, watching as she shuffled into view then shuffled away again. He winced as the volume continued to increase. 'Not sure how I feel about these mixed wards.'

'It's not a hospital, Andy, it's a hospice. Do you think they're bothered?'

'Fair point. Half of them don't even seem to know they're here.'

'They've been prodded and poked and medicated and tested... I don't think they care by the time they get to this stage. They're just glad of the comfort and care. You'll be the same when it's your turn.'

'No chance,' he said quickly. 'Not me.' He nodded at Dad. 'If I end up in this state I want someone to finish me off.'

'I'll do it,' Jess said without hesitation.

'Thanks, sis.'

'Your problem will be finding someone who still cares enough when you get to that stage. You've already pushed most of us away.'

He ignored her. He usually did when she was right.

The patients' combined din continued to escalate. Dad's jaw began to judder, as if he was ready to join in but couldn't make it past the first syllable. Up and down his bottom lip went, a tremble becoming a definite movement, until he swallowed involuntarily then coughed and retched. Jessica was up out of her seat and over him in seconds, tissue poised to catch the phlegm. Andrew looked away and sunk back into his chair, bilious. 'Disgusting,' he grumbled.

'He can't help it,' Jess snapped at her brother. She screwed up the tissue and dropped it into the clinical waste bin with all the others.

'It's gone quiet,' Andrew said, and he was right. Dad's sudden outburst had brought the cacophony to an abrupt end. A gluey full-stop. Calm was restored. Enid shuffled past again, this time without a word.

A nurse appeared at the foot of the bed, a wide smile on her face, eyes locked on Dad's vacant gaze. 'Everything all right here?' she asked, sounding brighter than she had any right to at half-past nine on a Monday evening.

'Fine,' Jess replied, trying to summon up a smile herself.

'He looks very peaceful tonight.'

'He always looks the same these days,' Andrew said. 'Think it'll be long?'

'Jesus,' Jess said when she realised what he was asking. 'Will you shut up.'

The nurse had heard it all before. Much worse, probably. 'No way of knowing,' she answered. 'Make the most of the time you've got. We'll keep him comfortable and warm. Make him feel safe.'

'You'll be doing well if you can make him feel anything.'

'Thank you,' Jessica said, talking over her brother, and she meant it.

The nurse moved on and the silence returned, but it didn't last long.

'What did you have to say that for?'

'Because it needed asking,' Andrew replied. 'This is just a waste of everyone's time, his especially.'

Jessica leant across the bed and lowered her voice. 'These are the last days of our father's life, maybe even the last hours. Can't you just stop thinking about yourself for a while and show some respect? What else would you be doing now anyway? Propping up some bar somewhere? In the all-night bookies? Slumped in front of the TV putting bets on with your phone?'

'Give it a rest. It doesn't matter what I'd be doing, point is I can't see what benefit anyone's getting from this. I don't care what you say, he doesn't know we're here.' He jabbed his finger in Dad's direction to underline his point. 'If he's not getting anything from this and we're not getting anything from this, why are we bothering?'

'Who said I wasn't getting anything from being here? Don't put words in my mouth.'

'Well, are you?'

Jess didn't answer at first.

'Does it matter what either of us wants? Dad's all

that's important at the moment. Like the nurse said, we need to focus on making the time he has left as comfortable and peaceful as possible.'

'Peaceful? In this place?' Andrew looked back over his shoulder again, making sure that Raymond wasn't about to kick off and berate another imaginary pupil, the noise of the patients' last combined outburst still ringing in his ears. When he was satisfied there wasn't about to be another interruption, he turned back to face his sister again. 'I'd hate this. I mean what I said, when my time comes, if it looks like I'm heading this way then I want someone to finish me off.'

'Well like I said, don't look at me. I'm not saying I wouldn't be happy to do it, mind.'

'Thanks for your support, sis.'

'I'll use your inheritance to buy you a ticket to Dignitas.'

'To what?'

'Never mind. Doesn't matter.'

Jessica paused, again wondering whether she should prolong this conversation, then deciding that she would.

'Seriously, though, who would look after you?'

'The state,' Andrew answered without hesitation.

'You mean no one.'

He pushed his chair back, looked down at his shoes. 'Haven't seen the kids for a couple of weeks. Shirley's being a dick about the maintenance payments again and —'

'You mean you've gambled your money away.'

'I pay my way.'

'Providing the right horse comes in.'

'Ease off, sis, I've got enough people on my back right now. I don't find all this as easy as you do,' he said, gesturing around.

'You think this is easy for me?'

'You're the one who's all smiles and happy voices all

141

the time.'

'When I'm here for Dad, yes. This is hell, though. This is really, really hard.'

More nurses appeared. Three this time, hunting in a pack. 'We need to reposition your dad,' one of them said. 'Should only take a couple of minutes. We'll give you a shout when you can come back in.'

They were barely out of their seats before the curtains had been whipped closed around the cubicle. Jessica paused on the other side of the faded screen for a moment longer than she should have, just listening. Funny, she thought, how the curtains brought about such an abrupt change in behaviour. She was still thinking about it when she caught up with Andrew in the family lounge. He'd already made himself a coffee. It was almost at his lips when she came in. He caught her eye then handed it over and fetched himself another. He noticed his sister was crying.

'What's up?'

'That's the most redundant question I've heard all day. What do you think's up? Our dad's dying, or had you not noticed?'

'Yeah, of course I noticed. But Dad's been dying for a long time. We knew the cancer was going to get him eventually.'

'That doesn't make it any easier.'

'I know that, but you weren't crying out there, were you? What happened?'

'Maybe I think about what other people might be feeling, has that ever occurred to you? Maybe I just don't want Dad to see me upset. Maybe I'm just struggling with this and the longer it goes on, the harder it gets.'

'Like I said out there, this isn't benefitting anyone.'

'That's not what I mean.'

'What then?'

'I don't know... it's the little things that get to me. Those nurses just now... they were chatting away to Dad, then they closed the curtains and started talking about him like he wasn't there, like he was a piece of meat. *You grab his feet*, one of them said. *Roll him over this way.* One of them called him a lump.'

'He is! Even now. He's lost a lot of weight but I'd still struggle to shift him. That's why it takes three of them to move him around and hose him down.'

'Andrew, please,' Jessica said, hiding her tears in her coffee.

'Look, I'm sorry if you think I'm being harsh, sis, but Dad's gone. He stopped being Dad when they wheeled him in here, whenever that was.'

'Seven and a half weeks ago.'

'Right.'

'I know. I've been here just about every bloody day since.'

'Okay, but the point is, he's had his time. His number's up. This is just delaying the inevitable.'

Wandering Enid drifted past the lounge doorway. Jessica waited until she'd gone then hissed at her brother, 'you just want to get your hands on his money.'

Andrew shrugged. No denial. Then, 'so do you.'

'I don't. I mean, it'll be nice and everything, but I'd rather have Dad than his money.'

'You saw him about as often as I did before he got sick.'

'You know how it is...'

'Always off on holiday or doing up the house.'

'If you're saying I should have seen more of him then yes, you're right. We both should have.'

'That's not what I'm saying at all. I'm saying I think you'd rather be debt-free than be visiting the old man here every day like this.'

'That's not true.'

'Come on, Jess, you forget how well I know you. I'm not stupid. I know roughly how much you're on, and your Brian can never stop telling me how much he picks up each month.'

'And?'

'And I know it's not enough to sustain your fancy lifestyle. Brian told me as much.'

'I don't have a fancy lifestyle.'

'Believe me, compared to me you do.'

'People who live on the streets have a fancy lifestyle compared to you.'

'You know exactly what I mean.'

'And what's Brian been saying exactly?'

'Last Christmas he was half-cut. He was bending my ear about you and your credit cards. He didn't say a lot, but it was enough to start me thinking. I reckon you're mortgaged up to the hilt. Probably got everything on credit.'

'Not everything...'

'You've dug yourself into a hole, haven't you? Big house, two nice new cars on the drive, couple of holidays abroad every year...'

'We work for everything we own.'

'I'm not saying you don't both work hard, I just don't think you actually own much of it.'

'That's none of your business.'

'You're right, it isn't. And what I do with my share of Dad's estate isn't any of your business either. When the money's gone, it's gone.'

'You're starting to sound like him now.'

'Christ forbid.'

'Okay, you're right – the money will make a difference. A big difference, if I'm honest.'

'How big?'

Jessica shuffled awkwardly in her chair and finished her drink. 'Doesn't matter.'

'You see, I'm just trying to get a feel for things, sis, because Dad's cash is going to make a massive difference to me, if I'm honest. It'll get a couple of people off my back for starters.'

'Oh God, what kind of people?'

'Not the kind you're probably thinking, but not the kind you want to keep waiting for money, either.'

One of the nurses appeared at the door. 'All done. You can go back in now,' he said.

When Jessica and Andrew returned to his bedside, Dad looked completely different. An orderly was still tidying, smoothing down the bedclothes. They'd washed Dad. Combed his hair. Changed his pyjamas and propped him up in a more comfortable-looking position. 'Looks lovely, doesn't he,' the orderly said, and she gently stroked his cheek. Jessica nodded and bit her lip to save more tears. Dad didn't react to anything. Breathing heavy. Eyes fixed ahead in that same vacant gaze.

Brother and sister re-assumed their positions on either side of the bed. 'I might get going soon,' Andrew said.

'I hate it when people say that,' Jessica replied.

'Say what?'

'I *might* do something or other when they know full well they're going to do it whatever.'

'Okay then, have it your way. I'm going to go soon.'

'That's better. Places to go? People to see?'

She sounded more vitriolic than she intended.

'Yes, as it happens. Not that it's any of your business.'

'What kind of people do you need to see at this time on a Monday night?'

'Jennifer Billings, come back here when I'm talking to you!' bed-bound Raymond yelled from across the way, startling them both. His physical frame might have

145

withered over the years, but an unquestionably authoritative tone remained to his voice. 'You're never going to amount to anything.'

And that was it.

'Help me, I'm sick,' Enid wailed on her way past the bay.

'I don't want to die,' Brenda moaned from next-door.

'Christ's sake,' Andrew sighed as their voices continued on a loop. 'I can't take much more of this.'

'You're never going to amount to anything.'

'Help me, I'm sick.'

'I don't want to die.'

Dad's mouth began to twitch again, and the twitch became a violent cough. Jessica rested a hand on his shoulder – stopping him from slumping to one side – then wiped a green-tinged dribble from his chin.

The man in the fourth bed in the room snored loudly, audible even over the combined patients' voices. 'How anyone can sleep through this racket I have no idea,' Andrew said, struggling to make himself heard.

'Help me, I'm sick.'

'You're never going to amount to anything.'

'I don't want to die.'

Several more repetitions and the voices eventually petered out.

'I don't know how much more of this I can take,' Jessica admitted.

'What, the noise?'

'No, all of it. Being here night after night...'

'Go home then. I am.'

'I'm going to stay a while longer,' Jessica said.

'But you just said —'

'I know what I just said.'

'You and Brian fallen out again?'

A pause, then 'yes.'

146

'Bought something you shouldn't have again?'

'We needed it.'

'But you didn't have the money?'

'Yes.'

She was crying again now but tried not to let her brother see.

'You need Dad's cash more than you're letting on, don't you?'

Another pause. Yet more tears. 'Yes.'

'Me too. I'm in trouble, Jess.'

'And me. Bloody hell, Andy, I don't know what I'm going to do.'

'It'll be okay, sis. We'll get it sorted. Soon as he's croaked we'll get the solicitors sorted. There's only you and me named in the Will and there's only the house and his car to sell. I've got a mate who knows a bloke who can put us in touch with a lawyer who'll see us right at a decent price. Won't be long now.'

Jessica nodded.

'Brian said he'd leave me if I didn't stop.'

'Didn't stop what?'

'Spending. I can't help it, though. Since the kids left home I get bored. It makes me feel better, spending a few quid.'

'It's an addiction,' Andrew told her. 'Believe me, I should know. Gambling's the same.'

'I can't see another way out of this mess.'

Andrew paused before speaking again. It was clear he had something more to say but wasn't sure if he should – could – say it. Deep breath. 'We could, you know, speed things up a little.'

Jessica wiped her eyes and looked up at him. For a moment she didn't know what to say, how to react. 'Tell me you're not serious...'

His face cracked. 'Had you going there, sis.'

Jess relaxed. Smiled. Shoulders slumped. Almost laughed.

'I thought you meant it.'

'I know you did. Let's be honest, we've both considered it, haven't we?'

Dad coughed again, louder this time. Jessica dabbed at the spit pooling in the corners of his gaping mouth.

'I feel terrible saying this,' Jessica admitted, 'but yes. And I know I was shitty with you earlier, but things would be a heck of a lot easier for all of us – you, me *and* Dad – if he just stopped fighting and let go.'

'He's hardly fighting. He's barely even breathing.'

'I'm sick. Help me.'

'You're never going to amount to anything.'

'I don't want to die.'

'Jesus, not again,' Andrew cursed, looking around. 'I wish these noisy bastards would just shut up. Don't they ever stop?'

'I'm sick.'

'You're never going to amount to anything.'

'I don't want to die.'

The three patients' voices were ringing in his ears, filling the hospice with noise.

'The staff never do anything,' Jessica said. 'Bloody useless, they are. It's making my head hurt.'

'We should complain. This can't be good for any of them.'

Dad's chin was going again. He retched. Jess was out of tissues. She looked around for another box.

Shuffling Enid appeared at the end of Dad's bed, frightening the life out of both Andrew and Jess. 'I'm sick,' she said.

'Fuck me,' Andrew said, clutching his chest.

'Go back to your bed, Enid,' Jessica told her, but she didn't.

Andrew was far less understanding. 'Nurse!' he yelled, 'One of your patients has escaped again.' But no one came.

Dad coughed again and Jessica found more tissues in his bedside cabinet.

'You're never going to amount to anything.'

'I don't want to die.'

'I'm sick,' Enid said, and then she drifted away.

'It's a bloody disgrace,' Jessica said, competing with the din. Her hands were sticky with Dad's mess and she got up to wash them. 'I mean, I know the NHS is stretched and under-resourced, but surely they can do better than this,' she continued from the sink.

'You're never going to amount to anything.'

'I don't want to die.'

'I'm sick. Help me.'

'I'd write to my MP,' Jessica said, 'but she's next to useless. Did you see her on the TV the other night, Andy? Andy? Are you even listening to me?'

Andrew didn't take his eyes off Dad, just gestured. 'Look.'

'You're never going to amount to anything.'

'I don't want to die.'

'I'm sick.'

'What's wrong?'

'Look,' Andy said again.

Dad's mouth was moving. Forming silent words.

'What's he saying?'

'Don't know, sis.'

'You're never going to amount to anything.'

'I don't want to die.'

'I'm sick.'

'Wish they'd just shut up,' Jessica hissed. She wanted to yell at the other patients to be quiet but she stopped herself. She sat down opposite her brother.

149

Dad's mouth was still going. Same movements. Same silent words. On a loop.

'You're never going to amount to anything.'
'I don't want to die.'
'I'm sick.'
'You're never going to amount to anything.'
'I don't want to die.'
'I'm sick.'
'You're never going to amount to anything.'
'I don't want to die.'
'I'm sick.'

'Is he copying them?' Andrew asked.

'Which one?'

'All of them? None of them? Can't tell.'

'You're never going to amount to anything.'
'I don't want to die.'
'I'm sick.'

And then, gradually, Dad's mouth began to match some of the words. He was picking out snatches of what Brenda, Raymond and Enid were each repeating tirelessly. The same few words every time.

And then his lips synced with the sounds.

'You're never going *to amount to anything.'*
'I don't want to die.*'*
'I'm *sick.'*
'You're **never going** *to amount to anything.'*
'I don't want **to die.***'*
'I'm *sick.'*
'You're **never going** *to amount to anything.'*
'I don't want **to die.***'*
'I'm *sick.'*
'You're **never going** *to amount to anything.'*
'I don't want **to die.***'*
'I'm *sick.'*

Different words combined. A single sentence formed

from fragments. On repeat.

'Fuck me,' said Andrew, pushing back his chair. Dad had definite eye contact with him now. First time since they'd brought him in here.

'I'm never going to die.'

'I'm never going to die.'

'I'm never going to die.'

'I'm never going to die.'

'I'm never going to die.'

'I'm never going to die.'

'I'm never going to die.'

'I'm never going to die.'

'I'm never going to die.'

EVERYTHING AND NOTHING

The writing of **Dog Blood**, the second **Hater** novel, was something of an ordeal. Having independently published all my previous books before **Hater** was picked-up by Thomas Dunne Books of New York, **Dog Blood** was the first time I'd worked with a professional editor. And one editor soon became two when the UK rights were sold to Gollancz. I tried to please both my new bosses and lost focus on the story for several months until I decided to ignore them all and start again from scratch. The end result was pretty much the book I'd originally planned, but I amassed a lot of additional material along the way. The book opens with an action scene, and the original opening chapters became this prequel. As a side-note, this is the first time this story has appeared in print, and the timing is perfect. The release of this collection coincides with the release of **All Roads End Here** – which is technically a sequel to both **Hater** and **One of Us Will Be Dead by Morning**, and therefore also a 'side-quel' to **Dog Blood**.

DRIFTING

When this war began, killing was everything. You did what you had to do, when you had to do it. The only thing that mattered was wiping out the Unchanged whenever you could, however you needed to do it. Those first days and weeks were a blur of blood and battles. The enemy was everywhere, and they were easy pickings. You chose your spot, you went in there, and you started killing. And you didn't stop until you were the only one left standing.

Things are changing.

There are fewer of them left now. Just last month I was killing more than ten a day on average. Even as recently as a couple of weeks ago I was still finding them regularly, and the hunt, the chase and the kill seemed to fill every hour of every day. But now they're getting harder to find. The gap between kills is increasing, and in the spaces between I'm left drifting: frustratingly purposeless and directionless.

My life has changed more than I could have imagined. I'm learning to live off the land now, picking at the flesh which hangs from the bones of what used to be here before and taking whatever I need from wherever I can find it. I see things now that I used to look straight past, taking chances and finding opportunities I would previously have missed. I understand and accept things which never used to make any sense. The old Danny McCoyne is long gone. I'm a thousand times the man I used to be.

Before all of this happened, life was simple and easy. We used to bitch and moan but we had it all on a plate and everything was there for you whenever you wanted it. We all took things for granted and expected that what was there today would still be there tomorrow. You went out to work and you were paid to do your job. You used that money to buy food and to pay for the roof over your head and the clothes on your back and whatever else you thought you needed. Today I hunt and fight for everything. I eat scraps to survive and I stop and find whatever shelter I can when I'm too tired to keep going. There's no certainty about anything anymore – no plan, strategy or routine – but I don't care. I'm free of the shackles of my past. The war has taken everything I ever had, but it's given me so much more. Now all I have is the clothes I'm wearing and the weapons in my hands, and that's all I need. Everything and nothing.

It poured with rain earlier this afternoon but the sky cleared a while back and the sun broke through. Now night's coming and the light is fading. Long shadows are stretching across the land all around me. It's been a frustrating and uneventful day, with just a single uninspiring kill so far, first thing this morning. I keep telling myself the Unchanged are becoming harder to find because we're winning. I've killed hundreds of the fuckers, and if everyone like me has done the same then there should hardly be any of them left. But there's no way of knowing for sure. Communication between us is virtually non-existent and the uncertainty and lack of information is sometimes hard to handle. All I know for sure is what I see for myself, and I've got no choice but to keep fighting because until every last trace of their kind has been completely and unequivocally wiped from the face of the planet, this bloody war won't end.

Finally now, after hours and hours of nothing, something has happened to relieve the frustration of this long, dragging day. I think I've found a nest. Most people wouldn't have given this place a second glance, but I'm not most people. To me it's obvious. I stumbled across this village by chance. It's little more than a short stretch of road with a handful of large houses scattered haphazardly on either side of the central strip, but I sensed something as soon as I got here. As this war has dragged on, people like me have become increasingly nomadic, drifting from fight to fight, never staying in any one place for too long. So if there is anyone left here and they're dug in, then they're almost certainly Unchanged.

One of the houses looks different to the rest. There's a car on the sweeping drive that's been clamped to prevent it being taken. The house itself has been deliberately made to look empty. I've been watching it for a while now from the safety of the branches of a sturdy old oak tree across the road. The ground floor doors and windows have all been blocked and boarded up, but the upstairs windows are still intact. Surely both floors would have been damaged if this place had seen as much violence as the rest of the surrounding area? Credit where credit's due, whoever's here has done well to survive for this long, but it's all been for nothing. They think they're making a stand and protecting what's theirs, but all they've done is back themselves into a corner. They're just delaying the inevitable.

And now I can see one of them, and I know I'm right.

In their old lives, when the Unchanged were teachers and lawyers and doctors and dentists and lovers and parents and children and whatever else, all they had to worry about was what was for dinner or what time the next episode of their favourite reality TV programme or soap opera was on. And when their world began to fall apart around them, most of them just carried on and stuck to what they knew for as long as they could. They never learnt how to run and hide or forage for food and water, or how to cover their tracks. It's the simplest thing that's given the location of these people away. The flat roof on top of the double garage (which looks bigger than my entire apartment used to be) is covered with buckets and pots and pans to collect rainwater, and one of the Unchanged – a dumb, arrogant, long-haired fuck-er – has just climbed out of a window and is passing the water back to someone inside the house. Idiot's not even making any attempt to keep out of sight. Thinks he's su-perior and above it all. It's all I can do not to jump down from this branch and run at the fucker right now, but I force myself not to. It sticks in my gut but I'll bide my time. They're dead whatever happens. Waiting will only make what I'm going to do even easier.

Another half-hour and the light levels have faded sub-stantially. How many of them are in there? I'm not con-cerned about numbers; I just want to plan my attack. The house is huge and there could be as many as ten or twen-ty of them. No matter. I've taught myself to be fast, quiet and hard. I'll get in and keep fighting until there's only me left standing.

I'm hungry and tired. No more waiting. Time to move. I climb down from the tree then sprint across the road. I jump up onto the bonnet of the car on the drive then run along its length and launch myself off the roof and up onto the garage. My body rattles as I smash into the top of the door but I ignore the pain and manage to swing my legs up and over. Now I'm standing on the flat asphalt, surrounded by the recently emptied buckets and pans. I accidentally kick a saucepan over the edge and it drops and hits the block-paved drive below with a bell-like clatter. Damn. They'll know I'm here now. No matter. Their fear and anticipation will make them that much easier to kill.

I press myself against the wall to one side of the frost-ed-glass window that the Unchanged man disappeared inside through. The house is dark and I can't see any movement. Taking my hand axe from its holster on my belt, I smash the glass. I can immediately hear them panicking inside as I climb through the window and I manage to stand upright just as the long-haired man bursts into the narrow, shadow-filled space. I hit him before he can even focus on me: a single strike of the axe, right between the eyes, so hard that the blade is left wedged deep in a vertical split in his skull. He drops to the ground at my feet, his dead bulk propping the door open, and the adrenalin rush is immense. First kill of the day or the hundredth, it doesn't matter. It's like the perfect drug and for a few precious seconds everything feels right.

An ear-piercing scream brings an end to my brief moment of bliss. I look up and see a scratty, pencil-thin woman standing at the other end of a galleried landing, frantically backing away from me, then half-running, half-falling down the staircase. I jump the corpse in the bathroom and run after her. The whole house is dark and cluttered, filled with these people's supplies and their accumulated waste, and the place smells foul. The woman manages to make it into another room and slams a door in my face before I can get close enough to catch her. I break it down easily with just a couple of kicks and find her cowering in the corner at the far end of a massive lounge. I move towards her but a figure comes at me from out of nowhere and shoves me away. It's a kid, tall and gangly, mid-teens. He hits me hard, but it's a desperate, last-ditch defence and I know he doesn't have the balls to attack. Idiot just stands there, waving a carving knife around in front of him like he's conducting an orchestra, too scared to stab. The end of the blade shakes wildly in the brief pauses between unconvincing swipes, revealing the true extent of his nerves. He hesitates, not knowing what to do next, and in that mo-

159

ment of indecision I rush him, grabbing his wrist with one hand and his neck with the other and pushing him all the way across the room, slamming him back against a grubby patio window. I smash his wrist hard against the glass so he drops the knife and it lands with a dull thud, point down in the carpet. The woman in the corner screams again and the kid tries to shake me off. Just for a second it seems like he might actually be about to put up a decent fight, but I know that no matter how hard he tries, he doesn't have a hope in hell. I dig my fingers into his flesh and tighten my grip around his throat, then pull his head forward and pound the back of his skull against the glass again and again until it cracks, feeling his weak, starved body judder and rock helplessly with each violent impact. He's already unconscious but I slam him into the glass a few more times to make sure he's dead before letting go. He slides down the window like a passed-out drunk, leaving a long smear of blood behind him.

Apart from the howling woman, I don't sense anyone else here. She gets up and launches herself at me, but her attacks are insignificant and barely even noticeable. I catch her fists and throw her back across the room. Her legs buckle.

'You're an animal!' she screams at me, looking up from down on the carpet. 'A bloody animal!'

I pick up the knife and run towards her. She shuffles back across the floor until she hits the wall and there's nowhere left to go. I crouch down at her level and look deep into her vile, tear-streaked face. These people's hatred of us used to terrify me, but now it's empowering. She spits at me and I casually wipe her sticky saliva away, refusing to break eye contact for even a second, refusing to show any emotion.

'What have we done to you?' she sobs, her words barely discernible. I won't lower myself to answer her pointless question, but I do at least think about it as I thump the knife down hard and end her pathetic existence. The truth is, I don't have any choice but to do this. The whys and wherefores of our opposing individual situations are unimportant and irrelevant. All that matters now is the end result: their extermination and our survival.

The woman lies dead at my feet, pools of blood glistening in the last light of the day. Other than my panting and my empty stomach grumbling, the house is now silent. Relieved, I step over the corpses and head for the kitchen. Whoever these people were, they'd been rationing themselves carefully and there's still food left in the cupboards. I take off my trench coat, wipe enemy blood from my hands and face, then eat. I'll stay here and rest tonight, I decide, then move on in the morning.

I collapse heavily onto a comfortable leather sofa. By torchlight I flick through a couple of uninteresting magazines, remembering how pointless the world and everything in it used to be, then switch off from everything for a few precious minutes with a Sudoku.

ADAM

It's early – maybe too early – but my sleep pattern's screwed and I'm already wide awake. It takes me a few seconds to make sense of my surroundings. I'm in a long, narrow bedroom filled with so much clutter that it looks like a junkyard. The walls are bare, the decoration minimalist save for a huge black and white canvas print of the family I slaughtered hanging on the wall above the bed I've just slept in. I killed three of them but there are four people looking down at me with smug, self-satisfied grins fixed on their now dead faces. There's another boy in the picture, a little older than the one I killed last night.

It feels strange being in a place like this again, wrong almost. These days I sleep rough most nights, catching a few hours' rest whenever the opportunity arises. It's oddly unsettling lying in a proper bed in a relatively secure house with a kitchen and bathrooms and walls and doors and windows and... and I don't like it. It reminds me how things used to be before the Change, when everyone lived their lives hidden away from everyone else, locked in private little boxes like this. The idea of allowing myself to be so restricted, so inhibited and controlled, is unthinkable now.

I'm comfortable, but I force myself to move. I head for the bathroom where, with one foot on either side of the greying corpse on the floor, I dunk my head into the half-full tub of water they'd managed to conserve. It's ice-cold and the temperature takes my breath away, numbing and revitalising in equal measure.

I look down at the long-haired dead man by my feet and remember the ease with which I killed him last night. I remember how both this guy and the boy downstairs held back, almost too afraid to attack. And that, I decide, is one of the crucial differences between them and us, a difference which will help us win this war. The Unchanged are too concerned with what might be, too tangled up worrying about the consequences of their actions to be able to fight freely. In comparison, we're uninhibited. While they're still thinking about it, we've already done it.

I crouch down beside the corpse and go through the ritual of stripping it of anything of value. He has nothing I need and anyway, my definition of value has changed completely over the last few months. Today I'm looking for food, water and weapons. The chunky gold watch on this foul bastard's wrist, the decorative chains around his neck and the rings on his fingers aren't worth anything to anyone anymore.

Christ, that watch is an ugly thing. I take it off the body and stand over by the broken window to get a better look at it in the light. It's completely over-the-top and damn heavy. It's studded with diamonds and it probably cost more to buy than my last car. And I bet this idiot was damn proud of it too. He probably only wore it as a status symbol, a way of showing everyone just how much he had, how much he was worth. Even when it mattered and I used to have a routine to follow I never wore a watch, but if I'd wanted one I'd have got one that was cheap and functional. Where's the sense in spending a fortune more than you need to just to find out it's twenty past five on the morning of June 11? *Thing is,* I silently tell the corpse lying at my feet, *when it came down to it, what good did all of this do you? You had the expensive house, a flashy car, lots of jewellery... but did any of it actually help you? No amount of cash could have helped you survive. Look at us both now, pal. I know who I'd rather be.*

June 11. That date rings a bell.

I stand on the landing looking down over the banister and try to work out why. I spend so little time thinking about what's gone now that I almost have to force myself to remember who I used to be. Then it starts coming back to me. June 11 last year was the day I started work at the PFP – the dead-end council department I was transferred to after being shoved and shunted out of various other equally dull and pointless offices. And then, once I've managed to lock on to one shred of detail, the rest of what happened a year ago begins flooding back. I sit down at the top of the stairs and remember.

I was late. First day in the new job and I was late. But it wasn't my fault. Any rational person would have understood that, but five minutes in the company of Tina Murray, my new supervisor, left me in no doubt that the PFP was not staffed by rational people. Some dick had left a shopping trolley in the middle of the train line into town, and with all the bullshit bureaucracy and health and safety red tape which used to slow everything down in the pre-war world, it had taken a ridiculous length of time to get it shifted. Tina Murray seemed to enjoy the bollocking she gave me. She delivered this cliché-filled lecture about how 'my reputation had preceded me' and how I'd just used up my 'one and only chance'. I'd already been disciplined by the council because of problems I'd had with my previous supervisor and I knew I was living on borrowed time, but I couldn't help myself. Once I started arguing I knew I was digging myself a deeper and deeper hole, but I couldn't stop. I started getting sarcastic, and that was when I knew I was really in trouble. I asked her if she'd thought I'd put the trolley on the line myself, or whether she thought I was late because I was keen to make an impression? The bitch reported me to her boss, Barry Penny. She said I needed to take a long hard look at myself and change my attitude. I remember wanting to tell her to go fuck herself, but I didn't. Like an Unchanged coward I said nothing.

Back to reality. I get up and go downstairs, mooching through the wreckage of the house, still daydreaming about what happened this time last year. I remember standing in the toilet at the end of my first day at the PFP when Barry Penny walked in and started taking a piss next to me. I did all I could to ignore him, but he made a point of talking to me, telling me how disappointed he was and that I needed to think carefully about how I conducted myself at work. All I remember thinking at the time was that I wasn't about to take any advice from a man who had his dick in his hand. I remember wanting

164

to hit him, wanting to smash his face into the wall and leave him lying bleeding on the piss-stained floor. But I didn't. I *couldn't*. I held the anger and frustration inside and let it eat at me and fester. Things would be different if I'd had that conversation today. Today I'd rip the fucker's head off in a heartbeat and think nothing of it.

I step over the bodies in the living room and seeing the corpses again makes me think about my family last June 11. I got home that night thinking Lizzie would understand my frustration and tell me they were all out of order, but she didn't. In some ways she was even worse. She kept banging on at me about how I needed to face up to my responsibilities and start looking after the kids instead of acting like one of them. Then she offloaded with the usual spiel about us needing to get out of the flat and get a bigger place to live and how everything depended on me working hard and being promoted, not demoted. We ended up having a massive row in front of the children, and she didn't talk to me for days. All that responsibility, heaped onto my shoulders.

None of that matters now. Today I feel no pressure at all. Today I'm free and the contrast between this year and last is incredible. Tina Murray, Barry Penny, Lizzie... where are you all with your advice now? Probably hiding in some desolate shit-hole, if any of you are still alive, that is. You're sitting there, quaking in your boots, waiting for someone like me to track you down, flush you out and kill you. Wish you could all see me now...

Wait.

What was that?

Thought I heard a noise. Cursing myself for getting distracted, I grab a knife and stand in the middle of the cluttered kitchen floor, listening. Then I hear it again, a distant, muffled thump coming from another part of the building. At the far end of the room I notice a utility area I didn't see in the darkness last night. There's another door at the end of it, secured by three thick wooden crossbeams and a heavy-duty padlock and chain. Why would this particular door be so important? Supplies? No other part of the house has been barricaded like this, and it isn't even an external door. My curiosity aroused, I move the wooden beams and check the three corpses for the keys to the locks. I find them on a bunch attached to a belt around the dead man in the bathroom's waist. Funny how insignificant people used to like to exaggerate their importance with big bunches of keys. I open the locks and take a step forward into the gloom, my knife held ready.

I'm in a wide, stale-smelling garage space. There's an expensive-looking, metallic pale-blue sports car parked directly in front of me, and I can hear something moving on the other side of it, just out of sight. I creep around the back of the car, ready to fight, then relax when I see a shape lying on an untidy nest of dirty bedding. The family pet? I walk closer, expecting to see a malnourished dog (and trying to understand why anyone would waste food on animals at a time like this?) but I stop when I'm near enough to see that it's a kid. Male, late teens or early twenties, half-dressed in grubby clothes that look several sizes too big, a curtain of knotted, straw-like hair covering his face like a veil. He lies almost completely still, barely even breathing. I use the tip of my knife to tease his hair away from his eyes and I immediately see that he's like me. Poor bastard stinks. I reach down, gagging at the stench, and try to move him. Both his right hand and left ankle are badly injured – the bones are broken and the flesh is lumpy and deformed – and he's shackled. He has a chain around his neck like a dog collar, and other chains around his good foot and wrist. His face has a vacant expression: his eyes are open and staring, but unfocused. I think he's been drugged.

'You okay, mate?' I ask, not sure what kind of reaction (if any) I'm going to get. His eyes slowly lift towards me, then droop shut. I shake his shoulder and he looks up again before trying to move. I help him up, doing my best not to overreact at the godawful stench. He's been lying in a pool of his own waste for days. It takes him several minutes to sit up straight. The light from a small, square window illuminates his weary, hollowed face. I recognise him. He's is the fourth person in the picture on the bedroom wall.

'You killed them...?' he starts to ask, but he doesn't have the energy to finish his question. He slumps to one side and drifts back into unconsciousness.

It's taken almost two hours for the kid to come around fully. I managed to undo his chains and move him into the living room and lay him on the sofa. His eyes are wide open and bright now. He's staring at the bodies.

'Your family?' I ask. He nods and his head drops, more through a lack of energy than emotion. He looks at his right hand, examining his injuries with curious fascination. His broken fingers stick out at sickening, unnatural angles.

'Did they do this to you?'

He looks up and nods again.

'Dad did it. Said it was for my own good. Said he wanted to stop me fighting, but I know he only did it 'cause he was scared of what I'd do to him. He couldn't let me go 'cause he knew I'd kill them all, and he didn't have the balls to kill me himself. So he smashed up my hand and foot with a lump-hammer to stop me getting away and stop me attacking them. Mum made him chain me up. She even had me eating out of a bowl.'

'You must have been going out of your mind stuck in

there with them so close.'

He shakes his head.

'Didn't know a lot about it, to be honest. Mum was a vet. She put stuff in the food to knock me out. Thing was, I had to keep eating it, didn't I? I knew what they were doing, but I had to try and stay strong so I could fight when I had to.'

I watch him as he tries to straighten a smashed finger. The pain's too severe and he winces, but he doesn't complain. He stares around the room then looks back over his shoulder to try and see out of the boarded-up window behind him.

'What's your name?'

'Adam,' he answers. 'You?'

'I'm Danny.'

'So what's happening in the world, Danny?'

'What do you know?'

'Not a lot. The view's pretty limited when you're chained to the garage wall.'

Where do I start? It's hard to know what to tell him. Over the last few weeks I've come to realise how much we used to rely on the TV, radio and Internet. Other than what I've actually witnessed for myself, I know surprisingly little.

'I can only tell you what I've seen.'

'So tell me.'

'More violence and killing than I ever thought possible. I've spent my time fighting, hunting down those evil bastards.'

'How many have you killed?'

'Hundreds, I imagine. The numbers aren't important. All that matters is that you kill and keep killing until every last one of the Unchanged are dead.'

'So what are you doing here?'

'Just passing through.'

'And where you going next?'

'Wherever the next fight is.'

'Take me with you, Danny? Come on, you can't leave me here like this.'

He's wrong. I could walk out now and not give him a second thought. Without my help this poor bastard's going nowhere. The last thing I want is to be slowed down by a cripple, but I have to admit the idea of company is welcome. If he can kill a few Unchanged along the way, then the effort required to take him will have been worthwhile, and having someone to talk to will fill the ever-lengthening gaps between kills.

'Get yourself cleaned up,' I tell him. 'Start slowing me down and you're on your own.'

EVACUATION

The world feels huge out here today. It's a bright, warm and dry morning and as I follow the curve of the road up and around a steady incline, the landscape opens up on either side making me feel small and insignificant. Can't help feeling uncomfortably exposed too, out here in Adam's dead dad's sports car.

Up above us, everything's as it always was. The sky is deep blue, dappled with bulbous white clouds. The tops of trees sway in the gentle breeze and birds flitter through the air without a care. Down at ground level, however, the scars of war are everywhere. The road stretches away in front of us and, even out here in the middle of nowhere, it's littered with human debris. Jutting out into the centre of the road is the wreck of a burned-out car, complete with the roasted remains of a long-dead family still trapped inside. I slow down as we approach it, conscious that Adam is staring, his eyes wide and unblinking. I don't think he expected the scale of the devastation he's seen since we left the house. It's sobering to think how quickly this has become the norm to everyone else.

'Unbelievable...' he mumbles.

I force the car up the kerb and around the back of the wreck. Just ahead is another corpse. As we near it I see that it's only half a body – a pelvis and a pair of broken legs sprawled on a grass verge. The rest of it – everything from the waist up, complete with a stunted and bloody spinal cord tail – has been dumped a little further down the road. The vacant eyes of a deservedly butchered Unchanged face stare back at me as we drive nearer. I'm impressed with the brutality of what we're seeing. Whoever was here before us did good work.

'Have you actually killed anyone yet?' I ask him. My question is bizarre, but he doesn't bat an eyelid.

'The people next door,' Adam explains, still staring out of the window at the carnage. 'They were loading up their car, trying to get away. I killed the lot of them.'

'So how come your dad managed to get to you?'

'He was an arrogant fucker,' he says. 'When all this started he said there was no way anything was going to happen to him. Said if anyone tried anything, he'd kill them before they got anywhere near him. But when it came down to it and he realised it was me he was going to have to kill, he couldn't do it. Lost his nerve. Bastard caught me off-guard while I was trying to get back into the house to look for him and Mum though. Came up from behind and smacked me round the back of the head. Next thing I knew I woke up in the garage with him standing over me with his fucking sledgehammer.'

He looks down at his broken hand and shakes his head.

'They're dead; you're still fighting,' I tell him. 'Just remember that.'

'It's not that,' he says, suddenly sounding despondent. 'How am I supposed to fight like this? Makes me feel like a fucking failure before I've even started. Fighting's all I've got left now.'

I put my foot down and accelerate. I sympathise, but there's nothing I can do or say to help. Kid should just be thankful he's still alive.

There are little more than fumes left in the tank. This expensive, fuel-guzzling car wasn't designed for this kind of stop-start driving. The twisting roads are littered with rubbish and wreckage and it's virtually impossible to build up any speed.

'You know where you're going?' he asks.

'No,' I answer honestly. Navigation is frustratingly difficult these days. I never was that good at map-reading and most of the road signs we pass are either obscured or unhelpful. Anyway, what good are place names when you don't know where those places are?

'So are we just going to keep driving indefinitely?'

'Looks that way.' I'm getting annoyed by his constant questions.

'Great.'

'Well if you've got a better idea, let's hear it.'

I take a sharp corner too fast and have to brake hard to avoid hitting the back of an abandoned silver Peugeot which straddles the width of the road immediately ahead. We screech to a halt, leaving black rubber skidmarks on the tarmac. I lock my arms and push myself back into my seat, heart thumping, amazed I didn't crash. I can't see any way through.

'Can you move it?' Adam asks.

'I'll have a look.'

I get out and climb up onto the bonnet of the silver car, denting the metal with my heavy boots. This is strange.

Up ahead the narrow road has been completely blocked by several more abandoned vehicles.

'Problem?'

I turn around and see Adam struggling to get out. He stops, half-in and half-out of the car, propping himself up on a long metal walking stick he brought with him from home. It looks like a ski-pole or something a hiker might use. It had a rubber protector on one end which he threw away, and now it's sharp enough to skewer and kill.

'Road's been blocked,' I tell him as I climb up onto the roof of the silver car and look around, 'but I can't see why.'

Other than a couple of low buildings a short distance away, there's nothing obvious here. There's no way of telling how recently these cars were dumped. Might have been here for weeks or...

'Hear that?' Adam says.

'What?'

I listen carefully but can't hear anything at first. I gradually become aware of muffled noises up ahead. Someone yelling orders... engines being revved... a panicked scream... The crack of a single gunshot startles me, and the windscreen of the car I'm standing on shatters beneath my feet. I throw myself back down onto the road and scramble towards Adam.

'Fuck me,' he says, head ducked down, 'that was close.'

I don't answer. My mouth is dry and my pulse is racing at a hundred times its normal rate.

Another car swerves around the corner and smashes into the back of Adam's dad's car. I manage to get out of the way, yanking Adam back with me. He yelps with sudden pain as his broken foot drags along the ground. The driver of the second car scrambles out and I know immediately that he's not like us. Before I have time to think I snatch my knife from my belt, throw myself at him and shove the blade up hard into his throat. I pull it out again and leave him on the ground at my feet, gurgling blood, his life spilling out over my boots.

'What's happening?' Adam asks, staring at the twitching corpse.

'Not sure,' I answer as I look around for a way out. Adam grabs my arm and points up into the sky. A huge military helicopter is approaching, moving at an incredible speed. It thunders overhead and begins circling. There's a gap in the hedge just before the first car in the road block and I pull Adam towards it. We slip and slide down into a boggy, waterlogged field. There are several other people here scattered across the wide expanse – people like us – and they're all heading in the same general direction, converging on the buildings I saw. And then it dawns on me what this is.

'What?' Adam asks again, sensing that I know something he doesn't.

'It's an evacuation,' I tell him. 'Someone told me they'd seen something like this.'

'Evacuating who?'

'Unchanged. Who d'you think?'

'But how...?'

Before he's even finished asking his question I drag him away. I put my arm around his shoulder and start moving him forward in the same direction as the ten or so other fighters I can now see nearby. The temptation to leave him behind is great but I keep helping him, telling myself that the closer I'm able to get him to the enemy, the more of them he'll kill.

'Over there,' he says, pointing with his broken hand in the direction of the grey buildings. I can see Unchanged soldiers out in the open now, taking up positions on the low roof to try and hold us off. I glance across at Adam and see that his face is suddenly ghostly white. He's soaked with sweat.

'You okay?'

'Just keep moving,' he gasps, grunting with effort.

A sudden staccato burst of gunfire rings out, and a woman drops heavily to the ground a few metres away from where we are. With the final burst of energy she can muster, she tries to get up and run on but the effort quickly overtakes her and she collapses dead into the mud.

Adam's still trying to move but he's slowing. I haul him closer to the hedge at the side of the field to give us some cover, but he's having none of it. The ground is increasingly wet and uneven.

'Go on,' he shouts at me as he slips and almost falls. He tries to steady himself with his walking stick but the sharp metal point just sinks deeper into the mud. I help him yank it free, then leave him leaning up against the trunk of a tree. 'I'll catch you up,' he says optimistically.

I sprint up a low embankment, my mouth watering at the prospect of killing again. The mud beneath my feet turns to gravel and I barge and shove my way through the ever-growing crowd of fighters arriving from all directions. What the hell is this place? Beyond the large single-storey grey concrete building I can see the smashed remains of row upon row of metal-framed glasshouses. Some kind of garden nursery or farm, perhaps? Above us the helicopter drifts lazily away then comes back around.

I use the people around me as cover as, directly ahead, armed Unchanged militia fighters burst out through double doors on one side of the building and start shooting indiscriminately into the crowds like the clumsy, panicking, barely-trained dumb fuckers they are. Above them soldiers continue to prowl along the edge of the flat roof, picking people out of the advancing masses with single sniper shots. I change direction and take cover behind a massive steel waste bin. I peer around the edge and watch as our assault continues. A huge hulk of a man charges towards the enemy, seemingly oblivious to the barrage of bullets which tear through the air all around him. He takes several hits to the chest but the impacts barely register. His momentum carries him forward until he drops just short of the door. There are already more fighters swarming close behind, following in his substantial wake. By the time his dead bulk has hit the deck, they've jumped his corpse and have attacked the gunmen. I watch in awe as one of the enemy is dragged out then thrown back again, smashing into a wide, plate-glass window with such force that he's almost thrown completely through. His broken legs dangle uselessly through the shattered glass, skin slashed to ribbons.

Now that the shooting from the doorway has been momentarily silenced, I follow the lead of several others and leave the cover of the waste bin, sprinting over to the building and pressing myself flat against the wall. As the fighters furthest forward disappear inside, I follow them in through the now unguarded door. It's dark in comparison to the early morning brightness outside, and for a few disorientating seconds I can't see anything. I trip over upturned tables and chairs and trample fallen bodies as we charge *en masse* through a wide open-plan café and seating area. There's more gunfire up ahead as a handful of enemy soldiers attempt to herd a panicking wave of Unchanged civilians out into the open.

I drop down behind an upturned table as another hail of bullets thuds along the wall behind me, smashing through plaster, bricks and tiles and filling the air with deafening noise and choking dust. Many other people are doing the same, desperately ducking down and waiting for a break in the firing, but still more continue to charge towards the enemy, refusing to stop until either they've killed Unchanged or they've died trying. Outside, the helicopter swoops low again, its muffled roar filling the building until it's all I can hear.

The Unchanged soldiers funnel the civilians towards another exit. All around me people begin to sprint after the rapidly disappearing crowd and I do the same, tripping through an unending mass of fallen bodies, some still groaning, others still trying to get up and fight. There are countless casualties from both sides here but who and what they were is unimportant now.

The incredible noise around us continues to increase, so loud that the building itself seems to be rattling, shaking like it's about to collapse. I'm trapped, stuck in a bottleneck, trying to get out. Can't move forward or backwards – can hardly move at all. With a sudden hard shove the person in front of me finally shifts and we spill outside. I barely manage to stay on my feet, but then I have to throw myself down as the enemy begins firing on us again. I crawl on my hands and knees, looking for cover behind an abandoned car, feeling the wreck rocking and shaking as it's peppered with bullets. I lie flat and look underneath the chassis and can see that the Unchanged are being led across the road now in a single mass, a ring of soldiers surrounding and protecting them like dogs herding sheep. Christ, there must be more than fifty civilians. I haven't seen them together in these kinds of numbers for days, maybe even weeks.

Still hovering overhead, the helicopter banks away then drops down out of view. I get up and, alongside huge numbers of fighters, I run after it. The enemy soldiers have given up trying to fight and are instead concentrating on reaching the helicopter which I can now see landing on the far side of a field across the road. Before the helicopter has even touched down, a heavy door at the tapering rear end of its matt khaki fuselage drops open and more troopers appear from inside. They fan out and begin firing, concentrating on the attackers moving towards them from either side. The bunch of refugees stranded between them and us prevent the soldiers from aiming directly at the rest of the chasing pack.

My lungs are empty, the muscles in my legs and arms burning with the effort of the run, but I can't slow down. I don't want to slow down. We're gaining on the Unchanged, our fastest runners already pouncing on their slowest and dragging them to the ground. Unnecessarily large numbers of fighters join in the attack on each individual Unchanged that falls, their adrenalin-fuelled desire to kill too strong to be ignored now that we can see enemy blood being spilled. I keep moving, jumping fallen corpses and dodging other fighters, determined to get to the fresh enemy targets who've almost reached the helicopter.

A huge explosion in the field just ahead of me knocks me off my feet. I'm suddenly flat on my back and I cover my face as dirt rains down all around me. More fighters run past, one of them unknowingly planting a boot in my balls as they sprint over me, filling my body with nauseating pain. I curl myself up and protect my head with my arms as more of them power past. There's another explosion over to my left and I look up through the chaos in the opposite direction to see a soldier armed with a shoulder-mounted rocket launcher, trying to reload. Our people are onto him before he can fire again.

Some of the enemy have reached the back of the helicopter now, and those that have survived their frantic escape across the field are being brutally shoved, dragged, hauled and thrown on-board. Still more of our fighters continue to attack, many of them being picked off by controlled gunfire and by more violent grenade and rocket explosions. The surface of the land – green and relatively clear just minutes ago – is now a churned quagmire, covered with bodies and riddled with bullet holes and impact craters. The cargo bay door at the back of the helicopter begins to slowly close and I will myself to move even faster, desperate to get there before it shuts completely, desperate to get closer to the foul creatures I see stowed inside. The aircraft starts to lift, the wind from its rotor blades battering me and everyone else like a strangely swirling gale. One of the Unchanged dives for the back of the powerful machine, reaching for it with fingers outstretched. He misses and I catch him as he falls, stamping hard on those same fingers with a muddy boot. As the helicopter starts to climb higher, the wiry-framed, scrawny little bastard rolls away from me and manages to scramble back to his feet. He takes a few slipping, sliding steps before falling face-first into the dirt. I accelerate, adrenalin coursing through my veins. This one's mine. I reach down, grab his shoulder and flip him over onto his back.

'Don't,' he pleads pathetically, looking up at me with tears streaming down his face. 'Please don't...'

I wrap one hand around his throat, then clench my other hand into a fist and smash it into his face, so hard it hurts. His nose is broken and blood starts gushing out of a deep gash. He's out cold, but he's still alive. Eight more increasingly fast and increasingly hard punches finish the job and I relax and drop him down. Killing like this feels so good, so right.

The noise from the helicopter increases yet again, its impossibly loud engine suddenly sounding even louder, but it still hasn't lifted more than a couple of metres off the ground. Do they have a problem? Too many refugees and soldiers on board? With the fighting on the ground now beginning to slow down and dissipate as the last of the stranded Unchanged are massacred, I stand back and watch as the helicopter struggles to climb. Some of our people are hanging off its wheels like they're trying to pull it back to the ground.

I quickly kill another straggler who'd been trying to get away. She was crawling through the fallen bodies, keeping low, thinking no one had spotted her amongst the dead. As I dump the corpse I turn around and see the helicopter drop back down and bounce up off the grass, crushing several fighters who refuse to let go. The cargo door starts to open again. What the hell? As soon as the gap is wide enough, desperate Unchanged begin throwing themselves out, falling the short distance to the ground where people like me immediately pounce and kill. The door opens further and now I can see why they're panicking. Some of our people have got on board. I can't see how many there are or how they got inside, but the details aren't important. The door hangs fully open now, and people from both sides tumble out as the pilot attempts to take off again. Others are still trying to climb in through the cargo door, clinging on and hauling themselves up as the helicopter finally begins to ascend. It climbs at an unnatural, awkward-looking angle, its tail sagging down, more bodies falling out of the open hold and hitting the ground with thud after sickening thud. But the fighting inside continues. I catch a momentary glimpse of several of our people who are on-board, holding onto anything they can, climbing along the walls to get closer to the pilots and kill them.

I stumble back across the field as the helicopter continues to rise. Still flying at a bizarre angle, it skims the tops of a mass of tangled trees, occasional bodies still dropping. Then it tips over to one side and seems to hang for the briefest of moments before plummeting from the sky like a stone. Noise briefly fills the air, but then everything becomes silent and a twisting column of dirty black smoke rises up through the trees.

For a while I just stand there, breathless, and survey the carnage all around. The Unchanged are dead and the only people left moving now are people like me. The world immediately feels strangely calm, the chaos abruptly ended as if someone just flicked a switch.

'Oi, Danny,' a voice shouts at me as I head back towards the road. I look around and see that it's Adam. He's sitting on the back of a fresh Unchanged corpse, panting with effort. He's soaked with blood and grinning like a madman.

'You all right?'

'Fucking brilliant,' he answers. 'Now that,' he says, nodding in the general direction of the battlefield, 'was awesome.'

Saddled with Adam again, I head back to the buildings where the enemy were hiding, moving infuriatingly slowly. Most of the other fighters have already left in search of the next fight, but Adam's in no state to go anywhere for a while. I take advantage of the break to check the place over for food but I barely find anything. Almost everything has already been taken. Even the still-warm bodies here have already been fleeced.

'So if they were trying to evacuate, where were they taking them?' he asks me as I search through the contents of a small, windowless storeroom.

'How the hell should I know?'

'So what do we do now?'

'You do what you like, mate. I'm going to get moving.'

'Sounds good. Where you going?'

'Wherever I need to go,' I tell him. 'Wherever the next

fight is.'

'Why not stay here?'

'What?'

'Think about it, if they were holing up here before being evacuated, still more of them might come. This might be some kind of rendezvous point. We could just sit here and wait for them and get some rest, then take them out as soon as they arrive.'

He might be right. I doubt he is, but I'll give it a couple of hours and see what happens.

A few hours turns into half a day and this place remains silent as the grave. No one's coming back here now, and even if they did, the carnage all around the building would put them off long before they got close enough for us to attack. It's time to go.

'What's up?' Adam asks as I get ready to move.

'We need to get out of here,' I answer.

'You taking me with you, then?'

'Looks that way.'

Not wanting to prolong the conversation, I leave the room where we've been resting and head for the main entrance, picking my way through the chaos. I stand outside and listen. Everything remains still and deceptively calm. Apart from the muffled curses, grunts and crashes as Adam tries to follow me, there's nothing. Absolute silence. Using the bullet-ridden wreck of a car as a step-up, I climb onto the low roof of the building to look around and try and get my bearings. I can't see anything remarkable. There are trees and fields on all sides, and the smoke from the downed helicopter continues to drift up from the crash site over the way.

Wait.

What's that?

I see something over to my right that makes me catch

my breath. At first it's nothing – just more trees amongst many – but as I stare out into the distance, my eyes focus on something I never expected to see. It's The Beeches, a distinctively shaped clump of years-old trees which stands on the top of an otherwise barren hill. My legs weaken unexpectedly with nerves as I continue to stare. Adam staggers out into the open, still using his metal walking stick for support. He looks around, then spots me up on the roof.

'What you doing up there?'

I don't answer. I can't answer. I climb down and run back inside to the small office I turfed through earlier. I was looking for weapons and supplies then; now I'm just trying to find an address, something to confirm our location. I snatch up a piece of paper and stare at the letter heading. The disorientation of these last few months has been extreme, with days and battles and locations and kills merging into each other in a blur. Place names and road signs lose their importance when you're drifting and I genuinely had no idea where I was or how far I'd travelled. I must have covered hundreds of miles but now I've come full circle, almost all the way back to the start again. *I'm almost home.*

Adam appears in the doorway, breathless and looking pissed-off. 'Will you slow down and tell me what the hell's going on?'

'This is Burcot.'

'And?'

'Up on the roof... I saw something I recognised... I know this road...'

'You're not making any sense, mate. What are you on about?'

I don't bother answering. I don't expect him to understand.

I'm almost home.

My head is suddenly filled with vivid memories of the family I thought I'd lost, that I'd forced myself to forget. They might be close. More importantly, *Ellis* might be close. I need to know what happened to my little girl. She's like me and we need to be together. I thought she was gone forever.

How could I have been so close and not realised? This world feels so unfamiliar and strange, but knowing where I am seems to have changed all of that in an instant. It's brought everything back into focus. Now a couple of days' travel might be all that separates me from Ellis.

Whether she's there or not, I know I have to go back home. I might find nothing when I get there, but if there's the slightest chance of finding her then I have to take it. She's everything to me. Apart from the war, she's all I have left.

ALMOST FOREVER

I have a passion for watching odd, forgotten, and just outright weird films. I'll come clean at the outset – **Almost Forever** was inspired in part by one such film, **The Asphyx**. If you can track down a copy, it's well worth a watch. In it, a scientist finds a way of preventing death by capturing a person's spirit at the moment it leaves the body. Now I'm not one for ghosts and spirits and souls and all that – I prefer quasi-scientific explanations in my stories, no matter how far-fetched. But ultimately, it's never the scientific achievements that matter in tales like this, it's what people do with them. This story about the ultimate body modification has a deliberate B movie feel to it. It was written for **The Mammoth Book of Body Horror**.

'Immortality! You're just taking the piss out of me now. Come on, mate, you know as well as I do, that's just science-fiction bullshit.'

'Okay, so what exactly *are* you talking about?'

'You haven't been listening, have you? I'm not talking about living forever, I'm talking about massively improved cellular efficiency leading to substantially increased longevity throughout the body. I'm talking about doubling, even tripling our lifespan.'

'And you think that's achievable? Still sounds like science-fiction to me.'

'Which part of this don't you get? I know it's achievable. I've already done it. *It works!*'

'Am I going out on my own tonight?'

'What?'

'I asked if I'm going out on my own,' Deanna repeated, sounding less than impressed. 'Jesus, John, get off your backside and stop staring at the phone.'

I still didn't move. I couldn't stop thinking about what Morgan had just told me. In the fifteen or so years I'd known him, he'd continually infuriated and inspired me in equal measure. There was no doubt he was brilliant and gifted, and if he said he'd made a ground-breaking discovery which would change medicine forever, then I knew he almost certainly had. His qualifications and intellect were undoubted; everything else about him, less so. Back when we'd first met at university, I'd initially hung around with him because I'd thought I wanted to be a rebel too, but I soon discovered the real reason. Being with Morgan kept me on the straight and narrow. At times his life seemed like a constant succession of bad decisions. He took chances where I'd overthink the odds and took risks I thought were way too great to even consider. He pissed money up the wall and got himself into more scrapes and dodgy situations than everyone else I know combined. He showed me how not to do it. It turned out my best friend was everything I didn't want to be.

'So what's he done this time?'

I watched Deanna as she sat in front of the mirror, fixing her make-up and hair. She looked stunning, as usual – the result of ninety minutes spent bathing, epilating, moisturising, and Christ alone knows what else. We were only going out for a meal, nothing special. All I needed was five minutes in the shower. A piss, a comb through my hair and a squirt of aftershave, shove some clothes on and I'd be done.

'He says he's made a miracle breakthrough,' I eventually remembered to reply.

'Another one? As good as his last half-baked scheme?'

I hesitated. Much as I wanted to deny it, everything he'd told me had made sense.

'No... it's different this time. I might regret saying this, but I think he might actually be on to something.'

Deanna got up, snatched her handbag from the dressing table, then breezed out of the room, leaving nothing behind but the smell of her perfume.

'You're a bloody idiot,' she shouted after me, her voice fading as she disappeared downstairs. 'You'll believe anything he tells you.'

I followed her out and leant over the bannister. 'No, Dee, seriously, I really think he's got something this time.'

She stood in the hallway, coat half on, staring back up at me.

'Morgan infuriates me. You don't hear from him for months, then he clicks his fingers and you come running.'

'That's not fair, Dee...'

'Isn't it?'

'No.'

'So when are you going?'

She had me there. 'Tomorrow.'

Morgan's father's house was a couple of miles out of town. Despite his dad having died several years ago, I still found it impossible to think of the large, imposing and increasingly dilapidated building as belonging to Morgan now. Being a homeowner inferred some level of responsibility, and Morgan was regularly the least responsible person I knew.

'It's about time you got here,' he said as he opened the door. 'You were supposed to be here hours ago.'

'Got stuck at work,' I said, staring at him. 'Complications with a patient.' I stopped and stared some more. 'For fuck's sake, Morgan, what have you done to yourself?'

He was half-dressed, with his long, greasy black hair pulled back in a straggly ponytail which stretched down his back. His painfully thin torso and arms were a mass of tattoos, so many that I couldn't see where one ended and the next began.

'That's no way to greet a friend.'

'You do realise you're stuck with those tattoos?'

'My dad's dead, mate,' he said, grinning, 'and I didn't advertise for a replacement.'

He walked further into the house. I followed at a cautious distance, picking my way through the carnage. The grubby carpet was tacky beneath the soles of my shoes.

'Oh, wait,' he said, stopping suddenly, 'if you like the tattoos, you'll love this.' He stuck his tongue out at me. The end of it had been split, and the two sides twisted over each other as he made shapes with his mouth. There were many things I didn't understand about Morgan, and his apparent addiction to bizarre body modifications was one of them.

'What did you have that done for, you bloody idiot? You're going to look stupid when you get old. I can't wait to see it, actually. Saggy old man tits, trousers hitched up to your navel, wrinkly skin, bald head and all those tattoos. And what have you done to your earlobes? Jesus, I could get my finger through those holes. You look like one of those Amazonian tribesmen.'

'Brazilian,' he said, correcting me, walking away again, heading down the steps to the basement.

'Anyway,' I shouted after him, 'I was forgetting, you're going to live forever, aren't you.'

He stopped outside the door to his lab and looked back at me, face deadly serious. 'Not forever, just for a very long time.'

Later Morgan sat opposite me in his overgrown back garden, smoking a foul-smelling herbal cigarette. On his lap was a tame grey rat which curled playfully around his fingers as he fussed it. I couldn't take my eyes off the thing. I'd watched him inject it with enough poison to kill a horse less than ninety minutes earlier. For a while it had become lethargic, hissing with pain, then appearing on the point of death. But then it had slowly recovered, coming around as if it was just waking from a particularly restless sleep.

'So you're convinced now, then?'

I looked from the rat to Morgan then back again, desperately trying to find a hole in his theory, a way to disprove the impossibility I'd just witnessed. But I couldn't.

'More convinced than I was when I got here.'

'Look,' he said, suddenly sounding marginally more serious, 'there's no bullshit here, mate, no trickery. I'm completely on the level. This works! Like I said on the phone, it isn't immortality, not yet, but I reckon it might double your projected life span.'

I watched him for a while longer, my head swimming with a thousand different thoughts. Morgan looked like a stoner, a drop-out or a roadie for a band, as far from an influential, game-changing genius as you could get. Beneath the cocky façade, though, he was a troubled and lonely soul. We'd been through a lot together and much as it sometimes pained me to admit, he was like a brother. An annoying, lazy, bad mannered, but frequently quite brilliant brother.

'So what are you going to do with this?' I asked. The rat scrambled up his open shirt and perched itself on his shoulder.

'Nothing. I'm keeping it to myself for now.'

'But think of the people you could save...'

Yeah, and imagine the problems this will cause. Fuck's sake, John, we can't have a world of people living past a hundred and fifty, can we? The planet's overstocked as it is. There's no more room.'

'That's not for you to decide.'

'Actually, it is. My discovery, my rules.'

'But you can't create something like this then keep it to yourself. That's immoral.'

'It's all a bit dubious whichever way you look at it.'

He leant back in his chair and nuzzled the rat, then finished his cigarette and flicked the stub into the bushes.

'So why did you do it?'

'Because I could. To prove a point.'

'And why did you contact me? If you're so intent on keeping this to yourself, why bother telling anyone?'

He paused before answering. I'd already suspected what was coming next.

'I haven't finished yet. I need to try the procedure on a person. I've got a volunteer, but you know what I'm like, mate. I've never been one for official channels and ethics committees and all that bullshit.'

'Again, why involve me?'

'I need your help. You're medically trained and you're my closest friend. You're about the only person I still trust. Face it, mate, who else am I going to ask?'

'You should have seen her, John, she looked awful. She was literally having to hold her breath to get it on. And when she finally managed to do it up, there were bulges where there shouldn't have been bulges, and the fastenings were straining. Honestly, she was twenty years too old and several stone too heavy for that dress, but it was the most expensive thing in the store so there was no way she was leaving without it... are you even listening to me?'

'What?'

'I give up. What's the bloody point? Did you leave your brain back at Morgan's today?'

I reached across and grabbed Deanna's hand. 'Sorry, honey. Got a lot on my mind, that's all.'

'I remember when the only thing on your mind was me,' she grumbled. 'Now I have to compete with whatever nonsense Morgan's been filling your head with. Bloody hell, if you're like this now, how will you be when I'm as old and ugly as Hilda Daniels?'

'Who?'

'Hilda Daniels, the woman with the dress. Christ, you really weren't listening, were you. I was just telling you about her. A gross old crone with loads of cash but no taste.'

'I don't get you. I just—'

'Forget it,' she said, and she snatched her hand away from mine and got up.

'Dee, please, I'm sorry.'

She stood with her back to me, and I cursed my insensitivity. The longer the awkward stand-off continued, the more I knew I'd really upset her. Then, very slowly, she turned back around. I cringed, ready for the torrent of abuse I was sure she was about to let fly.

'You're a bastard.'

'Sorry.'

She unbuttoned her blouse and let it fall from her shoulders. 'What exactly do I have to do to get your full attention these days?'

I was back at Morgan's within the week. I knew very little about his volunteer, save for the fact he had an incurable muscle-wasting disease. He'd been a friend of Morgan's for some time, I understood. I feared their friendship wouldn't last much longer; either the disease would finish him off or Morgan would.

The two of them were in the kitchen. Morgan's friend was in as unfortunate a condition as I'd expected. Although similar in age to us both, his body appeared unnaturally small. He was wizened and contorted, crammed awkwardly into a high-backed wheelchair. His neck was twisted to one side, his face fixed into a permanent strained grimace. One claw-like hand – the only part of his body over which he seemed to still have any real control – was stretched out, fingers wrapped around the stubby black joystick which operated the chair, holding on for dear life.

'This is Colm,' Morgan said, putting a reassuring hand on the other man's bony shoulder. 'And not to put it too crudely, without my treatment he's fucked.'

'Jesus, Morgan, is this supposed to happen?'

The emaciated man on the bed in front of me began to violently convulse. As quickly as the horrendous spasms started, they stopped. Morgan checked his vital signs, seemingly unconcerned. 'He's fine.'

Phase one of the treatment had begun hours earlier with an initial dose of chemicals followed by an intense but brief bombardment of radiation. Morgan explained that the irradiated serum had to work its way around the patient's entire body for the procedure to be successful. These convulsions were the first indication that it was almost time for phase two to begin. I stood at the back of the cellar lab, redundant, as Morgan lined up a series of injections.

'There's only a small window of time to administer the second stage,' he said, watching Colm intently.

'And if you miss that window?'

'Then the effects of the first stage medication will kill him.'

The room was silent save for the metronomic bleeping of Colm's heart-rate monitor. And then I thought it missed a beat. Then another. The beats became increasingly irregular and slowed until there was an awful, overlong, gut-wrenching gap between one beat and the next. I instinctively moved forward to help but Morgan blocked me. He waited a second longer, then sprung into life. He thumped the needles deep into Colm's motionless chest, administering the drugs one after the other in quick succession, then stepped back.

And he waited.

It felt like forever, but it could only have been half a minute before the heartbeat trace returned, weak at first, but picking up pace. Soon it was stronger and steadier than before.

I stayed long enough to be sure that Colm's condition was stable, then went home. I heard nothing more from Morgan for over a week. I'd given up on him, deciding that his experiment must have failed, when he finally called. I was out with Deanna at the time, and we immediately drove over together. My uncertainty increased when I rang the doorbell and there was no reply.

'Listen,' she said. 'I can hear him in the garden.'

We let ourselves in through the side gate and there, playing football on the lawn, was Morgan and another man. It took a while before I realised it was Colm, and a while longer for me to fully accept what I was seeing. The pitiful wreck of a man, who'd been unable to move without assistance last week, was now playing football! He remained painfully thin and occasionally unsteady, but the change in his condition was remarkable.

'You're bloody good, I'll give you that,' I told Morgan that evening as the three of us ate dinner together. Colm had skipped town a short while earlier, leaving his wheelchair and his old life behind. He'd decided to head off and start over again somewhere no one knew him - somewhere he'd just be Colm, not the man who'd made an impossible recovery from an incurable disease.

'I always knew I was bloody good, just not *that* bloody good. I've surprised myself.'

'I still can't believe what you've done, Morg,' Deanna said. 'And there's honestly no trick or deception involved, just your treatments?'

'It's that simple,' he said, trivialising the medical breakthrough of the century. 'It's the ultimate body mod.'

'So what's next?'

Morgan didn't answer her at first. He chewed his food thoughtfully.

'I'm satisfied that Colm's treatment was a complete success,' he said. 'I want to see what effect it has on a healthy subject next.'

'But there's no way you'll find anyone who would—'
I began to say before he interrupted.

'I've already started,' he said. 'I've administered the
first stage treatment on myself. I couldn't say anything
beforehand, because I knew you'd refuse to help.'

What? I don't understand...'

'I asked you here to help with Colm so that you'd see
the entire procedure. Now I need you to finish my treatment.'

I laughed. 'You're not serious?'

'Never more so.'

'I won't do it.'

'Then that's me screwed, isn't it? Thanks mate.'

'What are you saying, Morgan?' Deanna asked.

'He's blackmailing me, Dee,' I explained, getting up
and walking away from the table. 'You're a manipulative
bastard, Morgan.'

He shrugged his shoulders and carried on eating,
completely unfazed.

'I still don't understand,' Deanna said.

'If I don't carry out the second phase of the treatment,
Morgan will die.'

What else could I do? I had no option but to help, but
I vowed that would be the extent of my involvement. I
watched the life drain from his body – first unconsciousness, next the convulsions, and finally cardiac arrest –
then I sunk the syringes into his flesh as I'd seen him do
to Colm. Once his heart had restarted, Deanna and I left.
That stupid, selfish fucker could look after himself, I decided, leaving his semi-conscious body on the slab in his
cellar laboratory.

We heard nothing further from him. Deanna mentioned Morgan frequently, but I did all I could to block
him from my mind. He'd be all right, I told her, he al-

ways was.

It was almost two weeks later, in the middle of a vicious summer storm, when he appeared at the door of our house, soaked through and clearly not giving a damn.

'This is incredible,' he said when I opened the door. 'It works, John. It really works!'

'Fuck off.'

I went to slam the door shut but he stuck his hand out and caught it.

'Morgan!' Deanna shouted, pushing past me and wrapping her arms around his scrawny, scruffy frame. She took his hand and led him into the house. 'I thought you'd killed yourself, you stupid bastard.'

'Far from it. Honestly, Dee, this is incredible. I mean, I'm not Superman or anything like that, but I feel...'

'What?'

'Different. More alive than ever. I can't explain, but I've never experienced anything like this before.'

'Me neither,' I said, taking my wife's hand from his and going through to the living room. Morgan sat down opposite us, soaking the sofa and dripping onto the rug. 'You're an utter shit, you know that? What makes you think you can just waltz back in here like nothing's happened?'

He ignored my question. 'We should all go through this,' he said, babbling excitedly. 'I'm serious. The three of us should do it.'

'What if I don't want to?' I said. 'What if there are side-effects? Christ, Morgan, you could drop dead tomorrow.'

'That's not going to happen, John. Think about it... my body's stronger than it's ever been. Listen, I might only have just told you about this, but I've been working on it for years. There are no side-effects. I know exactly what

I'm doing.'

My anger towards Morgan slowly subsided. I watched him for weeks, checking him over every couple of days, monitoring his health. And what I saw was remarkable. One afternoon, he caught his hand on a jagged piece of metal in his scrapyard-like garage. A couple more centimetres and he'd have severed several fingers. It was a deep and vicious injury and yet, incredibly, within a couple of hours it was healed. I went to change his blood-soaked dressing and discovered that the wound had almost completely disappeared, just a faint red marks remaining where the flesh had been sliced open.

The following day both Deanna and I were off work. There was much we should have been doing, but we chose to do nothing instead. It was almost midday, and we lay in bed together like a pair of teenagers. She climbed on top of me, still naked from the night before.

'You can't want more,' I said, half-joking. 'Bloody hell, Dee, it's only been a couple of hours.'

'Don't you fancy me anymore?'

She slid off and lay beside me again, running her hand over my chest.

'You know I do. I'm spent, that's all. The spirit is willing, but the flesh is weak.'

'You're getting old. That's your problem.'

'Maybe I am. Anyway, I didn't know I had a problem.'

'You've forgotten how to relax and have fun.'

'I haven't. I just don't have enough time.'

'Well we can do something about that.'

'How?'

'Maybe we should try Morgan's treatment.'

'Don't be stupid.'

'I'm not being stupid,' she said, offended. 'I'm serious.'

'It's out of the question.'

She moved her hand lower.

'Just imagine it, John. Making love all night, every night, forever.'

And the things she did to me beneath the sheets made it impossible to argue.

I lost a patient this week.

How ill she'd been and how hard my team and I had worked was irrelevant; the fact remained that a seventeen-year-old girl who'd been in my care was dead. Her family were devastated and so was I because I hadn't been able to save her. As I'd struggled and fought to keep her alive, all I'd been able to think about was that fucker Morgan and his damn treatment. Could I really be expected to keep what I'd learnt to myself? His discovery, which he seemed to think of as little more than a party trick, could potentially alleviate untold amounts of pain and suffering. I decided to confront Morgan when I next saw him, and I didn't have to wait long. He was at the house when I finally got back.

'What's up with you?' Deanna asked. The two of them had been drinking.

'Bad day. A patient died. She was only seventeen.'

'I'm sure you did all you could,' she said, sounding less than interested.

'Don't trivialize this,' I shouted, surprising myself with the depth of my pent-up anger.

'Calm down, John,' Morgan said, standing up and moving towards me. I pushed him away.

'Calm down! For Christ's sake, Morgan, I think I've got every right to be a little pissed off, don't you? You're sitting on a discovery that's going to revolutionise medicine forever, but you refuse to share it. If you'd seen what

I'd seen today... if you'd been the one who had to tell that girl's parents that their daughter was dead...'

'We've talked about this. You know I can't just let this out into the public domain. Society can't cope with people living twice as long, or even longer.'

'And what would you know about society? What are you afraid of, Morgan? Do you think that we'll all become selfish, self-obsessed shits like you? Or is it a power thing? Does it make you feel like a god?'

I stared at him, wanting the argument to continue, but he didn't answer. I glared at him with his long hair and his stupid bloody patchwork quilt of tattoos covering every visible inch of skin, and those goddam things in his ears, and the split in the tip of his tongue...

'You're *not* a god,' I told him, 'you're a fucking freak.'

Morgan remained infuriatingly calm. He picked up his coat.

'Sorry, Dee,' he said as he left, squeezing her hand when he passed her. The silence after the front door slammed shut was deafening.

'You bastard,' Deanna said, barely even looking at me. 'You totally underestimate him.'

'You think? I've been out there trying to save lives today, Dee, and what's he been doing? Playing Superman and pissing what's left of his inheritance up the wall, no doubt.'

'You're wrong. He was here tonight because he wanted to talk to you. Have you ever stopped to think he might be struggling with all this too? He needs your help. You're all he's got, you insensitive prick. He knows the importance of what he's discovered, and he can't handle it on his own.'

'Well he wasn't on his own, was he,' I snapped, not thinking. 'He's got you.'

I tried to apologise but it was too late. Deanna pushed

past me and went up to bed.

When I woke next morning, she wasn't there. I knew where she'd gone, though. I drove straight to Morgan's house and hammered on the door until he let me in.

'Where is she, Morgan?'

I didn't wait for him to answer. Deanna was in the kitchen, sitting staring out of the window. She glanced back over her shoulder at me, then turned away again.

'What do you want?'

'To talk.'

'Morgan needed to talk last night.'

'Come on, Dee, I'm sorry. I wasn't thinking straight last night. It's just that I could have saved that kid yesterday if I'd had access to Morgan's treatment.'

'I know that,' she said, still not looking at me, 'but Morgan's right, isn't he? The world's barely limping along as it is. If he shares the information he's got, we're all screwed.'

'It's an impossible situation,' Morgan said. I turned around and saw him standing right behind me. 'Damned if we don't, damned if we do.'

'We?'

'We're all in this together now, John. But I'm seeing things from a different perspective to either of you. We need to get back onto a level playing field.'

'What the hell are you talking about?'

'Let me tell him, Morgan,' Deanna interrupted, and I felt my legs weaken momentarily. Tell me what? Were they having an affair? In the heat of the moment that, stupidly, was all I could think. 'I want us both to have the treatment, John,' she eventually admitted.

'You can't be serious...'

'Deadly,' she said, and it was clear that she was. 'Thing is, we need time to make sure we handle this properly, and Morgan can give us that.'

'No way.'

'But it's so much more than that,' she continued. 'You're an ass at times, John, but I love you. We've been together for twelve years, and they've been twelve incredible years, haven't they?'

'The best.'

'And you'd be the first to admit, we've both been busy and haven't had as much time as we'd want.'

'Yes, but...'

'But imagine another hundred years like that. Morgan's treatment will make that possible.'

'Come on, mate,' Morgan said. 'You've got nothing to lose and everything to gain. If someone told me I could have a hundred years with someone like Dee, I'd take it in a heartbeat.'

He was right, of course. I was about to say as much when Deanna spoke again.

'Thing is, sweetheart, I've already started my treatment. Morgan administered the first stage medication before you arrived. There's no choice now. I have to see it through.'

When Deanna's reaction began in earnest, I was terrified. She'd been talking normally a few seconds earlier but had suddenly sunk into deep unconsciousness. And now she lay in front of me on Morgan's operating table, her body convulsing. The heart-rate trace kept time, and I didn't realise how much reassurance the constant noise provided until it stuttered, then stopped. I stepped back as Morgan moved forward, fighting against all my instincts to push him out of the way and resuscitate her myself. He held back for what felt like forever, then plunged the syringes into her naked body and waited for her to reanimate.

Every second felt like an hour.

'Morgan, is this normal?'

'It sometimes takes a little longer,' he hissed at me defensively. 'Just wait.'

And then, finally, the heart-rate monitor began to bleep steadily again and I leant back against the wall with relief.

'See,' he said. 'I told you it would be okay. She just'

He stopped speaking instantly when the noise of the machine turned to a sudden, high-pitched whine. I reached out for Deanna but he blocked my way.

'Her body's reacting to the treatment!' he screamed.

'Get out of my way!'

On the bed in front of me my wife's naked body began to convulse. Her spine arched as I fought to get closer, then she dropped back down hard like a piece of meat on a butcher's counter.

No noise.

She was completely still. No movement.

Absolute silence.

I shoved Morgan away and tried to resuscitate Deanna, my head spinning, my hands numb with shock. I refused to give up, even when I knew she was gone and there was no hope. Morgan pulled me away from her lifeless body and I collapsed in the corner of the room, barely able to breathe.

The love of my life was dead, and my reason for living had died with her.

The pain was like nothing I'd ever felt before. It consumed me. Tore me apart. It never faded, never eased. If I lived to be a hundred I knew it would still be as raw as the moment Deanna had died. Morgan had taken everything from me, and I needed him to suffer. That night he sunk quickly into a drink-fuelled haze, and I took full advantage. I anaesthetised him while he was sleeping and took him back down to his lab where I operated alongside Deanna's corpse. The various procedures took many hours to complete but that didn't matter; we had plenty of time.

I kept him sedated for several days to ensure he made enough of a recovery. It was remarkable – anyone else would have taken many weeks, but in no time at all his wounds had almost completely healed. I strapped him to a chair then sealed the cellar door with the three of us inside, blocking it with as much equipment as I could.

He tried to move when he came around, but then realised he couldn't.

'Don't panic, Morgan,' I said, 'you're safe. We're in your lab.'

He tried to speak, but that was impossible as I'd removed his tongue. When he realised this he started to panic again.

'Please don't struggle, Morgan, it really won't do you any good. You've destroyed my life, and now I've destroyed yours.'

He shuffled furiously on the seat and I stared at what was left of him. His bare but colourfully inked skin, his long hair, those bloody holes in his ear lobes, the stumps where his arms and legs had been...

'I need you to try and understand what you've done. You're a selfish fucker, so I don't expect you'll grasp the full enormity of the hurt you've caused straightaway, but you're a man with plenty of time now. I've done what I can to give you the perfect conditions in which to reflect uninterrupted.'

What remained of Morgan gave a little shudder.

'I hope you don't mind, but I've made a few body modifications of my own to help keep you focussed. You'd be amazed if you could see what I've done to you, except, of course, you can't because I've removed your eyes. And that split tongue of yours? Gone too. I didn't want you shouting out for help when you should be thinking. But the biggest change is your arms and legs. I've amputated them. Don't worry, I did a good job. Everything seems to have healed nicely.'

The bizarrely decorated torso twitched and fought against its binds, then slumped forward with resignation. I got up and lay down on the bed next to Deanna, then held her cold body tightly.

'The door is sealed, and I doubt anyone will come looking down here for a long time,' I explained.

I injected myself with a lethal dose of Morgan's chemicals, relaxing as I felt them coursing through my veins.

'I'm ending my life now, Morgan. See, I still have the power to do that. You, on the other hand, are stuck here forever with nothing to do but think about what you've done. Well, almost forever.'

THE LAST BIG THING

One of my favourite bands is **Everything Everything**. Their lyrics are often remarkable: crammed with unique images and oblique references. This story was inspired in part by the end of one of their songs, **The House is Dust**: *"I wish I could be living, at the end of all living, just to know what happens."* That's quite an image, being a spectator to the end of history itself, and that got me thinking. I listen to music all the time – couldn't survive without it – but I can't sing and I can't play a damn note. I wish I could. I'm filled with envy when I see the effect a musician can have on their audience. Who knows, maybe I've still got time to learn? Question is, if the stakes were as high as they could possibly get, how long would I keep playing? This story was written specifically for this collection.

'That was shit.'

'What are you on about? Were you at the same gig as me? That was brilliant, Nick,' Dougie said.

'No, it wasn't. No one was listening.'

'No one was *there*. Open mic night and we were first on the bill. That's how it goes. Luck of the draw.'

'Face facts, we're terrible. What the fuck are we doing? We're just a bad covers band.'

'No, we're a fucking great band, playing bad covers. There's a difference.'

'You think? It all sounds shite to anyone listening. Not that anyone is.'

'Musically we're actually pretty good,' Kathy said.

'You are,' Nick said. 'You're a classically trained pianist, for crying out loud.'

'Yeah, and do you think I'd waste my time playing with you losers if I didn't think we made a half decent noise together?'

'We don't even have a name for the band.'

'I thought we were going with *Dead Against It*?' Dougie said.

Gavin swigged the dregs from his bottle of beer and chucked it over the fence. 'Fuck that. Stupid. DAI. I put that on my kick drum and people will just think I'm Welsh and that's my name.'

'Since when did you get a say?' Nick goaded. 'You're not even a musician. You just hit things with sticks.'

'Fuck that and fuck you.'

'I like the name,' Dougie said, ignoring the banter. 'It's a Bowie reference. *The Buddha of Suburbia* was an important album.'

'To you, maybe,' Nick said.

'No, to Bowie. You could hear him loosening up on it. Got him out of his middle-of-the-road corporate rock phase. All that *Glass Spider* bollocks in the mid-eighties.'

'Loving the irony. Middle-of-the-road corporate rock bollocks is all we've got.'

'Until we get the EP out.'

'And when's that gonna happen? We've only got three decent songs.'

'And the beginnings of a handful more.'

'And how exactly are we supposed to record this landmark EP?'

'I told you, I'm waiting for a guy to call me back about getting some time in his studio.'

'And how long have you been waiting?'

'A couple of days.'

'What, since you first made contact?'

'No, since I last chased him up.'

Nick shook his head. 'I think we should use the name Gav came up with.'

'What, *Nowhere Fast*?'

'Yeah, 'cause that's exactly where we're going.'

'Hilarious,' Dougie said, unimpressed. 'Come on, mate, where's your ambition?'

'It's just about all gone. I lose a little bit more of it every time we play to an empty room.'

'Dougie's right,' Kathy said. 'We can't give up now. We've invested too much in this band, whatever we end up calling it. If we can get a couple more songs finished and get something recorded, then I think we've got a decent chance.'

'See,' Dougie said, vindicated. 'I don't know what she sees in you, Nick, but Kathy's smart. She gets it. We keep at this and we'll end up on top of the fucking world.'

THREE

It didn't take long in the end, just a couple of weeks. The door to success hadn't been fully opened – in fact it had been left only slightly ajar – but for the first time since they'd formed the band it at last felt like it wasn't locked, bolted and nailed shut.

It was Dougie who made the deal. He called the others from outside his parents' house, buzzing with excitement. A gig. A proper, fully paid, gig. It was a friend of a friend of a friend who'd seen them play in the back room of a pub a while back. The friend's friend's friend been due to get married early next month, and the band they'd got lined-up to play at the evening reception had split up. Right place, right time: *Dead Against It*, or *Nowhere Fast*, or whatever the hell they eventually decided to call themselves, had been booked to fill the vacant slot. Okay, so it wasn't a record deal and a headlining tour, but it was a start and right now that was all that mattered. It meant that someone thought the band was worth listening to. That was more than Dad thought. He'd had another full-on fit at Dougie this morning before he'd left for work, the usual 'get a job and get a grip or get out' sermon. 'You've got to get all this bullshit about being a rock star out of your head,' Dad had yelled at him. 'Stop sponging and start working.' Miserable bastard hadn't even heard them play. How could he make a statement like that when he hadn't even heard them play?

Dougie sat on the wall at the end of his parents' drive and soaked up the feeling. He felt euphoric. His mind was racing, thinking he'd chase the guy about the studio again in the morning. It would be great if they could get the EP recorded and give copies of it away at the gig (sorry, the wedding reception). He'd demoed the skeleton of a new song with Kathy at the weekend and it had real potential. It was called *Not Without You*. No chorus as such; it just built and built to a completely fucking perfect crescendo. This song was going to blow people away, he was sure of it. It would be their anthem.

Dougie knew they were onto something big. This was going to wipe the smile off Dad's face, he thought. All that cliché-filled parent bullshit he'd been forced to put up with since the gap year he'd taken mid-way through his uni course had become gap *years*. Dad was permanently on his case: *if you'd spent as much time on your studies as you spent playing that bloody guitar, you might have made something of yourself*, all that crap.

The house was quiet when he unlocked the door and let himself in. Mum and Dad were in their usual positions in their respective armchairs, both seats angled towards the over-sized TV which dominated the room, their pride and joy. Dougie walked through the narrow gap between them and positioned himself in front of as much of the fifty-five inches of screen as he could.

Deep breath.

'We've got a gig! A proper, paying gig! It's on Saturday the fifth at the Albany Suite. It's only a wedding reception and I know you're probably thinking I should slow down and not get too excited, but I've got a really good feeling about this. The more people that see us play, the better. We're gonna try and get some flyers printed and maybe even get something recorded that we can give away. It's gonna be amazing!'

Dougie looked into his parents' faces, illuminated by the TV flicker.

Nothing.

He'd half expected this. Whenever he talked about the band they lectured him on getting a proper job. 'It's one thing having your music as a hobby,' Mum was always saying, 'but it's never going to bring in enough money to put a roof over your head or food on the table.'

'He can't even afford a bloody table,' Dad would grunt.

But today Dougie couldn't hide his disappointment.

'Shit, is that it? The biggest thing that's happened to me in, like, ever, and neither of you have got anything to say?'

Mum was crying. Dougie could see tears rolling down her cheeks.

'You two been fighting again?' he asked.

'I'm sorry, son,' Dad said.

'Sorry for what?'

He nodded at the TV and turned up the sound.

The headline at the bottom of the screen was only three words long. Dougie laughed out loud when he read it.

WORLD ENDING WEDNESDAY.

'This is a joke, right?'

Mum shook her head. 'No joke, love,' she said through her tears.

'Three days?'

'Half eleven on Wednesday morning,' Dad told him. 'Two and a half days.'

Dougie laughed again. Nervous this time. 'Bit precise, don't you think?'

'Watch the bloody news if you don't believe me.'

Dougie sat on the arm of Mum's chair, same as he used to when he was a kid. The newsreader's immediately recognisable voice filled the room, but there was something about her tone tonight which made him uneasy. He'd seen her reporting on all manner of stories over the years, keeping the nation informed about anything and everything of note: wars beginning and ending, earthquakes and floods and the humanitarian disasters which inevitably followed, countless political changes at home and abroad, an endless parade of celebrity births, deaths and marriages. Gone tonight was the plummy BBC confidence and perfect diction, and in its place... was that honesty? Sincerity? A trace of vulnerability? Raw emotion? Dougie sat between his parents and watched and listened, because there was nothing else he could do.

He felt numb.

Empty.

'It's my sad duty to again confirm the devastating news we've heard this evening. A rogue satellite, Phion P2R, has entered our solar system on a direct course with Earth. Its velocity and direction are such that it is expected to collide at approximately eleven-thirty on Wednesday morning.' The presenter paused. Checked herself. Swallowed hard and wiped her eyes. 'Scientists around the world have confirmed that this will result in the total destruction of our planet. The government has advised all citizens to—'

'This is bullshit,' Dougie said, getting up and turning his back on the screen again. 'It's one of those drama-documentary things, it has to be.'

'It isn't,' Dad said, and he flicked through the channels to prove it. Same news, just about every station.

'I'm sorry, love,' Mum said through her tears.

'Why are you apologising?' Dad asked her. 'It's not your fault. It's not anyone's fault. Luck of the draw...'

Dougie still wasn't convinced. 'You're seriously buying into this crap?'

Dad got up and put his arm around his son's shoulder. A physical closeness they never normally shared: a little more than a handshake, but nowhere near a hug. 'It's real, mate. We've got less than three days.'

'It's got to be a wind up,' he said, shaking Dad off.

'You go online and check. It's all over the Internet.'

'So I'm supposed to believe this planet or satellite or whatever just appeared out of nowhere, and it's going to hit us like someone's playing a frigging game of intergalactic snooker? Come on. Surely they'd have known about it earlier.'

'They did,' Dad said, 'but they thought there was no point saying anything. Said there's nothing anyone can do. They said it would have just caused panic.'

'They wouldn't have said anything at all if it hadn't been for him,' Mum said, pointing at a man on the TV. He was an unshaven, scruffy-looking thirty-something wearing a faded band tour T-shirt. His hair was all over the place and his eyes were wild, yet he sounded calm, lucid, considered... completely plausible.

'His name's Paul Rafferty,' Dad explained because he didn't want to waste precious time sitting through the whole report again. 'Absolute hero, that man is. If it wasn't for him, we'd have never known anything.'

'I think that might have been better,' Mum said.

'We've already been through this, Jean.'

'So what happens now?' Dougie asked, sensing an argument brewing and quickly heading it off.

'We're going to see if we can get to your grandmother's in the morning,' Mum said.

'We haven't decided yet,' Dad interrupted.

'But I need to see Mum before...'

'And I need to see Richard and Sonya. And Phil, if we're travelling in that direction.'

'Why?' Dougie asked. 'You haven't seen your brothers for years.'

'I need to say goodbye.'

'What difference will it make?'

Dad made no attempt to answer. 'We're leaving in the morning. Richard, then Phil, then on to your gran's.'

'We'll be spending all day in the car at this rate,' Mum said.

'I don't see how else we're going to do it. It's that or

nothing. Few hours each way. We can bring your mum back here. Or stay there, maybe?'

'I'm not going anywhere,' Dougie said. 'My friends are all here.'

'We're a family and we're sticking together,' Dad said, and he stormed out to the kitchen before anyone could argue. Dougie went after him.

'I mean it, Dad, I'm staying here.'

Dad threw his empty coffee mug across the room and it smashed against the wall. 'Then you'll die alone son. Stop being so bloody selfish and grow up before it's too late.'

Nick and Kathy sat together on the end of the bed in their cramped bedsit. They'd been there for hours, staring at the screen. 'I still can't take this in,' Kathy said. 'Doesn't matter how many times I hear it. It's just too big... too much...'

'So what now?' Nick asked. 'We've got a couple of days left to cram in everything we ever wanted to do.'

Drinking had started to soften the blow. She took another swig from the two-thirds empty vodka bottle. 'Honestly, I don't know where to start.'

'We could get married if we can find a vicar who's on duty.'

'Are vicars ever off-duty? I thought they were supposed to be permanently on-shift? Anyway, you haven't asked me yet. You've never talked about getting married before. Why now?'

'Why not?'

'Fair point.'

'There's loads of places I haven't been. Things I haven't seen.'

'I thought we were supposed to be thinking about what we want to do, not what we'll never do.'

'I guess we could pick one country.'

'What, and walk there?'

'No, fly.'

She shook her head. 'You're so naïve, Nick.'

'I'm not.'

'You *are*. Are you going to work tomorrow?'

'No bloody way. Even if this turns out to be a hoax. It'll be frigging madness out there.'

'Exactly. So do you reckon the airline pilots and customs officers and baggage handlers are going to turn in?'

'They have to.'

'Not anymore, babe.'

Momentarily derailed, Nick took the vodka from her, slugged back a gulp, then tried again. 'Okay, let's do something stupid then.'

'Like what?'

'Break the law. Rob a bank.'

'And use the money for what exactly? Where's the fun in robbing a bank that's closed if the police won't even bother chasing us?'

'I don't know. Okay, let's go out naked or cook ourselves dinner in a fancy restaurant or take over a penthouse in the swishest hotel in town and spend our last days fucking.'

'And these are serious ambitions of yours, are they?'

'The last one is.'

'Yeah, I suppose I could go for that...'

And Nick put down the booze and they collapsed back on the bed together.

The hammering from the garage was incessant. The executive houses on the development were well-spaced, but sound still travelled in the relative stillness of the night. Barry Parker marched up the drive and kicked the metal door.

The drumming stopped.

A pause, a click, the whir of a motor and then the door opened.

'What?' Gavin said. Sweat-soaked, stinking of beer, wearing only his boxers.

'It's the middle of the night. Keep the bloody noise down.'

'Why? You think anyone's sleeping tonight?'

'It's the middle of the bloody night!'

'Stop shouting then.'

'You've always been a waste of space, sponging off your father.'

'Thanks. You should tell him.'

'I will. Where is he?'

'Thailand with his missus. If you do see him, tell him I said hello. And goodbye.'

'Do you not realise the end of the world's coming?'

'Yep. I saw it on TV.'

'And you still think it's okay to drink and play drums at four am?'

'I think it's more appropriate today than it has been in a while, actually.'

'I should beat the life out of you, you obnoxious little shit.'

'I wouldn't bother, Barry. I'll be dead in a few days, apparently. We all will.'

'I just think it's sad, that's all, that even at a time like this you can't be motivated enough to do something with your life.'

'I am. I was having a nice evening, actually. Better to be half-pissed and banging on the drums at four in the morning than to be outside someone's house in your pjs moaning about the noise, don't you think?'

And he shut the garage door in Barry Parker's face.

By the time Barry had reached the end of the drive, the

drumming had recommenced with death-metal ferocity.

TWO

Dougie woke up on the sofa with a start. He tried to avoid remembering anything and go back to sleep but failed miserably. Half a thought about what he'd learnt last night and he was wide awake. Then he cursed himself for having slept at all. There were a million random thoughts running haywire at ridiculous speeds around his sleep-dulled brain.

Oh, fuck. Two days. Oh, fuck.
How much time did I waste asleep?
How much longer will I sleep?
How much more will I drink?
How many more meals?
How many more toilet trips?
Who will I see again?
Who won't I see?
How many more songs will I hear?
How many more songs will I play?
Does anything matter anymore?
Should I just sit here and wait for the end to come?
Would it be better if it happened today?
Did yesterday really happen?
Did we really get booked for a gig?
Nowhere Fast *or* Dead Against It?
Is there really a massive rock hurtling through space that's gonna wipe us all out?
Could it miss?
Have they got it wrong?
Is it a hoax?
Will they fire missiles at it or send up a spaceship full of retired astronauts like in the films?

Is it going to hurt when it happens?
Is Mum ever going to stop crying?
Dad appeared in front of him. 'Get up.'
'What?'
'I need your help, son. Get up.'
'What for?'
'Food and fuel. We don't have enough of either to get anywhere.'
'Okay. I need a shower first.'
'No time. Now!'
'I need a pee at least.'
'Quick,' Dad said, and Dougie got up and stumbled to the bathroom. The sound of the taps and water filling the bowl was initially all he could hear, but once he'd finished he became aware of other noises outside. He washed his hands and splashed his face with ice-cold water to try and wake himself up fully. The rest of the world didn't sound like it ought to at ten-to-eight on a Monday morning. The usual traffic noise sounded different. Stop-start. Fractious. Revving engines and blaring horns. Bad-tempered. Completely disordered.

Dougie had seen more than enough post-apocalyptic movies to know what typically came next, but it was still a shock when he saw it with his own eyes and at the end of his own street. The dual carriageway which snaked through the suburbs and in and out of the city centre was clogged with traffic in both directions, none of which was moving. Cars nudged aggressively to join the line, but to no avail. Dougie walked to the end of the road. It was the same for as far as he could see in either direction. Then he went further, all the way to the footbridge over the motorway. Same thing again. Six solid lanes of unmoving, bad-tempered, terrified people stuck in their vehicles.

'We're not going anywhere, Dad,' he said when he

made it back to the house.

Dad looked as if he'd been punched in the face. 'But we have to go...'

He went and looked for himself, either not believing his son, or just not wanting to.

Mum was outside now too. 'What's the matter, love?' she asked.

'We'll have to leave it a while. Hope the traffic eases up.'

'I'm guessing it won't,' Dougie said. 'Everyone's going to be doing the same thing, aren't they?'

'You're not helping,' Dad said through gritted teeth.

'So what do you want me to say? Shall we just pretend all this isn't happening? If that's the case I'll go and see my mates...'

'Dougie, don't,' Mum pleaded.

He stopped and checked himself. Dad looked scared. They all were. It was no one's fault. 'Okay. Sorry.'

'We need to get some food,' Dad said. 'Come with me to the supermarket, mate?'

'Sure.'

It had seemed sensible coming here when Dad first suggested it, but now they felt hopelessly naïve. What they found at what was left of the supermarket surpassed their worst fears. It wasn't even ten o'clock, and the place already resembled a war-zone. There were no uniformed staff or security to be seen, and people were running away from the building in all directions, arms overloaded with looted bags and boxes. Others were cramming whatever they'd managed to get hold of into their vehicles, only to find themselves unable to drive any further away than the swollen bottleneck where the mass of cars trying to escape the car park went up against many, many more still trying to worm through the gridlock and force their way in.

'This was a really bad idea,' Dougie said.

'We have to eat, though. There's hardly anything in the house.'

'I'll wait out here for you then.'

Dad scowled, took another few steps forward, then bottled it and stopped again. 'Forget it. We'll try later.'

'Think they'll have had a delivery by then?'

'Can't imagine any delivery drivers are still working today.'

'I was being sarcastic.'

'Don't get smart with me, Douglas, now's not the time. Maybe we should try somewhere else.'

'I think everywhere's going to be the same.'

Even from this distance they could both see more than enough of the chaos consuming the inside of the vast superstore. People were taking whatever they could get their hands on from the shelves and freezers, clearing them out, and if they were already empty they were instead snatching things from those who'd got there before them. And if that didn't work, they were just taking whatever they could lay their hands on, even if they didn't need it. One man ran past with a Christmas tree.

'A bloody Christmas tree in the middle of summer! Whole world's gone crazy,' Dad said.

'I reckon people are just showing their true colours,' Dougie replied. 'No need to follow the rules anymore. I think this is what it's going to be like now.'

Panic was spreading through the ill-tempered crowds like the most virulent of infections. Animosity could be seen jumping from person to person to person. Fighting had broken out in places and swarms of people were skirting around the violence but not getting involved. Dougie could see bodies, and that shocked him more than anything. Dad grabbed his arm and pulled him away.

They ran back to the house together but stopped again on the footbridge, distracted by a wall of noise which was coming up from the motorway below.

'That's that, then, no one's going anywhere now,' Dougie said as they looked down onto the chaos. Someone up ahead had tried to steer through a gap that wasn't there and had instead driven straight into the back of another vehicle, which had in turn been shunted into the back of another. More drivers had attempted to take evasive action, and more of them had collided. The madness had even spilled over the crash barrier thanks to an overturned delivery truck, and now the traffic on the motorway in both directions, which had only been crawling forward at a glacial pace anyway, now wasn't moving at all. Oily grey smoke began to leak from under the jackknifed truck. It was a few light wisps curling up into the daylight initially, but in no time at all something had caught and flames started to appear. Soon black clouds belched skyward. There was no way the emergency services were going to be able to get anywhere near, not that there appeared to be any of the emergency services left working this morning.

But Dougie and Dad weren't watching the fire.

Realisation had clearly dawned for those nearest to the crash, and they'd started to abandon their vehicles in huge numbers, grabbing what they could carry from overloaded cars. And as others began to realise what was happening, they too started to follow. In no time the trickle became a flood. Pedestrians filled the gaps between cars and were herding away from the crash-zone in a fast-moving wave in both directions. It was unstoppable, not that anyone had any reason to try and slow the sudden exodus down. Realising the futility of following the road, many of the people were now climbing the embankments on either side of the carriageway then scaling fences or simply pulling them down, spilling out into the suburbs in vast numbers. In the short time Dad and Dougie were watching, the fire in the road spread to more vehicles and the hundreds of fleeing people became thousands.

'Almost makes you hope that thing that's coming for us doesn't miss, don't it, son?' Dad said, and Dougie knew exactly what he meant.

'It would be impossible to undo all of this mess now,' Dougie agreed. 'We're screwed whatever, aren't we?'

'We'll get home, give it some time, then reassess.'

'Come on, Dad, be realistic. We're not going anywhere.'

'Like I said, we'll reassess.'

'But none of the traffic will have moved. All these people are stranded.'

'Don't care about anyone else. Not my problem.'

'I'm not so sure.'

'What d'you mean?'

'Where do you think they're going to go?'

Within hours the streets around the house were full of them. 'Scrounging bastards,' Dad called them, watching from the bedroom window as people went house-to-house, looking for charity or shelter... or anything. A great crowd of them broke into the primary school a hundred metres further down the road. 'Bastards,' he said again from behind the curtain. There were two ringleaders, from what Dad could see, a man and a woman. They were beckoning more people down towards the school. Some of them were carrying armfuls of food they'd obviously nicked from what was left of the supermarket. 'It's a bloody outrage.'

'What is, love?' Mum asked.

'Bloody looters. Looks like they've helped themselves. They've got more food than we have.'

'There are more of them.'

'That's not the point.'

'Then what is?'

'They're not even from round here! Look at them. Who the bloody hell do they think they are? Taking our food...'

Mum sat on the edge of the bed, her head in her hands. 'They're scared, that's all. They don't know what to do. We might have been in the same boat if we'd left here this morning and got stuck somewhere else.'

'It's a good job we stayed. They'd have broken into here if we'd gone. I saw a couple of them looking in through the downstairs windows.'

Dougie was going to say something about how quickly Dad had changed his tune, but he bit his lip and kept quiet instead. There weren't any easy answers anymore. Nothing was straightforward. Everything felt like they were taking the wrong option. Even the smallest decisions now felt like monumental (end of) life choices. Mum clearly felt the same way.

'All I wanted was to see the family again before... before it happens, but I can't. It's not fair, none of it is. It's like we're always having to choose the least worst option now. Say goodbye to the family or risk people getting into the house? Go hungry or risk our lives fighting for food? Tell you the truth, love, I wish we'd just got in the car and gone for it. The fact we're sitting here doing nothing makes everything feel a thousand times worse.'

'We wouldn't have got anywhere, Mum,' Dougie said. 'I bet the kind of thing we saw on the motorway is happening everywhere.'

'If you've nothing positive to say, don't say anything,' Dad said.

'There's nothing positive left, Dad.'

'Just shut up then.'

'Leave him alone, Geoff.'

'It's all right, Mum,' Dougie said, and he went to leave the room but Dad called him back.

'Keep the doors locked if you're going downstairs, understand? Don't want any of those fuckers out there thinking they can come in here and take what's ours.'

'There's hundreds of them, Dad. Face facts, if enough of them decide they're coming in, they're coming in.'

'Well we're not going to make it easy for them. Your mother and I worked hard for everything we have, and I'm not going to let anyone take it from us.'

Dougie knew there wasn't any point, but on his way out the door he said it anyway. 'You're going to lose the whole lot on Wednesday morning whatever happens.'

Early evening, a little over a day and a half until the end of the world, and Kathy and Nick's quest to find a hotel room in which to act out their hedonistic fantasies had so far been about as successful as Dougie and his dad's aborted supply run. When they finally managed to get themselves to somewhere decent the reception desk was unmanned. There weren't any staff left anywhere.

The lifts were out, and the couple only made it as far as the fourth floor before changing direction and going back down. They weren't the only people intent on indulging in a little clichéd, hotel-based fantasy, it seemed. A steady stream of furniture, TVs and, occasionally, people were being thrown from the windows out onto the street below. The couple were being dragged towards some suites to join the party, shoved away from others. Through room doors left casually open they saw things the likes of which they'd barely imagined before. Debauched, drink- and drug-fuelled behaviour. Out of control. Uninhibited. Nick didn't like it. He wanted out. 'You've changed your tune,' Kathy said. 'You're all talk and no trousers. You told me you were up for anything.'

'With you, yeah. Not strangers.'

'Makes you kind of wish we'd stayed in the flat, don't you think?'

Nick agreed. 'Let's check the Holiday Inn and the Hilton, then go back.'

'It's going to be the same everywhere.'

'You're probably right. I just have this stupid image in my head of you and me in a penthouse suite with an epic view, watching the end of everything.'

'You're right. It's a stupid image. This isn't a movie, you know.'

'I know that. It's always perfect in the movies. Things always work out.'

'Not always. Come on, babe, let's keep going.'

They didn't make it as far as the last hotels on their list. Getting there involved crossing Paradise Square, a vast, block-paved plaza in front of the Council House, right in the very heart of the city. This evening it was impassable. The place was being swamped by an enormous crowd of people which appeared to be getting bigger by the minute, more and more folks dragging themselves out of the shadows towards the light and noise. In front of the council buildings there was a raised platform made of scaffolding, and on it a woman was screaming into a microphone.

'How did they get all this set up?' Kathy asked.

'It's been here a few days. There's some kind of arts festival going on here next week, remember? Well there was.'

From a distance the noise of the impromptu rally was hard to discern, all mosquito-like buzzing and confusing echoes. But the size and the roar of the crowd had an impossible pull and the couple found themselves drifting towards its fringes, moving into range of the PA system. It was hard to argue with much of what the woman on stage was yelling.

'We deserve better than to be left in the dark and treated like children. What gives our government the right to treat us this way and take away our choices? Our final, most important choices at that.'

Cue a volley of cheers, enough almost to drown her out completely.

'We demand that the politicians in Whitehall and Downing Street – those who are still there and not hidden away in plush bunkers somewhere – show themselves. Face the public and tell us the truth. There's been nothing but silence from our so-called leaders, but there has to be a plan.'

Kathy nudged Nick. 'Hey, d'you think the royals are tucked away somewhere?'

'No idea. No point, by all accounts 'cause it won't make any difference. I bet they're still being pampered, though.'

'You reckon?'

'Hope so, for their sakes. Can you imagine any of them having to cook their last suppers for themselves?'

The woman on the stage continued. 'It looks hopeless right now, like there's no future for any of us, but maybe there's a way through this? Brothers and sisters, maybe we can survive? Our cities are a network of tunnels and passages. We need to get underground. Flood the subways and basements with people and take as much down there with us as we can. If we can stay down below until the surface is inhabitable again, who knows what might happen.'

The noise of the crowd shifted slightly: a toxic mix of fear and adrenalin now, a glimmer of hope colliding with a tidal wave of doubt and incredulity. The woman on the stage appeared oblivious to the noise coming from supporters and detractors alike.

'Thing is, we don't know what to believe, do we? Are they telling us the truth about what's coming? Is there more to this than we're being told? Is this just a rouse to terrify us and keep us under control? Does Phion P2R even exist? If it does, will it have the devastating effects we're being told? Will our planet really be destroyed? It's in our nature as a species to try and survive and we're not prepared to just roll over and wait for this to happen. Half a chance is better than no chance at all, so gather your friends, families and loved ones together and join us underground.'

As the woman stepped away from the mic to a volatile mix of indifference and cheers, tinny music was cranked up to a deafening volume. She left the stage, passing the baton to the next person in line. The atmosphere was beginning to feel increasingly fractious. Kathy pushed Nick on. 'Let's go. I thought this might be something serious, but it looks like it's just a parade of cranks and nutters. Give them a mic and they think they matter.'

'I agree,' Nick said. 'It all seems a bit desperate if you ask me.'

'Suppose. But if ever there was a time to be desperate, this is it, don't you think?'

And that desperation, it seemed, was increasingly manifesting itself now as fear and violence. Nick became aware of something happening over on the diagonally opposite side of Paradise Square, and he climbed up onto the rim of a dried-up fountain to get a better view.

It was like a mosh at the front of a gig, all pushing and pulling and people running into each other, but without security guards or barriers or goodwill it spiralled out of control with astonishing speed. Panic bred panic. These thousands of people, their lives already turned upside down and stripped of all future form and purpose without warning and through no fault of their own, had already been pushed right to the furthest edge of the edge, and it took hardly anything to push them over. Some people fought while others ran to avoid the fighting, but in the sudden disarray it was impossible to tell one from the other. Kathy pulled Nick back down from the fountain. 'We have to leave, babe. It's not safe here. We need to get away from everyone else and stay away.'

Each minute felt like a lifetime wasted. Though not as crowded as this morning, the street outside the house was still busy. Dougie's home felt like a prison to him now, though he knew things could have been far, far worse. For a time he and Dad had threatened to come to blows, Dad insisting that the family should spend their remaining day and a half in the cellar. He'd bought into the bullshit and had moved everything of value into the cellar in the vain hope they could somehow avoid oblivion by burying themselves six feet deeper underground. It had taken all of Mum's considerable Dad-wrangling and negotiation skills to make him see sense. She herself had stopped panicking and now seemed to be doing a decent job of accepting the inevitable. In the hours since the cellar plan had been abandoned, they'd drunk two bottles of wine between them, had become tearfully over-amorous, and had now gone to bed. Dougie had the TV on loud to drown the awful noises from the bedroom. Now he sat alone on the sofa, staring into space, the room drenched with light from that damn huge TV.

Is this it? It's the end of everything, and all I can do is sit here alone and watch TV while the seconds tick away. Pathetic.

Trouble was, what else was he supposed to do? Until a couple of days ago things had been very different.

Sure, he'd had an equal lack of direction and he'd been no more motivated, but back then it hadn't seemed to matter. His motto had been *why do it today when you can put it off until tomorrow?* Well now there was only one tomorrow left to defer things to.

But what was the point of trying to do anything? What would it achieve? His bucket-list – not that he'd ever seriously considered making one – would remain frustratingly un-ticked. If he wrote the best song in history tonight, would it even matter now that history was scheduled to end the day after tomorrow and no one would ever hear it? Nothing seemed to matter any-more and yet, at the same time, absolutely everything felt more important than it ever had. The floorboards creaked above his head and he turned up the TV sound even louder as the olds started acting up again.

Most channels had stopped broadcasting, many of them now simply showing feeds from webcams and other static cameras, images from every corner of the globe. Some TV stations were still showing something resembling normal programming, mostly just pre-pro-grammed re-runs and repeats on a loop, but it just didn't feel right watching them. More than that, it actually be-gan to feel wrong, like he was spying on a world he was no longer a part of. It was like when he used to skive off school, watching endless hours of crap daytime TV, knowing all the time that he should have been in les-sons. Tonight those feelings were massively multiplied. Dougie was worried that if he allowed himself to be-come distracted by banal rubbish, his final hours would evaporate even more rapidly. He stuck initially to the static feeds instead and it was interesting, he thought, how the same thing appeared to have happened every-where. Across every continent and country, irrespective of languages, borders or beliefs, people's reactions were broadly similar: a wave of confusion, fear, and ultimately pointless panic.

London – rioting in the streets. The Houses of Parliament in ruins. Buckingham Palace over-run by commoners. Big Ben burnt down to a stump.

Several cities in the United States appeared to have been wiped completely off the map, looking like Phion P2R had already hit.

St Peter's Square in the Vatican was swamped, but there was no one left preaching.

A Boeing full of passengers had crashed in the centre of Shanghai and huge swathes of the city were burning. Dougie thought that the people on the crashed plane had been dealt a particularly cruel hand. It was like tripping and breaking your ankle in the twenty-fifth mile of a marathon and being unable to finish: they'd almost reached the end of everything, only to be taken out at the last gasp by pilot error or pilot panic or a passenger revolt or the absence of air traffic controllers... Or had the pilot simply refused to land? Did they think they might have stood half a chance of surviving if they'd still been in the air when Phion P2R impacted?

Then again, maybe the people in the plane and on the ground near the crash site had caught a break? Dougie thought it might actually be preferable to be spared the prolonged agony of the next day and a half. Nothing was going to change the end result, it seemed, and he could only imagine the pressure increasing exponentially as the end of the world neared. He almost wished time would fast-forward so he could get it over with.

The area around the Sydney Opera House looked like a 1970s-style love-in on an impossibly grand scale, as if the entire population of the city had decided to kick back and chill out together for the little time remaining. It was daytime there, and people were out in their hundreds of thousands.

It was hard to believe all this would soon be gone.

When he'd worked his way through the limited TV channel options, Dougie switched to the Internet. The online world had always been a fertile breeding ground for paranoia and conspiracy theories and Jesus Christ, the cranks were out in force tonight.

'That one's a bloody nutter,' Dad said, making Dougie jump. 'I've heard him going on before.' Evidently the shuffling around upstairs had been the end of something, not the beginning, and with the TV so loud Dougie hadn't heard him come down. Dad was half-pissed and his earlier nervous aggression appeared to have been negated by the booze. The guy whose pixelated face now filled the screen was talking at a thousand miles an hour, punctuating his constant tirade of anti-authoritarian rants with regular Jesus, God and Satan namechecks and suggestions of hellfire and damnation for those who didn't believe in the same things he did. 'Bit late for all that garbage now.'

Dougie laughed. 'Yeah, he's always been banging on about the end of the world. Now it's confirmed and all he's talking about is how to save yourself!'

'Bloody nutter,' Dad said again, and he went to fetch another bottle of wine for him and Mum.

The next feed was mildly better. At least this fellow appeared outwardly to be holding his shit together. His face was unfocused, far too close to the camera, and he spoke in a strangely hypnotic, mid-Western drawl. Calm. Far too calm for Dougie's liking. 'I'll say it again people, one more time, dig down and dig deep. We don't know if it'll work, but it's the only option we have right now. Take as much food and water as you can carry and get your loved ones as far below ground as you can. Basements, caverns, mines... whatever's nearby.'

Dougie switched to another feed.

This one was too professional. Too slick. The frantically animated host of the cast was so energetic as to be almost unwatchable. The myriad of shock headlines and graphics which appeared on the screen said it all: government conspiracies, hoaxes, mind control, erosion of civil liberties...

'Change it, son,' Dad said, pausing on his way back from the kitchen. Dougie obliged and switched again.

A stark contrast this time: a single steady black and white image coming from some satellite up there somewhere. A simple, noiseless transmission from NASA which said more with its silence than the combined bombast of all the preceding broadcasts. It was unfiltered, uninterrupted footage of Phion P2R's unstoppable approach. "Time to Impact" and "Distance from Impact" graphics ticked away at the bottom of the screen, both figures counting down to zero with no fanfare but with unsettling speed and dogged inevitability.

All thoughts of delivering Mum's wine temporarily forgotten, Dad sat down next to Dougie, transfixed. No matter how long they watched, Phion P2R didn't seem to be getting any closer. Strange to think it was hurtling towards them at thousands of miles per second.

'Think we can see it yet?' Dad asked. He sounded more excited than he should.

'You know that thing's gonna kill us, right?'

Dad wasn't listening. 'I read something online that said because of the angle it's coming in at, pretty much straight down, it'll be permanently visible from most of the Northern Hemisphere.'

'Permanent for the next day and a half. Lucky us.'

'Wait. I've got an idea.'

Dressing gown flapping open in the breeze, Dad dashed upstairs, handed Mum the bottle of wine, then started mooching around in the spare room. He came down again a few minutes later, arms loaded. 'You kept that thing?' Dougie asked.

'Your telescope? Of course I did.'

'I must have used it all of three times.'

'Yeah, I remember. You weren't interested. Your granddad bought it for you.'

'Because *he* liked astronomy.'

'I know. Funny old goat. Used to buy me toys that he wanted to play with, did I ever tell you that?'

'Only about a thousand times.'

Dad took the telescope and its tripod out into the back garden and set it up. Dougie followed him out and watched bemused as he looked up and scanned the heavens. Phion P2R was easy to spot without any help. The penultimate night on Earth was a clear one, and the approaching mass of rock glowed brighter than any star.

'Grandad would have been blown away by all this,' Dad said, bending down and squinting through the eyepiece.

'I know. Now it's us that's going to be blown away.'

Dougie swallowed down an unexpected sob. Dad heard it but focused on sky-watching instead. The sadness was contagious.

'Got it! Jeez, would you look at that!'

He stood to one side to let Dougie have a look. Christ, but the incoming destroyer was a beautiful thing. It had a brown hue with an ice-blue tinge, like nothing either of them had ever seen before.

'It's going to look awesome when it takes us all out,' Dougie said. His joking masked his fear, because now that he could see Phion P2R with his own eyes, the last shreds of doubt were gone. No longer could anyone cling onto the hope that this was some kind of fucked-up joke or toxic conspiracy theory. Instead this was, unquestionably, the end of everything.

ONE

Sleep was the furthest thing from anyone's mind, but exhaustion was as unstoppable as the impact of Phion P2R and it caught up with all of them in the end. Dougie woke up on his bed next morning, fully dressed. He could hear his parents talking downstairs. He got up and went down.

Everything he did reminded him that time was ticking away, and more unanswerable questions formed.

Will I keep these clothes on until the end?

Will I even go to bed tonight?

Will I eat anything today?

Will I see the band again?

Where will I be when it happens?

How close is Phion P2R now?

He stopped midway down the stairs and looked out of the window, one of his questions immediately answered. The rogue satellite was clearly visible. Dougie knew his telescope was as useless again now as it had been for the last ten years or so, because he no longer needed it to see the football-sized body hanging in the sky. And he knew it wasn't hanging, it just looked that way. It was actually hurtling towards him with phenomenal force and speed like an impossibly-sized wrecking ball. Regardless, it still looked like it was taking its time. He wished it would slow down. Take a breather. Give them all a few extra days together.

Mum was crying again. That didn't strike Dougie as strange. Surely everyone had reason to cry today? He still asked her why. She couldn't talk, but Dad explained. 'You remember Joanne from across the road?' he whispered so as not to upset Mum further.

'Pregnant Joanne?'

'She's not pregnant anymore.'

'Is everything okay?' Dougie asked, realising how re-dundant his question was.

'She had the baby last night. Everything's fine, but—'

'Everything's not fine,' Mum snapped. 'How can it be? Poor girl's just given birth and she knows she's going to lose her baby tomorrow. I've never seen anyone so conflicted. She was laughing one minute, sobbing the next. Over the moon and heartbroken at the same time. It's just all so damn unfair.'

Dougie froze. Didn't know what to do, what to say, what to think or what to feel. 'I can't stay here.'

'You're going nowhere, son. The family should be together at a time like this,' Dad said.

'Why? To sit and watch the clock ticking? To get all depressed together for a miserable last twenty-four hours?'

'It's too dangerous out there.'

'So? We're all going to die tomorrow anyway.'

'You're being stupid, Douglas.'

'And you're being blinkered, Dad. As usual.'

'Don't talk to me like that.'

'Don't talk to me at all.'

He headed for the door.

'Where are you going?' Dad shouted after him.

'To see the others.'

'Which others?'

'The band, of course.'

'Will you be back?'

'At some point.'

And Dad shouted something else then, and Mum too, but Dougie didn't stop.

He ran through the streets with an urgency the likes

of which he'd not felt before. Dougie felt totally alone, which struck him as strange because he could see people just about everywhere. He paid no attention to any of them, completely disconnected, completely focused on getting across town.

He found that some of the larger open spaces were virtually empty. The usually busy Paradise Square was desolate. There was more wildlife here than anything. Crows, magpies, pigeons and seagulls squabbled over scraps whilst a lone dog mooched through piles of stinking rubbish. It looked like the end of the world had already happened. The dog watched him with caution, its prime concerns being satisfying its hunger and making sure he wasn't a threat. Dougie envied the animal's ignorance. It was just another minute of just another day. The hound had no idea it was going to die tomorrow.

So where had everyone gone? The answer, Dougie discovered, was disappointingly simple. He found shuffling queues winding through the shadows as people bunched and pushed and queued and bartered and bribed, desperate to get underground. What did they hope to achieve? Surely they'd only be buying themselves a few extra seconds, whilst at the same time being denied a front-row seat to the most extraordinary heavenly display imaginable? And if, by some miracle, the planet wasn't completely destroyed and the people underground survived the impact, how long would they last without food or water when they eventually returned to the surface? It all seemed a bit fucking pointless, if you asked him. Not that anyone was.

Dougie decided he'd rather be up here where he could see what was going to kill him. Phion P2R was beginning to look pretty spectacular, hanging silently in the clear blue summer sky.

*

A blind man could have found his way to Gavin's house without any trouble. The noise coming from the garage was remarkable. Did he never stop playing drums? Dougie paused at the end of the drive and looked up at the grand executive-style house. He relaxed slightly, happy now he could hear bass and keyboards being played too. The gang was all here.

He had to wait for a gap in the beat to make his presence known. 'It's Dougie,' he shouted, though they wouldn't have been expecting anyone else, and he took a couple of steps back in anticipation of the door opening. Gav's dad's place had served them well over the years, the double garage giving them both a place to store their gear and a rehearsal space at zero cost.

The door motor clicked and whirred into life, and it rose like a metal stage curtain. Gavin stood up from behind his drum kit, stark naked. 'Put some clothes on, mate,' Dougie said. Gavin was a born exhibitionist, and though Dougie had seen it all before, he'd no desire to see it again.

'I'm through with clothes,' Gavin shouted at him.

'Then I'm going home,' Dougie laughed.

'You're not going anywhere!'

'You took your time,' Nick said.

'Yeah. I've been a bit tied up with the end of the world.'

'Crappy timing,' Kathy said. 'That's our big break fucked.'

'That's everything fucked,' Nick corrected her, and he started playing again.

'Home alone, Gav?' Dougie asked.

'Apart from these two, yep.'

'Where are your folks?'

'Thailand. Visiting Val's family.'

'You've heard from them?'

'Yeah, had a teary Skype call in the middle of the frigging night, Dad and Val calling home to say goodbye from paradise. They were on the beach, hand-in-hand and acting all lovey-dovey and I... er...'

He picked up his drumsticks before his emotions got the better of him.

'You okay, mate?' Nick asked.

'Yep. Are we gonna play some fucking songs now Doug's finally decided to turn up?'

And they played.

And they played.

And played.

They stopped briefly mid-morning. 'It's eleven-thirty,' Nick said. It was what they were all thinking. 'This time tomorrow...'

'You know when you were at school and it was the end of the holidays,' Dougie said, not entirely sure where this allegory was going.

'What about it?'

'It feels like that, doesn't it? Just a million times worse.'

'That's not as stupid as it sounds,' Kathy agreed. 'I used to think that. It always felt different when you'd got less than a day of the holidays left.'

'Come on, people,' Nick said, losing his patience. 'It's the end of the fucking world, for Christ's sake.'

He carried on playing, but he was on his own.

'Are we doing the right thing here?' Dougie asked. 'I mean, shouldn't we be finding better ways to spend our time?'

'Like how?'

'I don't know.'

Kathy shook her head. 'Stop thinking about it too hard. If you're looking for some kind of epiphany or meaning in your life, I wouldn't bother. We've always all been temporary, it's just that we're more temporary than we first thought. We should just carry on like none of it's happening.'

But Dougie couldn't let it go. 'I had all these huge plans for the band. I'd got us touring the world, selling out stadiums. It's not fair.'

'You're right,' Nick said, 'but there's fuck all any of us can do about it. Feeling like this is completely natural.'

'Natural? What's natural about any of this?'

'I did psychology, remember?'

'You flunked psychology, I remember that much.'

'Doesn't matter. You ever heard of the Kübler-Ross model?'

'No.'

'It's all about grief. There's five stages, apparently: denial, anger, bargaining, depression and acceptance.'

'What exactly are you saying, Nick?'

'I'm saying we're so short on time we need to skip straight to the last phase. We're fucked. Just accept it and make the most of the little time we've got left.'

'Play another fucking song is what he's saying,' Gav told him, and he counted them in.

The remains of the morning, the whole afternoon and half the evening disappeared in a haze of music and booze. They stopped for food, yearning for one last takeaway but knowing the moment had already gone. 'Good job Val still treats you like a kid, eh Gav?' Kathy said. The four of them were sitting around the granite-topped island in the middle of the vast kitchen.

'Do you hear me complaining?' he replied, swigging more beer. 'There's enough food left in that freezer for a month, and we've only got until tomorrow.'

It was a throwaway comment, but every mention of the looming oblivion cut each of them to the core.

'Still feel like we should be doing more than this,' said

Dougie, playing with his food, hardly eating it.

Gavin was having none of it. 'Then you're a fucking idiot.'

'Thanks, mate.'

'No, Doug, I mean it. You just don't get it, do you? What's the point getting all hung up on it all? We've got, what, about fourteen hours left, and you're gonna waste it worrying about who you should be seeing or what you should be doing?'

'Jesus, Gav,' Nick said. 'You're still the only person I know who makes more sense when they've had a drink.'

'I'm a frigging oracle,' he told him. 'You lot dismiss me because I'm just the drummer, but there's more to it than you think.'

'Yeah, right.'

'See? There you go again. Frigging music snobs. You try playing if I'm not there.'

'We have, remember. Pretty much every other rehearsal back in January when you were all loved-up with that girl.'

'Okay, okay. The point I'm making is we're better when we're all playing together, right? You lot do all the fancy stuff, and I keep us moving at the right speed. I'm a fucking conductor, me.'

'You're a fucking idiot,' Nick said, and Gav skimmed the remains of a burnt pizza at him like a frisbee. 'Remind me, why does any of this matter anymore?'

Gav shrugged his shoulders. 'It doesn't, I guess. Maybe it never did.'

'Now you've really lost me.'

'Why did we do it? Why did we do any of it? Why did Kathy spend years studying piano and why did you two pick up your guitars and start strumming? Why did I start drumming?'

There was a pause. It felt like an impossible question

that should have been simple to answer.

'Because we love it,' Dougie eventually replied.

'Exactly. No one else gives the tiniest of shits, really. If we'd had another five or ten years then maybe we'd have gone on to be the next big thing, and maybe people would have listened. No one had a chance to hear us, though, and I'm all right with that because I fucking loved every second of what we did together. Even today, the last full day before the end of the fucking world, when the four of us were playing together, nothing else mattered. If I could bottle that feeling and take a fucking huge swig of it when we all get blown to hell tomorrow morning, then that's exactly what I'd do. And yeah, my dad won't be around and neither will Val, and there's loads of other people I haven't said goodbye to and fucking loads of things I haven't done, but... but I'm not too bothered, truth be told. Even if we'd had a year to get ready for Armageddon, we'd all still have been sitting here tonight getting all maudlin about the stuff we'd missed.'

'Wise words, Gav,' Kathy said without any sarcasm whatsoever.

Gavin wasn't finished. 'What I'm saying is I don't know about you lot, but when the shit hits the fan tomorrow I want to be sat behind my kit, playing the fucking drums.'

ZERO

The light never completely disappeared all night. Something to do with the sun reflecting off the surface of the enormous rock hurtling towards Earth, Dougie thought. Tinged with an alien blue-green hue, everything felt and looked weird. It didn't feel like home to him anymore, like him and everyone else were just visitors, just stopping over on their way to somewhere else. It was because their time was running out, he decided. Guests, not owners. It was easier to think about it in terms of them just passing through, rather than having to believe that all this would soon cease to exist. Dougie could just about accept that his time was coming to an end, but it was still a struggle to believe that within just a few hours, all of this would be gone forever. Every scrap. Every living thing, and every inanimate object too. The tallest building, the highest mountain, the deepest ocean... *everything*. It made him feel about as significant as a frigging dust mote.

Since he'd left Gavin's house he'd noticed that people's behaviour was different this final morning. They were either at one end of the scale or the other, very little in-between: scores of people were quiet and reflective, trying to come to terms with impossible emotions and share their last hours with those who mattered, whilst a vast number of others, it seemed, were off their fucking heads. Many appeared to have overdosed on their drug of choice – alcohol, violence, sex, cocaine, whatever – anything to help detach themselves from their undoubtedly short but probably painful and definitely terrifying immediate future.

Dougie had spent the first few hours of his last ever morning moving from place to place, coordinating. It had felt good to have a purpose. A distraction. He tried, and failed, to look down as much as possible, because whenever he looked up, all he could see now was Phion P2R. It was eating up the sky, growing larger by the minute, so big and so fast now that it seemed to be swallowing the blue in huge, ever-increasing gulps. But all the work was done now and Dougie had only one thing left to do. It was great that he'd been able to persuade Mum and Dad to come here with him. He felt nervous playing in front of Dad, like he had something to prove. Dad said it didn't matter, but at the same time it mattered more than anything. Dad brushed it aside with the awkwardness of a man who'd always struggled to say the right thing, even when it mattered most. He made a joke instead. 'No point staying at home on my own,' he told Dougie. 'I was just hanging around to use your telescope, son. Don't exactly need it anymore.'

As the sun had appeared for the final time, many of the mole-people had re-emerged. Dougie thought he'd likely have done the same. Imagine not seeing this... But then again, perhaps it was just the noise that had drawn them back out of their tunnels and holes? First the noise of the generator, then the music. Some random bloke had appeared when he'd seen Nick and Gav struggling with the equipment. His name was Henry, apparently, and he'd been something to do with the team that set up the sound system for the aborted Paradise Square festival, but he hadn't been able to get home before everything had gone to hell. Like Dougie, he too was glad of the distraction. He fixed the power, then showed Gav how to connect his phone to the mixing desk. Not everyone liked a lot of the stuff Gav had on his phone, but most people seemed happy with the noise. It gave some of them something to dance to, others something to moan about, others something to lie back in the sun and listen to; a replacement for the fractious, panicked soundtrack of the last couple of days. Whatever it was, it gave them all *something*.

It was strange how, even now, the pre-gig ritual kicked in and took over, the four of them setting up their gear with the minimum of fuss. Roadie Henry helped with the amps. 'Won't be the best set-up,' he told them, 'but you'll make a decent bit of noise.'

'Oh, we'll make some noise all right,' Nick said.

'Couldn't tell you whether or not it'll be decent.'

Kathy didn't know whether she'd be able to play. Her hands were shaking with nerves. It often happened before a gig, but this wasn't *a* gig, it was *the* gig. Her heart was racing, and it seemed to speed up every time she caught a glimpse of Phion P2R. The rock was close now, looming so large that she could clearly see its rotation. Over and over it span as it rolled towards them. It filled a large swathe of the morning sky. The sun was still visible in the deep summer blue, but it wouldn't be for long. Kathy knew that the next time it went dark, it would stay that way. She slammed her hands on the keys, filling the whole of Paradise Square with noise, then turned to face the others. 'We ready, boys? We need to move quick. We're running out of time.'

It was gone half-past ten. Less than an hour to go by all accounts.

They cranked up the volume and started to play to the hundred or so folk scattered across Paradise Square.

They'd done this so many times before in Gav's Dad's garage and in half-empty pubs and clubs that there was no need to talk. It was instinctive. *Birdsong* was their usual opening shot, five minutes of *Sturm und Drang* which ended in a squall of feedback which might have been capable of drowning out the noise of the impending apocalypse if they'd kept it going long enough.

Half an hour, Dougie thought. *We've got around half a bloody hour left to live.*

The crowd was indifferent. Other than Dougie's mum and dad, hardly anyone seemed to be listening.

Another song. *You and Me and One Makes Three.* This was Dougie's favourite. He remembered when they'd written it in the space of a single autumn afternoon last year. And he started to think, *no more autumn, no more birthdays, no more Christmas, no more anything...*

The music distracted him and kept pulling him back. Focused him. He felt every note, every beat. The energy of their collective noise coursed through his veins, keeping him alive as time ran out.

Shame it wasn't having the same effect on everyone.

With Phion P2R getting closer by the minute, panic was spreading. Its proximity gave the illusion that it was accelerating and folks were losing control. Some were running for cover. Others were fighting. Bad-tempered bottlenecks were forming around the various routes back underground.

When the song finished, Henry, who was sitting on the edge of the stage swinging his legs and soaking up the last few minutes of sun, called up to Nick. 'Bit self-indulgent, don't you think?'

'What?'

'Playing songs no one knows at a time like this.'

'He's right,' Dougie agreed. 'We need some dad rock.'

Nick was appalled. 'What? You want to end your days playing fucking cover versions?'

'I just want to end my days playing.'

Kathy knew exactly what he meant. She flexed her fingers, took a deep breath, then played an unmistakable progression of notes which cut through the years. She looked up and couldn't help but smile when she saw the immediate reaction. People had literally stopped in their tracks. Many of them had turned around and were edging forward again, moving closer to the stage. Dougie knew there was no point him going anywhere near the mic. The crowd were going to do the singing.

Mama, just killed a man...

It felt so clichéd, and yet it also felt so fucking right. The band played on, and the steadily returning crowd sang on. A (generally) note- and word-perfect rendition of *Bohemian Rhapsody*. Corny as hell, haphazard and hackneyed, but loved by every last one of the frightened masses who yelled their lungs out in the shadow of the ever-approaching rock which filled the sky. The noise when the song finished was deafening. Dougie thought it might be loud enough to repel Phion P2R and stop it from crashing down.

'Keep going,' Dougie said, and Kathy obliged.

We Are the Champions.

'Seriously? We're going to die a Queen tribute band?' Nick yelled in his ear as the crowd filled in the chorus.

'There's worse ways to go out. Besides, we don't have to stick to Queen. We've got fucking loads of covers we can play.'

REM next. Gav's idea. He couldn't resist it, and Dougie couldn't remember the words, but that didn't matter because the crowd went crazy at the chorus. *It's the end of the world as we know it, and I feel fine...* When they reached the end of this song the crowd, which seemed twice as big as it had been, kept singing. Why not? It was the perfect anthem for this final summer morning.

The band gathered in a huddle around Gavin's drumkit as the noise continued. 'Our credibility is completely fucked, you do realise,' Nick said.

'Everything's fucked, remember?' Gav immediately replied.

'It doesn't matter,' Kathy said. 'Listen to them. *Look* at them!'

People were being drawn to Paradise Square from all directions. They were surging along streets, flooding in from all angles, dragging themselves up from subways and basements, hanging out of the windows of buildings. Hundreds of them – probably more than a thousand now – bunched together in front of the stage.

Probably around fifteen minutes to go.

'Biggest crowd we've ever played to,' Kathy said.

'Then let's keep playing,' Dougie replied, and he started the next song. *Sex on Fire.* 'I don't even like the fucking Kings of Leon.'

'No, but they do,' Nick said.

The crowd did the heavy lifting, yelling the words while the band did their best to play along.

'Focus on the choruses,' Dougie said as the end of the song approached.

'Straight into *Mr Brightside*,' Nick told them, and five minutes later that was followed with *Don't Look Back in Anger*. Halfway through the Oasis song, the sun disappeared, blocked out by the asteroid. The volume of the crowd reduced momentarily as a collective breath was taken. The acoustics of everything changed. The air pressure seemed to increase, as if a weight had been dropped, but the band kept playing.

By the end of the song the eclipsed sun had left the world shrouded in a bizarre mid-morning dusk. It was like nothing any of them had experienced before or ever would again.

Dougie stepped up to the mic.

'Looks so close you could touch it,' he said, glancing up at the endless rock overhead, not knowing if anyone was listening. 'I don't reckon we've got long left, but we'll keep playing as long as you keep singing. That okay?'

He was hit by a wall of sound. There must have been many thousands of them now, he thought. Although the light was limited, all he could see was people stretching out in front of him. And every last one of them was clinging onto every last note of every last song.

'If only we'd hit it big like this a couple of years back,' Dougie said, off-mic.

'At least we got to do this,' Kathy said. 'Wouldn't have missed it for the world.'

'What now?' Nick asked.

'Time for one more, I think,' Dougie said as the wind began to howl.

'Got anything in mind?'

'Yes, as it happens. And I finally came up with a decent name for the band too.'

In the crowd the emotion was unbearable. Minutes to go, maybe only seconds. Everything gone. Just these moments left. Nothing anyone could do. And yet the four people on the stage kept playing... giving up their own last moments to bring together everyone else for their last moments.

The people filling Paradise Square now were wedged together, shoulder to shoulder, welcoming the closeness of neighbours. Hugs and tears. No more arguments, no more fighting. Stereotypical British frigidity and reserve all forgotten. There were kids on shoulders, reaching up to try and touch the asteroid bearing down. Other folks watching from windows and roofs.

Just seconds left now.

Phion P2R passed overhead before smashing into the planet somewhere near Belarus. A vicious yet directionless wind began to howl, ripping tiles from the roofs of buildings. The ground shook, and the guitarist steadied himself as he stepped up to the mic one final time.

'Good luck everyone, and thanks for spending these precious minutes with us. We've been *The Last Big Thing*.'

They didn't know how long the music would last in the maelstrom, but the band played on and the crowd sang on until everything was over.

ABOUT THE AUTHOR

A pioneer of independent publishing, **David Moody** first released **Hater** in 2006, and without an agent, succeeded in selling the film rights for the novel to Mark Johnson (producer, **Breaking Bad**) and Guillermo Del Toro (director, **The Shape of Water, Pan's Labyrinth**). Moody's seminal zombie novel **Autumn** was made into an (admittedly terrible) movie starring Dexter Fletcher and David Carradine. He has an unhealthy fascination with the end of the world and likes to write books about ordinary folks going through absolute hell. With the publication of a new series of **Hater** stories, Moody is poised to further his reputation as a writer of suspense-laced SF/horror, and "farther out" genre books of all description. Find out more about his work at www.davidmoody.net and www.infectedbooks.co.uk.

"Moody is as imaginative as Barker, as compulsory as King, and as addictive as Palahniuk." —*Scream the Horror Magazine*

"Moody has the power to make the most mundane and ordinary characters interesting and believable, and is reminiscent of Stephen King at his finest." —*Shadowlocked*

"British horror at its absolute best." —*Starburst*

Lightning Source UK Ltd.
Milton Keynes UK
UKHW041443060119
335024UK00002B/32/P